A WELLS LANDING CHRISTMAS

"What are you thinking about?" Zeb settled down next to her, close, but still far enough away that she would have to lean in order to touch him. That was fine. Good, even. She had no business touching him in any way.

"I've always loved Christmas," she said. Her voice sounded dreamy and far away, as if she were floating above instead of tethered to the ground.

"Me too."

She took another drink of her cocoa, not because she really wanted it, but because she needed something to do. "Where's Dawdi?"

Zeb shook his head. "He was mumbling something about shirts and combs. I figure he either had to do a load of laundry or he was getting ready for bed."

"Maybe both."

He laughed. "Maybe."

They sat quietly for a moment. Ivy watched the flames, but she could tell that Zeb was watching her. This was no good; no good a'tall.

She could turn, lean in a bit, and she would be able to press her mouth to his. It was something she had been thinking about since the first time she had seen him back in Wells Landing. Even before. Truth be known, she had never stopped thinking about his kiss, how secure she felt in his embrace, and how warm and happy his attention made her . . .

Books by Amy Lillard

The Wells Landing Series
CAROLINE'S SECRET
COURTING EMILY
LORIE'S HEART
JUST PLAIN SADIE
TITUS RETURNS
MARRYING JONAH
THE QUILTING CIRCLE
A WELLS LANDING CHRISTMAS

The Pontotoc Mississippi Series
A HOME FOR HANNAH
A LOVE FOR LEAH

Amish Mysteries
KAPPY KING AND THE PUPPY KAPER
KAPPY KING AND THE PICKLE KAPER

Published by Kensington Publishing Corporation

A WELLS LANDING CHRISTMAS

AMY LILLARD

ZEBRA BOOKS
KENSINGTON PUBLISHING CORP.
http://www.kensingtonbooks.com

ZEBRA BOOKS are published by

Kensington Publishing Corp.
119 West 40th Street
New York, NY 10018

All Kensington titles, imprints, and distributed lines are available at special quantity discounts for bulk purchases for sales promotion, premiums, fund-raising, educational, or institutional use.

Special book excerpts or customized printings can also be created to fit specific needs. For details, write or phone the office of the Kensington Sales Manager: Attn.: Sales Department. Kensington Publishing Corp., 119 West 40th Street, New York, NY 10018. Phone: 1-800-221-2647.

Zebra and the Z logo Reg. U.S. Pat. & TM Off.
BOUQUET Reg. U.S. Pat. & TM Off.

First Printing: October 2018
ISBN-13: 978-1-4201-4572-4
ISBN-10: 1-4201-4572-X

eISBN-13: 978-1-4201-4573-1
eISBN-10: 1-4201-4573-8

10 9 8 7 6 5 4 3 2 1

Printed in the United States of America

*To everyone who loves Christmas and
second chances as much as I do*

ACKNOWLEDGMENTS

Christmas is a magical time filled with love and miracles. Sometimes my miracle is getting from chapter one to the end without losing my focus or my mind. I never manage it alone. There are several people who hold my hand the entire way.

Thanks to God for miracles and blessings. Without Him none of this would be possible.

Thanks to my editor and all the fantastic folks at Kensington. Writing for these great people has been a blessing and a pleasure.

Thanks to my best friend, partner in crime, research buddy, and all around "wing man" Stacey Barbalace. If I told you all the things she does to help me it'd make your head spin. Love you, Stace!

Thanks to my family who are always a great support, demanding food and clean clothes and making me take a break from the people in my head. Thanks for understanding those times when I can't. You guys are the best and I love you!

Thanks to Patti Koski who did her best to help this Southern Baptist navigate the waters of Catholicism. Any mistakes are mine and mine alone. I hope I did right by her and Mother Mary.

Thanks to my Street Team who help me spread the word about my books. Your support for my writing and Wells Landing is staggering. Truly a blessing to me.

Thanks to you, the reader, for making it all possible. Welcome back to Wells Landing.

Chapter One

"Irene Jane, you cooked too much food. Way too much." Her grandfather's gaze chastised her over the top of his wire-rimmed glasses. Those eyes were sharp and blue. They seemed to have lost none of their brilliance, but the brain behind them . . .

"Ivy, Dawdi," she corrected gently. "I'm Ivy." She didn't bother to remind him that Irene was her mother and had left months ago to live with her new husband in Indiana. Her grandfather would remember it or he wouldn't. Either way, she didn't want to start an argument. Not today. "It's Thanksgiving," she said with a bright smile.

"I know that. Bah." He scrubbed his hand over his head the way he did when he hadn't remembered, but didn't want to say it out loud. The action made the strands of his cottony, white hair stand out from his head like they had been shot through with static electricity.

Ivy allowed herself a small smile. She loved this man dearly, but as time went on, he seemed to be more and more forgetful. She was certain the day would come when he wouldn't remember who she was at all. When that happened, she wasn't sure what she would do.

"Don't just stand there," her grandfather chastised. "Sit

down and let's eat before it goes to waste. Too much food to let it rot on the plate."

"*Jah*, Dawdi." She slid into the seat opposite him and bowed her head for their prayer. Thanksgiving. It should have been a happy day. So why was she in such misery?

Because after Thanksgiving came Christmas, and this one would be even worse than last year. Last year, it hadn't been that long since Zeb had left. Last year she was still pretending that nothing mattered, that she didn't care, that she wasn't heartbroken. This year the charade had grown weary, or maybe it was her. But she couldn't let everyone know that she did care, she had always cared. What good would that do now?

Her grandfather stirred in his chair and Ivy lifted her head, her prayer, such as it was, complete.

"Everything looks good, Irene." He reached for the platter of turkey, forking a large helping from the top before passing it across to her.

Ivy bit back a sigh. "Ivy," she gently corrected.

He nodded as if that were what he had said from the start. "I know that."

She had lost count of all the times he had called her by her mother's name. It was a recent development. But it worried her all the same. She supposed she looked enough like her mother. They had the same heart-shaped face, sky-blue eyes, and slim build, but whereas Mamm had smooth, brown hair and even smoother white skin, Ivy's hair was the color of flames, her skin marked with so many freckles she almost looked tanned. Almost.

"You shouldn't have done so much for just the two of us." Dawdi nodded toward the laden table. She had cooked more than usual, but tomorrow was promising to be a busy day at work; the whole weekend was, as a matter of fact. The turkey would keep them both in sandwiches until next week and her grandfather wouldn't have to turn on the stove or the oven in order to feed himself while she was gone. That in itself was a stress reliever. Not that she wanted him to know that.

"I love leftover turkey. Don't you?"

He swallowed the bite in his mouth and nodded. "Almost more than first-day turkey."

Ivy laughed. There was her *dawdi*. The man she had loved her entire life. The man who was now worrying her more than she liked.

At first she had chalked up his slipping memory to the fact that he had more to do around the farm since her mother and father had moved away. Stepfather. Alan Byler had come down from Indiana to look at some horses over at Andrew Fitch's and hadn't gone home. Her mother claimed it was love at first sight. Ivy could only smile and agree. After all, her mother deserved happiness. Ivy's father had died a few years back from pneumonia. It was a sad and lingering death. Her mother had done everything possible to nurse Ivy's father back to health, but the illness just proved to be too much.

Ivy wanted her mother to be happy. She wanted it more than anything, but . . . she wasn't sure Alan Byler was the answer to her mother's lonely life. But it wouldn't do to voice her opinion. Her mother wasn't the kind to listen to the advice of others. Was it any wonder Ivy had taken the road she had?

"I'll clean up the dishes," Dawdi said. "That way you can get on over to the wedding."

Ivy stirred her potatoes around on her plate, her appetite suddenly gone. "I don't have a wedding today."

Her grandfather took a bite of his buttered roll and thoughtfully chewed. "When I was in the post office I heard Maddie Kauffman talking to Esther Fitch about Rachel Detweiler's wedding. I thought you two were good friends."

They had been, once upon a time. Before Zeb left, before

she decided to hide her broken heart in a wild *rumspringa* filled with jeans, cars, and *Englisch* friends. The Amish were forgiving people, but Ivy hadn't asked for forgiveness. She stubbornly refused. She hadn't done anything all that wrong, and yet she was treated like a leper. Well, the joke was on them. She wasn't contagious. She couldn't make Amish boys forget their raising or turn Amish girls from pious to jezebel. And she hadn't been invited to Rachel Detweiler's wedding.

Ivy gave a careless shrug. "I guess we just lost touch." That was one way of putting it.

Her *dawdi* nodded. "I guess that happens."

All Ivy could do was nod. It had happened all right. And now that it had, there was nothing she could do to change it.

Ivy scrubbed the cotton swab between the buttons on her cash register and sighed. So much for today being busy. She hadn't counted on all the "Black Friday" sales and people gearing up for Christmas. She'd simply been thinking about everyone being tired of leftovers already and coming in to get something different to cook. She supposed everyone was tired of cooking as well. She peeked out the front window of the Super Cost Saver grocery store to the fast-food restaurant across the street. The line for the drive-through wrapped around the parking lot and spilled out into the street. Yet the store was so quiet she was certain she could hear the fruit going bad. She wasn't sure what Black Friday meant, but it certainly spelled out no customers for the Super Saver.

"Ivy, you have a call on line two. Ivy, line two."

She started at the sound of her name, the voice coming through the store speakers, tinny and hard to recognize. She had a phone call? From who? And how was she supposed to answer it, since she was stationed behind register one?

Bill, the store's assistant manager, had sent everyone home but a couple of stock boys, her, and Sue Ann, who answered the phones and kept the books. She had to be the one summoning her. It could be no one else.

"You can take it in here," Sue Ann said, suddenly appearing at the door of the business office. She motioned for Ivy to step away from the register. "I'll watch it for you," she added when Ivy made no move. "It's not that busy, and this sounds important."

Ivy nodded and made her way to the office. She must have been distracted by the mere fact that she had a call. It took that long for her to realize that she didn't know anyone with a phone—and what reason would a stranger have to call her?

Sue Ann eased toward the registers as Ivy stepped into the office. She picked up the receiver and pushed the flashing button with the *2* above it. "Hello?"

"Ivy? It's Daryl Hicks."

Her closest *Englisch* neighbor. Okay, so she knew one person with a phone. But it still didn't answer the second question.

"Your grandfather is in the field across the road from my place."

It seemed to take a full minute before his words hit home. "What?"

"Your grandfather—"

She shook her head, though she knew Daryl couldn't see her. "Why is he in your field?"

"I'm not sure I know the answer to that. He's just there."

"I would appreciate it if you could take him home." *And lock the doors behind him.*

"Ivy, I don't have any problem taking him home, but he's talking crazy. About not getting involved in wars and the like."

Not exactly a proper afternoon conversation, but not a problem either. Right? But somehow she knew it was more than that. "Spit it out, Daryl." Her voice came out sharper than she intended, but his stalling tactics were getting her riled up, nervous, anxious.

"He's talking about Vietnam."

She chewed her bottom lip. He had done this once before—forgotten what year it was. It had happened three times, if she counted the one when he forgot what day of the week it was and missed an auction. But that could happen to anyone, right?

It was different than calling her by her mother's name and forgetting to put on socks. He didn't know *when* he was, and it confused him. The more confused he got, the more he seemed to slip into whatever time he had chosen.

"You need to come home," Daryl said.

He didn't need to tell her that. She knew it. Just as she knew that she couldn't leave work.

"Ivy?"

"I'll be there as soon as I can." She hung up the phone and glanced out the office door. Sue Ann hovered around register one, looking toward the office every so often. When she saw Ivy was off the phone, she headed toward her.

"Is everything all right?"

Ivy shook her head and swallowed hard. "I need to leave. It's an emergency."

Sue Ann blinked once, but made no other move. "Bill's not going to like this."

She knew that, as clearly as she knew there was nothing she could do to help her grandfather short of going to Daryl's, coaxing Dawdi out of the field, and taking him home. "I'm sorry," she said. "It can't be helped."

Sue Ann nodded as if she understood, but the slant of her mouth was anything but understanding. She nodded toward

Bill who was approaching from aisle six "Clear it with the boss."

Ivy pulled her tractor to a stop in Daryl's driveway. The day had turned out bright and sunny for late November, but the cheery sunshine only mocked her inner turmoil.

She had explained the situation as best she could to Bill, who had pursed his lips and given a single, stern nod. When she clocked in for work tomorrow, she would most likely have her hours cut if they couldn't find a way to fire her outright.

She bit back a sigh as she swung down. Her grandfather was barely visible in the slightly overgrown field. He was lying on his stomach, his head barely lifted off the ground. Did he think he was in some battle? She had heard about military men who returned from one war or another and never left it behind. Had her *dawdi* ever fought? She couldn't imagine. They were Amish: conscientious objectors. They didn't fight battles or go to war. But there he was sprawled out as if hiding from some unseen enemy.

"Dawdi," she called as she strode across to the field.

He raised up just enough to see who had called him, then lowered his head with a loud *shush*. "You keep hollering that way and you'll scare off all the deer."

Ivy glanced around the field. It was the perfect place for deer to come and munch on the stalks of crops harvested months ago, but there were none out now, in the middle of the afternoon. Deer fed at dusk and just before dawn. She didn't know a lot, but that much she knew for certain. But the thing that concerned her most was the idea of him toting a gun out here. What if he thought something was a deer and it wasn't?

"Dawdi," she started again, slower, more gently. "There aren't any deer."

He pushed to his feet. "Of course not." He snorted in disgust. "Not after you came over here hollering like a banshee."

"I'm sorry," she murmured as he brushed the dried grass from his clothing. Sorry for what? That she was yelling when he was trying to "hunt"? Or because there never were deer to begin with?

He dusted himself clear to his ankles, then straightened. The knees of his pants and the front of his blue shirt were stained with water, as were his elbows.

"Where's your coat?" The sun might be shining, but it was still winter. The wind was cold, and in Oklahoma, it never stopped. The recent rains had left the ground soggy. Wet and cold were not a good combination.

"It's the middle of June," he said. "Don't need no coat out here."

"Dawdi, it's November. Remember? Yesterday was Thanksgiving. And you can't hunt deer in June."

He stopped, mulling over her words as one studies a foreign language they are trying to learn. "Bah!" he said. He took his hat from his head and scrubbed his hand across his already frowsy hair.

"Come on," she said, running one arm through his. "Let's go back to the house and get you some dry clothes."

He looked down at himself then, as if just realizing that he was wet and he wasn't sure how he got that way. "*Jah.* Dry clothes," he said, though his confusion was tangible.

What was she supposed to do? She couldn't let him go on believing things were the way he imagined, and she didn't want to frustrate him by telling him the truth.

But the worst thought of all was the possibility of coming up on him on a day like today and not being able to convince him of the real time and place. What would she do then?

She thanked the neighbor and apologized to him once

again, then she hopped back onto the tractor and pointed it toward home. Daryl lived less than a quarter of a mile from her and Dawdi, but when she thought about her grandfather walking it alone, thinking heaven knew what, alone, and without a proper coat . . . So many things could have happened.

Thank the Lord none of them had.

They rode home in silence. Ivy would have given almost anything to know what her grandfather was thinking, but she knew if she asked him he wouldn't give a straight answer.

She parked the tractor and hopped down, her grandfather already striding toward the house. She knew he was embarrassed. Maybe that wasn't the word. He was frustrated, confused, and uncertain. As uncertain as she was herself.

"*Dawdi*," she called to his retreating back.

"Bah." He waved a hand behind himself, dismissing her questions without giving her a chance to ask even one.

He should have called, maybe written a letter. He should have told them he was coming.

And what difference would that have made?

They could have braced themselves for his return . . . ?

Did they need bracing? Heaven knew he did. Zebadiah Brenneman had never planned on returning to Wells Landing. In fact, he wasn't entirely sure what led him to come home now. Christmas, he supposed. But that was still over three weeks away. He had missed Thanksgiving by a couple of days. Not that it was a big holiday at their house. Four bachelor men living together, they were lucky to get a hot meal, much less a planned feast.

Three bachelors, he corrected himself. His brother Obie had married Clara Rose Yutzy earlier in the year. Zeb could have come home then, but he hadn't. Should have for certain, but he didn't. Because returning home would mean facing all the mistakes he had made. Mistakes that only one other person knew about. Ivy Weaver.

So why am I here now? he asked himself as he hitched the strap of his duffel bag onto his shoulder. It wasn't the kind of bag an Amish man took on trips, but it was handy and sturdy. Zeb figured if it was good enough for the Army, it was good enough for him. Or maybe some of that old rebellion was raising its head again. Who in Wells Landing carried a government-issue duffel bag? No one but him, he was certain.

He looked around him at the run-down bus stop. It looked the same as it had almost two years ago when he'd boarded the bus to Florida. He needed it to be changed. He wasn't the same person as when he left. He had moved on. Having everything the same suggested that maybe he hadn't. If everything was the same, then leaving and coming back were just small hiccups in his life. Like that book he'd heard about where a man went back in time and lived for years only to return to the present and find out that he had only been gone for two minutes.

He didn't stand out. No one would call him different. Here, in Wells Landing, he was the same old Zeb, brother to Benjie and Adam, twin of Obie, and son of Paul.

It wasn't that he wanted to be different. Somehow, he simply knew that he was. Like he had been given a message before he was born. *You will be . . .* something. Something more? Something else? Something unrelated? He wasn't certain. That was why he went searching. That was why he traveled to Pinecraft, Florida, and lived in a tiny beach house with three other Amish boys, all from different parts of the country. Pinecraft was as far as he could get without dropping off into the ocean. So he'd traveled there and stayed.

Yet why was he here now?

He could blame it on one of his roommates, who decided to go back to Ohio. Or maybe even the one who fell in love with an *Englisch* girl and left the church for what he called a once-in-a-lifetime love. Zeb had thought he'd had one of those, but it wasn't meant to be. How could two people be meant for each other when they had such different goals in life?

With a last glance around, he adjusted his bag once more and headed for the sidewalk. The wind was cool, and he shivered against its chill across his skin. Florida had been eighty and sunny. Yet again he wondered why he had come home.

Zeb sucked in a big gulp of that cool air and let it out slowly. He was here now, for whatever reason, and when he got whatever it was sorted out, he would leave. And that was all there was to it.

He looked toward town. The bus station was at one end of the little community. He couldn't see much of it as he stood there—just enough to know that two years hadn't changed much. Kauffmans' Family Restaurant. Esther's Bakery; the narrow park that ran down the center of Main. And across the street, the little shops lined up like good little children, unshifting, unmoving, unchanging.

Two days past Thanksgiving and they had already hung the Christmas decorations. Crisp green wreaths tied with fluttering red bows graced the tall black lamp posts. All they needed was snow to look like something off a Christmas card. But there wouldn't be a white Christmas in Wells Landing. Some winters brought no snow at all to Oklahoma.

Snow. That might be the thing to drive him back to Pinecraft. He had become something of a beach bum in his time there, if there was such a thing as an Amish beach bum. He worked, cleaned his part of the house, and did life's other little chores, but his free time had been spent next to the water. There was nothing like it. There were those who didn't believe in a higher power. He wondered if they had ever stood on the shoreline. How could anyone look upon the ocean and deny God? He found the feat beyond comprehension.

The town showed more signs of Christmas. Holiday music slipped out of the doors of the shops he passed. Lights were strung, even if they weren't blinking in the afternoon sun. At night the entire place would be sparkling like the stars in the sky, except these stars would be all different colors, some steady, others blinking to the tempo of recorded music. A large pine tree at the end of the park had been decorated as well. He didn't remember that from before, and the one change gave him hope that maybe it could be different. But the feeling was short-lived. He couldn't allow it to take root and leave him open for more heartbreak. He simply couldn't.

He reached the end of Main, where it shifted and wound through one of the oldest neighborhoods in town. He glanced back, over his shoulder. He felt like he'd been gone forever and he felt like he had just left. The mixed emotions tumbled inside him, each one fighting for dominance. One left turn and three more miles, then he would be at the road that led to his house. His father's house, anyway. Maybe even Obie's house. No one had told him what had happened after Obie and Clara Rose had married, and he hadn't bothered to ask. At any rate, whoever lived there now would surely take him in for the night. He had no beef with anyone there. Just Ivy.

"Zeb?"

As if he had conjured her from his thoughts alone, there she was, sitting on a tractor waiting for him to return her greeting.

"Ivy." He nodded to distract from the choked sound of his voice. He hadn't seen his family yet, hadn't spoken to anyone in town, and she was the first. Always Ivy. Was it some kind of cruel omen?

"What are you doing out here?" she asked.

"Going home." It was a simple enough answer and yet it wasn't simple at all. "You?"

She jerked a thumb over her shoulder toward the Super Cost Saver "I just got off work."

"You work at the grocery store?"

She nodded. "At least I did."

He cocked his head to one side and waited for her to continue. "Oh, *jah*?"

"Dawdi . . . he keeps forgetting—" She broke off with a shake of her head, pressing her lips together as if she regretted telling him even that much. "I could give you a ride," she said, the change of subject swift and unexpected.

"*Jah*. Okay." He wanted to tell her no, but the words wouldn't come. He found himself nodding like a fool at her feet. But hadn't it always been that way? He climbed up next to her, standing on the side and holding on to the back of her seat for balance.

She shifted away, just barely, but he had expected that much as well. They had been close once, but not now. Never again.

Funny how some things changed and others remained stubbornly the same. He could remember every freckle on her cheeks, but not the frown that pulled at the corners of her mouth. Her eyes were just as blue as the sky, her hair like fire pulled back and somehow tamed under the cover of her prayer *kapp*. She looked the same, she smelled the same. Perhaps she was a bit thinner than he remembered, but everything had to change a bit. Nothing could remain entirely the same.

He held himself stiffly, willing his knees to hold him back, not lean into the vanilla warmth that was Ivy Weaver.

Oh, how he had missed her. Not that it changed anything. Not one thing.

The sound of the tractor engine made conversation next to impossible. They could have hollered over the roar. They had done that more times than he could count. But not today. That Ivy and Zeb were gone, leaving new ones in their place. Two years older, and hopefully wiser. Whatever had been between them long ago had died out, leaving the ashes of what could have been love.

Could have been.

She didn't say a word as she turned her tractor onto the road that led to his house. There was no catching up on the community. No chitchat about who had a baby and who got married, who died, who still lived, or who made her happy these days.

Not that he cared. He and Ivy were long ago and never again.

The house looked the same as he approached; maybe even a bit better. The paint wasn't fresh, but it was a newer coat than had been there when he left. The yard was well maintained, even in late November. The garden plot was covered in black plastic. Mums had been planted in the front flower beds, their yellow faces reaching toward the sun, holding on to the fall as long as they could. They testified that there hadn't been a hard frost. Not yet, anyway. The barn was strikingly red, the laundry line laden with towels and sheets. It was the perfect scene of quaint Amish living, and it brought tears to his eyes. It hadn't looked like this since his mother died.

A small mobile home had been positioned behind the house. There was no *dawdihaus* and Zeb realized that this was the closest thing. Only it wasn't just for his father but his two younger brothers as well. It should have looked out of place, but it didn't. Somehow it fit with the landscape and the redone two-story where he had grown up.

He had thought perhaps he and Ivy would be the ones to make it a home again and not just a dwelling for four men who had too much on their minds to plant flowers and sweep the porch. But it had been Obie and Clara Rose, of that he was certain.

He hopped down from the tractor. Ivy kept the engine idling while he walked around the nose and stopped, turning between her and the house. "Thanks for the ride."

She dipped her chin, the gesture almost stern, then shifted gears and chugged back down the narrow lane.

Zeb looked back at the house. Good or bad. Right or wrong. Genius or folly. He had come home.

Chapter Two

Zeb cut his eyes to the side, doing his best to appear as if he was still looking forward though his attention was settled firmly on Ivy.

She had brought him home and immediately driven away, but never left his thoughts. Even here, at church, she was all he could think about.

Once he had knocked on the door of the house, he'd been dragged in by Clara Rose, who cradled three-month-old Paul Daniel in her arms. She'd called out the back door to Obie, and before he could wipe Ivy from his mind, he had been surrounded by his family.

There had been lots of hugs, assessments, and back clapping, but they had caught up. It had taken most of the evening to recount his trip back, what he had missed in Wells Landing, and what he had been doing in Florida. Not that he had told them all. He hadn't admitted to the reason why he had left or why he had stayed away so long. Just as he couldn't explain why he had come back, it was something he just didn't know.

Ivy moved, and he looked away as if she were about to catch him watching her. If anyone were to ask him tomorrow what the preacher had talked about today he wouldn't be able to give an answer, at least not one that would be accurate.

His gaze shifted, and she was in his line of sight yet again.

Just as he had thought the day before, she was slimmer now than she had been two years ago. Had she tried to lose weight? It wasn't like she was vain, or even needed to shed the pounds, but she had. Had she been worried? Sick? Worried sick?

Why did he care? She had made her feelings clear when he had left. Why should anything be different now?

The entire congregation shifted, and once again, Zeb turned his attention front. Time to go, last prayer.

They rose, turned, and faced the bench where they had been sitting. His gaze snagged Ivy's. Her blue eyes were like ice, her chin set as if she had been preparing herself for the inevitable confrontation. Then the moment was gone. She was kneeling, out of sight and out of reach.

Zeb knelt and bowed his head, but no prayers would come. The thing he wanted to pray for the most was the one thing he couldn't have. Ivy.

"She's trouble." Thomas Lapp sidled up next to him, and Zeb realized once again that he was staring at Ivy. He couldn't seem to help himself. No matter where she was his eyes seemed to follow her.

"Hi, Thomas."

The young man shook his head. "It's good to see you back."

Zeb gave the expected nod.

"You've been gone, so you don't know," Thomas said, casting his own glance in the direction Zeb had just been looking. Church was over and the meal had been served. It was a pretty enough day for late November, and only a coat was necessary to stand out and visit. Even after so much time in Florida, the day was mild and sunny.

"Know what?" he asked.

Thomas nodded toward Ivy. "I guess it was just after you left," he mused. "She just sort of went off the rails, so to speak."

This was the first he was hearing about this. What hadn't anyone told him? "What exactly does that mean?"

Thomas gave an elegant shrug. He was like that, fluid and graceful. As a member of one of the most prominent families in Wells Landing, Thomas had a delicate demeanor. All the Lapps did. Thomas wouldn't say anything bad about anyone unless the comment was one hundred percent true. "She's been running around with *Englischers*, driving a car, and wearing jeans."

"Wearing jeans?" He wasn't sure he had heard right. This wasn't like the Ivy he knew. Oh, she could be a little opinionated and a bit strong-willed, but she wasn't openly defiant. At least she hadn't been before.

"That's what bothers you most?"

Zeb shook his head and tried to get his whirling emotions to slow down enough that he could snag one and reply. He latched onto indignation, then let it go. "*Englischers*?" he finally managed.

Thomas nodded. "Luke Lambright, mostly."

But Luke Lambright wasn't really an *Englischer*. Sure he had left their district for all the freedoms and opportunities in Tulsa, but he was Amish born. It wasn't like he was a stranger.

Yet one look at Thomas's frown and Zeb knew that anything he said in Ivy's defense would go unacknowledged.

"Is that where she got the car?" he asked instead. She had been on a tractor when he had seen her before. But there was no mistaking what he was hearing now. A car! What was she doing? Did she want everyone in town to think she

was wild and unruly? That was all such behavior was worth
in their small community.

"I believe so, *jah*. But I didn't ask. I just thought you
should know since you had been gone and all."

Zeb nodded and thanked Thomas, another lie that
slipped into being so easily. Last night over supper Obie had
caught him up on all the happenings since he had been
gone, but he hadn't said one word about Ivy. And he hadn't
since last year when he took her on a hayride to make Clara
Rose jealous. Maybe that was it. Maybe Thomas was jealous because Clara Rose married Obie instead of him, and
Ivy just got caught in the middle. That seemed logical
enough, but somehow he knew it was more than that. There
was only one way to find out.

"Thomas." He nodded toward the man, and ignoring his
startled look, he walked away.

He would ask. It was as simple as that. It was a beautiful
day—a little chilly for his tastes, but beautiful all the same.
December was in the air, an expectant hush, despite the
playing children and chattering adults. Christmas. He didn't
know if he could make it that long. Funny thing was, no one
had asked him if he was going to stay. They had just assumed
he was—the prodigal son returned.

"Ivy." He spoke her name before he got too close. He
didn't want to startle her. Or maybe he just wanted her to
know that he was coming. He would talk to her, and anyone
within hearing distance would know if she spun and walked
away.

Her eyes widened at his approach, then narrowed. She
knew what he was doing. She was smart that way. Always
had been. She pasted a bright smile into place as she greeted
him. "Zeb Brenneman. So good to have you back. When did
you get into town?"

He stopped short. She knew good and well when he'd
arrived. She had been the one to take him home. Apparently

no one else knew that. It seemed strange to think that no one had seen them together Saturday afternoon as they chugged along, but he was sure anything was possible. "Yesterday." He forced the word out between clenched teeth and a forced smile of his own. "How have you been?"

"Good, good. And you?" She shifted, and he could tell that she would rather be anywhere than there, talking about everyday matters and nothing at all. But why?

"Oh, you know." He shoved his hands into his pockets and gave a quick shrug.

"No," she said quietly. "I don't."

A moment held in the air between them, and for a time, everything around them seemed to melt away. There they stood, like they had all those many months ago. Except it hadn't been this cold then. Ivy had been dry-eyed and stern, belligerent even as she raised her chin and told him to do whatever it was he had in his heart. If only she had asked him to stay . . .

"Nice talking to you," she said. "But I need to go see about Dawdi." Her gaze shifted to a spot over his left shoulder. Then she nodded in the same direction and brushed past him.

Zeb turned and watched as Ivy started toward the row of buggies. Yonnie Weaver, Ivy's grandfather, was walking around each one as if they were lined up for purchase. He made it around two more before Ivy caught up with him. Zeb was too far away to hear the conversation, but it seemed to him as if Ivy was trying to coax him back toward the milling throng of church members. He took a couple of steps toward the house, then started back toward the buggies. Ivy stopped him, then pointed in the general direction of the pasture where the horses had been let out for the afternoon. Next she pointed toward one of the buggies. It was as if she was saying, *Our horse is there. Our buggy right there*. But any other interpretation was lost as Obie sidled up next to him.

"You're staring," Obie said.

Zeb jerked his head in what might be considered a nod, then rolled one shoulder in a possible shrug. "Something's up."

"It's okay. I don't think anyone noticed."

Zeb turned to his brother. When they stood together like this, side by side, he wondered what others thought of them. Matching bookends with dark, rumpled hair? Mirror images with green eyes and crooked smiles? Once upon a time they were trouble in suspenders, always into something or another. But these days Obie was the model husband and father, and Zeb was . . . lost. "What difference does that make?"

Obie gave a shrug of his own. "Things have changed a bit since you were here last."

"Which means?"

"Ivy sort of . . ."

"I heard." He shook his head. "Thomas Lapp gave me an earful."

Obie chuckled. "I'm sure Thomas was kinder than most."

Zeb sighed and watched as Ivy escorted her grandfather to the pasture to pick up their horse. They were headed home. He wouldn't be able to talk to her again today. Was that a good thing or bad? "Why didn't you say something?"

"When?" Obie asked. "Last night at supper when everyone was so happy to have you back that they couldn't stop talking? Or this morning when Clara Rose was making breakfast and Paul Daniel was screaming his little head off?"

"Point taken."

Paul Daniel, Obie's three-month-old son, was the spitting image of his father. It was strange, seeing himself reflected in the child of his brother. It made him wonder about things best forgotten.

Zeb inclined his head toward the line of buggies. Ivy and Yonnie were still down there hitching up the horse as if they were headed for home. "Are they leaving already?" Things were really just gearing up. Some families left a little earlier than others. Elam and Emily Riehl headed out before others, as well as Abbie and Titus Lambert. But they were dairy farmers and had to do the milking done before it got too late. Yonnie Weaver was not a dairy farmer.

Obie looked to Ivy and her grandfather, then back to Zeb. "Ivy's sort of alienated herself."

Zeb growled in frustration. This had something to do with what Thomas had been trying to say, but Zeb was now getting the distinct impression that it was worse than Thomas had let on. Much worse.

Lots of Amish teens ran around with *Englisch* kids, sneaking rides in cars and going to parties. It all depended on their parents and what they would let the children get away with. Not that Ivy was a child. She was twenty-one now. Most of their friends were married and had started families. And her mother would never have allowed her to . . .

"Where's Ivy's mother?" Zeb asked.

"Indiana. That's what I've been trying to tell you. Irene got married and moved away about a month after you did. Ivy's been sort of wild ever since."

Sort of wild. The words knocked around in Zeb's head for the rest of the morning and on into the afternoon. *Sort of wild.*

It had been four years since Ivy's father had died. It was a strange and sad accident, and it had hit them all hard. Irene most of all. She had never been a particularly strong woman and Zeb wasn't surprised that she had remarried, only that it had taken her so long to do so. And now Ivy was "sort of wild."

He wasn't sure what that meant, but he knew one person who would tell him the truth.

"Clara Rose?" He spoke her name quietly, but still she jumped.

"Goodness, Zeb. You scared me." She was standing at the changing table, little Paul Daniel cooing and reaching for the strings on her prayer covering.

"I'm sorry." He leaned against the doorjamb and watched as she fastened the diaper into place. "I was hoping I could ask you about something."

"Of course. But I have to feed Paul Daniel in just a bit."

"It shouldn't take long."

Clara Rose smiled, her face lighting up like the full moon, glowing, beautiful, sweet. "Would you like to hold him?"

He couldn't say no. Not really. How could he tell the love of his brother's life that he didn't want to hold their sweet child? That he was afraid he would drop him. That he was simply afraid. He cleared his throat. "Uh, *jah*." He straightened as Clara Rose came toward him.

"Just support his head . . ." She handed the baby over, like Zeb could be trusted with such a small creature. He had handled newborn calves, colts, puppies, and kittens, but somehow this small human was beyond anything he had ever seen.

"His eyes are blue," he murmured.

"Most babies have blue eyes."

Did he know that?

"But they could stay that way," Clara Rose continued. "We'll just have to see."

Wait and see. This child he held in his arms would change, grow, evolve, and they would have to wait and see what he became. The idea was miraculous. And it filled him with thoughts of what could have been and what might be.

Clara Rose returned to the table where she had changed Paul Daniel's diaper and straightened the products she had there: powder, wipes, lotion. Babies needed a lot of stuff. More than Zeb ever dreamed.

Paul Daniel fussed and shook his tiny fists. Zeb bounced him as he had seen Clara Rose do the night before.

"What about Ivy?"

Clara Rose stopped. "Weaver? What about her?"

He cleared his throat. "I've heard some things . . ."

Clara Rose stopped. "What things?"

"Are they true?"

She turned back to her work with a small shrug. "I don't know."

"But you have an idea," he guessed. In his arms, the baby started to kick, his tiny face crumpling into what seemed might be a never-ending cry.

She pressed her lips together and shook her head.

Zeb bounced Paul Daniel a little more enthusiastically, with no results.

Clara Rose sighed and took the baby from him. "At first I thought they were." She shushed the baby, propping him on her shoulder and gently patting his back. His cries lost their shrillness and died away in a couple of hiccups and one small cough. Miracle.

"I'm not sure I understand."

She opened her mouth to explain, but Paul Daniel started crying once again. "I need to feed him."

Zeb wanted to protest, to tell her that he needed to know, that it wouldn't take long. But the baby took priority over everything, even broken hearts.

"*Jah*," he said with a resigned nod.

"Once I get him to bed we can talk, *jah*?"

Zeb nodded again and let himself out of the room.

Obie was out in the barn checking on one of his golden retrievers who was about to have a litter of pups. Zeb was proud of his brother and all he had built with his business, but right now babies, mothers, and the miracle of life were the last things he wanted to see. He wanted to know about Ivy and nothing more.

He prowled around the house, barely noticing the changes. Their mother had died when he and Obie were young, and their father wasn't the kind to run out and get married right away. Zeb often wondered if it was part of his defense mechanism from losing the wife he had depended on so desperately. Paul Brenneman hadn't wanted his boys to be lost without a woman, and instead of marrying another, he made them work through being motherless.

If that truly were the case, then Paul had succeeded in making his children more independent than most, but their house had suffered. Growing up, there were always hanging cobwebs and a thin covering of dust on most everything. But these days the house was spotless. A vase of fresh flowers even sat on the end of the kitchen counter. Since the blooms were out of season for Oklahoma, Zeb was sure that they had come from the small flower shop inside the Super Saver grocery store.

He wandered out onto the porch and immediately wished he'd put on a coat, or at the very least a jacket. With the sun down, the air was downright frigid. He'd heard talk of a cold front coming in. It was hard to tell if his chill was from that or from the fact that he had grown accustomed to more balmy temps.

The night was clear, and millions of stars twinkled in the dark sky, surrounding a fat moon that hovered lazily above the tree line. Despite the cool air, he lingered on the porch. If he was going to stay in Oklahoma through Christmas, he'd have to get used to the cold sometime. He said a small prayer of thanks that his family wasn't from farther north. He might not survive that kind of change.

"Zeb?"

He turned as Clara Rose eased out onto the porch beside him. "Did you get the baby down for the night?" he asked.

"*Jah.*" She stopped next to him, bracing her hands on the railing and gazing up at the clear sky. "So many stars," she murmured. Then she pulled her shawl a little closer around her shoulders. "About Ivy—"

He shook his head. "I changed my mind," he said. "I don't want to know." After only a few minutes in the cool night air he realized that Clara Rose's opinion was valuable, but it might also give him false hope. False hope where there was really no hope at all. He and Ivy were finished and done, nearly before they ever got started. Their relationship had begun all wrong, with them sneaking around and dating when she hadn't joined the church. If she wasn't a member, could he even call it dating? Whatever. It didn't matter now. She was doing her own thing, and he was doing his. Nothing was going to change that.

He turned to go back into the house, but Clara Rose stopped him, placing one hand on his arm. "I think she gets talked about a lot, but I don't think half of it's true. Which half?" She gave a quick shrug. "Who's to say?"

At one of the parties she had attended, one of those *Englisch* parties that Luke Lambright had taken her to, Ivy had heard a song about Mondays. The singer hated Mondays. *Monday, Monday.* She'd never understood that song.

Until today. Today she hated Mondays.

Just as she had expected, she had arrived at the Super Saver to find that she only had one shift. She usually worked four or five days a week. Not this week. They had cut her hours because she'd had to leave too many times to check on her grandfather. She understood that it was a business decision. Bill, the assistant manager, and Carla, the manager, had a store to run. And they couldn't run it if their employees weren't trustworthy. She was trustworthy, but her loyalty had to lie with her grandfather first. She was all he had left, and he her.

But still, the idea of losing her job over something she couldn't control didn't sit well with her, and by the time she clocked out to come home, she was inwardly seething. She worked hard to provide what she could for her and her grandfather. He bought and sold hay when he could, but these days his memory was getting the better of him. Sometimes she figured he simply forgot what he was supposed to be doing and missed the necessary appointments. She had been trying to come up with a solution, but hadn't devised a plan, as of yet. Now seeing as how she had all but lost her job at the grocery store, she was going to have to do something different. They were going to need the two incomes to make ends meet. Tomorrow she would go look for another job. Maybe if she worked a couple of days at the grocery store and a couple more somewhere else it would be like not having her hours cut at all. She could hope, couldn't she?

But first she had to deal with . . . this.

She pulled her tractor to a stop, set the brake, and turned off the engine.

Helen Ebersol sat on her front porch, as if she had nothing better to do than wait on Ivy to return home.

"Helen." Ivy nodded toward the woman. Why hadn't she noticed the rusty red tractor parked to one side of the big oak tree in the yard? Because she had been too busy thinking about her problems to realize they might be bigger than she even knew. "What brings you out today?" she asked.

Like that was really necessary. Helen was there to check up on her and Dawdi.

He must be gone, Ivy thought, or Helen wouldn't be sitting on the front porch with her cape flung over her shoulders to ward off the chilly air.

Helen stood as Ivy climbed the porch steps. "I came to check on your grandfather. I heard he ran into a little trouble last week."

Ivy nodded and took the key from her bag. Nothing like Sunday to recount the week and Monday to follow up. "He's fine. Really." She smiled as if to lend more credibility to the words, then froze as she tried to pull herself out of her own depressing thoughts.

"Where is your grandfather?" Helen asked. "I knocked, but no one answered."

Ivy popped the door open with one hard nudge of her shoulder and motioned Helen inside. It was too cold to be lingering on porch steps today. The weather had taken a turn, complete with heavy gray clouds and the promise of December.

"He's at an auction." She said the words with more confidence than she truly felt. But if God was listening and He answered prayers—and she knew He did—then she would surely be blessed. *Please let him be at an auction,* she silently prayed. *Please let him be where he is supposed to be.*

She put down her purse, took off her coat, and scooped her cat into her arms. Chester was a calico with short fur and a decided crook in her tail. Ivy had had her long enough that she couldn't remember why she had named her Chester. She simply had. She scratched the cat behind her eyes, smiling as the feline began to vibrate with a loud purr.

"Fred Conrad came by to tell me that he saw your grandfather out in Daryl Hicks's field Friday afternoon."

The mailman was as bad about gossiping as an old woman, but Ivy couldn't voice that thought. What good would it do anyhow? "Oh, *jah?*" She set Chester down, picked up her bags, and made her way into the kitchen. Helen followed close behind.

"Is that true?"

Ivy stopped unloading her bags from the store. She had picked up a few things after her shift ended. Better get them now, while she still had an employee discount. It was only ten percent, but it was better than nothing. These days she could use all the help she could get. She sighed. "Yes, but he was just a little confused." She closed her eyes.

"I'm not accusing," Helen said quietly. "I'm concerned."

Ivy met Helen's gaze once again. "He's fine." Maybe if she kept saying it, it would somehow become true.

Helen nodded, and Ivy knew. If Helen was concerned about her grandfather after one misstep, she had to be doubly worried for Ivy. If not more. "Ivy—"

Here it comes.

"—can we—"

Helen broke off as a knock sounded at the door.

Could it be her grandfather returned? Why was he knocking? Had he forgotten his key? She hadn't locked the door.

She stared at Helen for a moment more, then turned to answer the summons.

But it wasn't her confused *dawdi* lingering on the porch.

"We need to talk." Zeb Brenneman pushed past her and into the house.

Chapter Three

Zeb drew up short when he saw Helen Ebersol standing in Ivy's kitchen. "Helen," he said with a small nod of greeting. The oomph drained from him, his urgency leaking out like water through a sieve. He wanted to talk to Ivy. Alone. Maybe he could have coaxed her away from her *dawdi*, but how was he going to work around the bishop's wife?

"Good to see you, Zeb."

They stood there for a few moments, each one sizing up the other and what they needed to say. Finally Helen shifted. She pulled her cape a little closer around herself and moved toward the front door. "If you need anything, Ivy . . ."

"*Danki*, Helen," Ivy murmured.

Zeb stayed where he was, waiting for Helen to leave. He never took his gaze from Ivy, but he heard the front door creak open, then close.

He waited a heartbeat more before turning to Ivy.

"Goodbye, Zeb." She started toward him, her intentions clear. She was trying to force him toward the door the way a sheepdog herds an animal into a pen.

He planted his feet, refusing to budge. "I came to talk, Ivy."

She drew up short when it became evident that he wasn't about to back away. "There's nothing to talk about."

"I disagree."

She shook her head. "I don't want to talk."

"I've heard all sorts of talk, Ivy."

He didn't need to tell her what about. She tossed her head. "Talk is talk."

"I think there may be more to it than that."

She shrugged and stepped around him, prancing to the door and flinging it wide. "So sorry you can't stay."

"Ivy."

She gestured out the door. "It's really a shame you can't linger."

"We need to talk about this, Ivy."

"There's nothing to talk about." But he could see it in her eyes, the pain, the confusion, the doubts.

But she wasn't ready. He wanted to talk. He needed to get it out. He had returned to town and was faced with more memories and emotions than he cared to stare down, and he needed to work through it all. But she had remained. She had been there all along. She had faced it all and didn't want to turn back. He could understand that, but he couldn't honor it. There was still too much at stake.

"Leave, Zeb. I don't want you here."

He gave a solemn nod. "*Jah*. Fine. I'll leave but I will be back. There's still too much—"

"Goodbye, Zeb."

Suddenly he was face-to-face with the porch side of the front door. Just how had he gotten on this side? He wasn't quite sure. As always when he was around Ivy Weaver, he had gotten lost in her sky-blue eyes and forgotten nearly everything else. Including the conversation he had been mulling over for the last two years.

He raised his fist to knock again, but managed to lower

his hand before it met with wood. It had waited this long. One more day wouldn't matter.

"Helen Ebersol said you might be needing some help." Ivy resisted the urge to shift in place. Why was she so nervous? She had been on countless job hunts since she had turned fourteen. She had interviewed, gotten jobs, and started to work all in the span of an afternoon. So why did walking into Esther's Bakery feel like the biggest task she had ever undertaken?

Because it was important to her. Not just because she needed the work, but this, a job in the best bakery in town, was something of a dream come true. She might not like to sew or crochet or knit, but she could bake a pie that could bring a grown man to his knees. If she could work there, even if just through the holidays, she could show Esther and Caroline her baking skills. Hopefully, with a few prayers and God on her side, she would be working there for a while to come.

Esther Fitch nodded. "*Jah.* We are. Caroline can't work as much since Grace Ann was born."

Ivy nodded understandingly. Grace Ann was Caroline's third child, but the birth hadn't been easy on her. Not that anyone had told Ivy that directly. But she had heard talk. "With the holidays coming up I figured you might need some help."

"For certain."

"Esther, can I talk to you a moment?" Jodie Miller, the bakery's part-time help, wiped her hands on a towel, then motioned for Esther to step behind the counter.

The baker's forehead puckered into a frown, but she nodded and excused herself.

Ivy's stomach clenched. Jodie Miller wasn't in her youth group. Like she went to group functions these days. Most everyone had gotten married, and it was no fun being the only single person there. Even though, Ivy knew that Jodie didn't like her, working with someone who glared at her after church would be a small price to pay for having the job of her dreams. That was, if she actually got it. It seemed Jodie was against that as well.

She couldn't hear all of what was said. But she heard enough. She caught the words "no hope for redemption" and "bad for business." And there was nothing she could say in her own defense. She knew what everyone said about her, and she knew why. Not that it helped matters any.

"Everyone deserves a chance," she heard Esther explain.

Then Ivy remembered that Caroline herself had received a second chance from Esther. Not that Caroline's reputation had been in question. No, when she had arrived in Wells Landing, she was recently widowed with a baby on the way. Caroline and Esther had become fast friends as Esther allowed her to work in the bakery and make herself a name in the community. And Esther herself had had a second chance with Abe Fitch, marrying him after a short courtship. But Ivy's situation was a little different.

If only she could be allowed to do the same. To start over. That was what she would do.

Jodie said something else, but Ivy couldn't understand her words. Her tone, however, was unmistakable. She felt like Esther was making a huge mistake.

"*Danki*, Jodie," Esther said and with a nod of finality started back to where Ivy waited. "I appreciate your input."

"But you're still going to hire her." Jodie's words were flat.

"*Jah*. I'm hiring her."

Ivy fairly floated all the way home. Finally something was turning out. She would work harder than she ever had before. She promised herself and God that she would do everything in her power to deserve the chance Esther was giving her. And everything in her power to show Esther how worthy she was of the position. When doubters like Jodie Miller tasted Ivy's pumpkin pie, everything would change. At least it did in her daydreams. A girl had to have hope.

Ivy turned her tractor onto the short lane that led to the house she shared with her grandfather. She had more than her share of hope. She said a prayer each morning when she left, every afternoon when she returned, and again at night before she went to bed. She prayed that the Lord would take care of her grandfather in the time she had to spend away from him. And aside from the incident on Friday, He had answered her prayers. God was good.

Now she had a job with an employer who would understand and be more helpful if things went a little sideways. Right then, in that moment, she had more than hope. She had an air of anticipation like she had never felt before.

Then she saw his tractor. Zeb.

Her confidence deflated a bit. Or maybe it was just her elation.

What was he doing there? Well, she knew what he was doing there. She just wished that he wasn't. There.

How was she supposed to get over everything that had happened between them if he was always underfoot? It had been much easier when he was in Florida. Why hadn't he just stayed there?

She swung down from the tractor, her frustration and anger rising as she stomped toward the house. Zeb wasn't waiting on the front porch like Helen had been the day before, which meant her grandfather was home. That was good, she had to admit. She wanted him to be home, warm and safe. She just didn't want Zeb Brenneman there with him.

Anger mounting, she flung open the door and stepped

into the house, removing her scarf from her head as she did so. She felt her prayer *kapp* shift with the motion, and she straightened it a bit without the benefit of a mirror before storming toward the kitchen. If she knew her grandfather at all, he had invited Zeb in for a cup of coffee and some of the cookies she had baked last night. Worry over going to the bakery today and talking to Esther had sent Ivy into a baking frenzy. Any sort of large agitation could do that to her. The upside was a big problem could result in loaves of bread, dozens of cookies, and pies enough to share with their *Englisch* neighbors. The day her mother told her she was marrying Alan Byler, Ivy had stayed up all night baking everything she had a recipe for. In the morning she had enough food to host her very own bake sale.

It wasn't that she minded Zeb having a few cookies. On second thought, she did mind. He was the one who had run out. He was the one who left for nearly two years, then wanted to come back like nothing was amiss.

But if she stomped in there now, demanding that he put down the cookie and leave, her grandfather might get suspicious. If Dawdi was having a good day, that was. If he was having a super day, he might even put it all together and realize that Zeb was the one who had broken her heart. Well, almost. Thankfully, he'd left, taking only a small piece with him to the Sunshine State.

She pulled herself up short and took a deep breath to calm her pounding heart. She would walk in there calmly and act as if it were a normal occurrence, Zeb coming by to see her grandfather. Then she would excuse herself and head out to the barn to do her evening chores. With any luck and maybe a prayer or two, Zeb would take the hint that he needed to go home and that would be that.

Ivy swept into the kitchen as if she were breezing by without a care in the world. Nothing could be further from the truth, but neither man needed to know that. "Hi, Dawdi."

She bent to kiss his cheek and raised herself to coolly eye Zeb. "Zeb Brenneman. What brings you out today?"

"I came to talk to you."

Oops. Wrong thing to say. "Oh?" Nice recovery. She blinked at him balefully, then she shifted her attention out the window to keep from looking too interested.

"*Jah.*"

Her gaze strayed back to Zeb.

His green eyes were serious, and his hair was a bit messier than usual. He and Obie were the only people she knew who could brush their hair and still have it look as if it needed a good combing.

"That's unfortunate," she heard herself say. "I need to go out and do my chores."

"I'll help you." He was on his feet before she could utter one word of protest.

"That's a fine idea." Dawdi's eyes were clear of confusion. Leave it to him to pick today to hold his memory and mind together.

She shrugged as if she hadn't a care in the world. "Suit yourself." She made her tone as offhanded as possible when she really wanted to scream, stomp her feet, and tell him in no uncertain terms that he could not help with the chores and he should get on his tractor immediately—if not sooner—and leave.

She swept from the room and back toward the front of the house. Zeb's footfalls sounded behind her, but she wasn't about to look at him. She didn't want to see him following behind her as she had so many times before. All those times when they'd snuck off to Millers' Pond to swim alone. Picnics in the woods, even stolen moments in the hayloft away from prying eyes.

"What's wrong with your covering?"

Ivy's hands flew to her head. She couldn't go around with her prayer *kapp* crooked. She had straightened it before she went into the kitchen. Granted, it wasn't like she had used a mirror, but she had worn the covering since she was thirteen. She knew when it was on right and when it wasn't.

She stopped by the front door and peered at herself in the mirror. Everything looked fine to her. She turned her head from side to side. Nothing amiss.

"It's in the back," Zeb said, gently pushing on the back of her head. "There's a big hole right here."

"A hole?" Her eyes widened in alarm.

"Not a hole-hole. A dent, I guess I should say. Rough morning?"

Anger flooded her. The laughing light in his eyes looked less like jovial teasing and more like he thought he knew the secrets she kept. Well, he did. But that didn't mean she wanted to talk about them. "What did you say?"

Zeb eyed her cautiously now. "Nothing. Just that I want to talk to you. Alone." He cast a quick look over his shoulder, back toward the kitchen, where her grandfather sat, still enjoying his cup of coffee.

"That's unfortunate."

"You have chores to do. *Jah*, you already explained that. But I'll help."

"That's not necessary." Ivy donned her coat and retied her knitted scarf around her head.

"I think it is."

"Why?"

"I just think it is."

It was a lie, that much she knew. She had been lying so much about everything to everyone: her grandfather, Helen Ebersol, anyone she had come into contact with over the last couple of years.

"We can't go back, Zeb." The words fell softly from her lips.

Then she stepped out of the house and into the sobering, cool shelter of the porch.

"We can go forward."

She shook her head.

"Sideways?"

He was trying to make her laugh, and the last thing she wanted was to show that weakness. She started down the steps and across the yard. Her breath leaving little puffs of smoke in her wake.

"I said I'd help." Zeb started after her.

She didn't slow down. "I said it wasn't necessary."

"You are about the most stubborn person I have ever met."

"Sweet talker." She ducked into the barn and continued through to the corral on the other side. Zeb was behind her the whole way. One thing was certain: he was as stubborn as she was. Anything she said would be twisted and used against her. The more she protested, the harder he would dig in his heels. Her only hope was to ignore him. Pretend he wasn't there and go about her chores. He would either give up or he wouldn't. Nothing she could say would change it. It had always been that way between them. Why should this be any different?

"You're in early." Her grandfather peered at her over the rim of his glasses. He sat at the table, reading the paper while pots bubbled behind him.

"I had help," Ivy groused. She hadn't wanted help, but she'd had it all the same. And the worst part of it all? She had finished her chores in record time. She had been afraid that Zeb would hang around and want to talk. It had been hard enough to ignore him as he worked next to her, side by side, mucking out stalls, feeding the animals and giving them water. But to have him sit, look at her, and want to talk? No, thank you.

"Dinner won't be ready for another half hour." He turned the page in the newspaper and snapped it into place.

Ivy and Dawdi had an arrangement. She would take care of the outside chores while he took care of the inside ones. That was fine with her. She had never liked to cook. Baking, on the other hand, was a different matter altogether.

But he sat there, reading the paper while pots boiled behind him, looking like they needed to be stirred . . .

Maybe the division wasn't a good one. He couldn't burn the house down feeding the hens.

"Collard greens and venison stew," he said, turning his attention to his paper once more. "Everything's just simmering now. Plenty of time to make some corn bread."

He was hinting. He always said her corn bread was better than his. She thought they tasted the same. Yet he conspired to get her to bake it every chance he got. Same ol' Dawdi. Maybe she had been hasty in her worrying. He was reading the paper, teasing her, and their supper was gathering flavor on the stove top.

"Sure," she said, giving him a nod and a smile. She meant them both, so why did it feel so forced?

She moved toward the cabinet where she kept the cornmeal.

"That boy has a crush on you."

She stumbled, but somehow managed to catch herself. "Zeb Brenneman?"

"That's the one." Dawdi didn't take his eyes from the paper.

"I can't date," she protested with a wave of one hand. "I haven't even joined the church yet."

"About that . . ." This time he did look up, peering at her once again over the silver rims of his glasses.

"I will." She took the container of meal from the cabinet. She couldn't look at him, not and talk about the church and all her shortcomings. "When it's time."

"You don't think it's time?"

It was long past time. Yet too many things had happened. How could she bend her knee and pretend to be holy after all that she had done? How could she stand before the church and confess her sins? There were more than anyone knew. She was so unworthy . . .

Even thinking about such things at Christmastime seemed a sacrilege. "I didn't tell you the best news," she said, her voice overbright. She pulled out her large mixing bowl and started measuring the ingredients.

"*Jah?*"

She didn't look back at him as she spoke and wasn't certain if he was looking at her or the paper. "I got a job at Esther's Bakery. I start tomorrow."

"That's wonderful!" He was on his feet in an instant, the notion of her joining the church suddenly lost. "Forget the corn bread. Let's have cake to celebrate."

"Zeb? Is that you?"

He let himself in the house. "*Jah*, Clara Rose. It is."

His sister-in-law came through the kitchen door, Paul Daniel tucked into some contraption that snuggled him to his mother and still allowed her hands to be free. She carried a dust rag and a spray can of furniture polish.

"You've been to see Ivy." Her words were wise, not a question.

"Obie had no right to tell—"

She shook her head. "Obie didn't tell me anything."

"Then how—?"

"I have eyes, you know."

Was he that easy to read? Could she take one look at him and see through his every defense?

"It's easy to spot love in others when you're in love yourself."

"I don't love her." He shook his head. He didn't. He never had. They had potential was all. Maybe they could have had something. Maybe they could have loved one another, but that time had long ago passed.

"You just keep telling yourself that." She gave him that smile—the one women gave men when they thought they knew what was best for them.

He decided to leave that one alone. "Where's Obie?"

"Over with Gabe Allen. They've been partnering up. Obie sells the puppies. Gabe Allen makes the doghouses."

It was a smart plan.

It should have been yours.

He should be the one in business with his brother. But he wasn't. And all because of pride.

And a broken heart.

Broken hearts were bad enough, but they didn't "go before a fall." His own pride had been his undoing. His own pride had sent him to Florida, had caused him to stay there. His own pride was the reason his heart was broken in the first place. No one to blame but pride.

"Zeb?"

He roused himself out of his thoughts. "*Jah?*"

"I said he'd be back in a little bit." She shifted the baby and patted his little rump through the sling thingie. What he would have given to see Ivy standing there, holding a baby, telling Obie that he, Zeb, would be home soon.

He shook his head at himself. Christmas was making him nostalgic. Weak-minded. Or maybe that was seeing Ivy again.

"I'll be in my room," he muttered and headed for the stairs.

* * *

There was no way she could have said no. How could she turn down the opportunity to work a couple of extra hours? She couldn't. They needed the money. Plain and simple. But now that she was on her way home, the worry had settled in. *What if . . . ?* haunted her. What if her grandfather had lost his way again? What if he were "deer hunting"? It really was hunting season. He could wander through the woods and get shot.

She took a deep breath and said a quick prayer that he was safe. If only she had thought to go over and tell Daryl that she had started a new job. He was a frequent customer in the Super Saver. Most everyone in Wells Landing was. That was how he'd known she worked there. But she didn't have a clue how many times, if any, he frequented Esther's Bakery. He didn't know she worked there and wouldn't know to call her there if something happened.

She sucked in another breath, but this one didn't help either. Not even the prayer eased her mind and calmed her thoughts as she pulled her tractor to a stop. She tugged her coat a little tighter around her and rushed toward the house. She was being ridiculous. Paranoid, even. There was no reason she should believe that something had happened to her grandfather. So why did the thought burn through her like wildfire?

"Dawdi?" she called. She did her best to make her voice sound normal, or at the very least not crazy urgent. She might be alarmed over nothing, but there was no reason to get him worked up over the same. "Dawdi?"

No answer.

Her alarm rose. Had the front door been locked? She had grabbed her key out of habit, her thoughts whirling. Now she couldn't remember. Had there been an auction? Was he working? Was she being overly protective?

"Dawdi!" The urgency in her voice lifted a notch.

Then a small sound. From the kitchen. She raced toward it thinking she would find nothing, maybe her calico cat, Chester, wondering if she was half-crazy. She blamed Zeb. Everything had been okay until he had come home.

She knew that wasn't true. Everything had not been okay before then. Everything had been terrible. He'd just brought it all to the surface.

"Dawdi?" She eased into the kitchen and screamed. Her *dawdi* lay on the kitchen floor in a puddle of blood.

Chapter Four

Dear Lord, please help me. Father God, I beg you. Please let him be okay.

Ivy rushed to her grandfather's side, not caring about the blood as she knelt beside him. Chester sat on his chest as if guarding him until Ivy got back. She meowed at Ivy, then sauntered away as if her work was indeed done.

Ivy turned her full attention to her *dawdi*. There was a big gash on his head, his eyes were closed, and his breathing seemed low and labored. In an instant her mind went through the possibilities as she tried to formulate a plan. Heart attack, then fell and hit his head. Stroke and the same. Slipped on something and his head hit the counter. Thought he was fifteen again and jumping into Millers' Pond, hit his head on the way down.

Whatever happened, it seemed apparent that the blood came from his head. How he had fallen remained to be seen. She wasn't sure what was worse: thinking he was fifteen, with his mind in another time and place, or a heart attack. Doctors knew what to do for the heart. Did they know what to do when the mind went?

"Dawdi?" She cradled his head in her lap and lightly

tapped his cheek. She sniffed, only then realizing that she was crying. Had been for a while, if the moisture on her cheeks was any indication. "Oh, Dawdi." Why had she worked late? She should have been here. But another thought intruded, this one more important. How was she going to get him to the hospital? She couldn't lift him herself. He might not be a big man, but he was larger than she was. She couldn't load him onto the tractor and chug him on into town. Was it even safe to move him?

Her only other option was to run next door to Daryl's house and pray like everything that he was home and could help. But that meant leaving Dawdi alone, unconscious and bleeding. She bit her lip and did her best to come up with another option. But time was slipping away and she didn't know how much of it she had. He seemed to have lost a lot of blood. How much was too much? What if it was a heart attack and he needed immediate care in order to save him?

"Ivy?"

She jerked around as Zeb came barreling through the kitchen door.

"What happened?" He slid to his knees beside her.

"He was like this when I got here." She let go of his face long enough to wipe the back of her hand against her nose. She had thought herself a strong person, but now . . . now she knew the truth.

"Is there a neighbor?" Zeb asked.

"What?" Ivy looked at him, his words washing over her like a warm wave, not settling, just there and gone.

"Ivy." He took her by the shoulders and shook her like one shakes another to wake them from sleeping. "Is there someone who can help? A neighbor? Or . . . anyone?"

Slowly she nodded. "Daryl," she said, coming back to her senses. "He lives east. If he's home, he'll help."

* * *

It took both him and the neighbor to lift Yonnie into the back of the *Englischer*'s car. Thankfully Daryl had been home when Zeb came knocking. Home and ready to help.

Somehow they got Ivy into the back seat with her grandfather while Zeb rode next to the driver. They decided against the Wells Landing Medical Center. They dealt with small emergencies, simple broken arms, deep cuts, and cases of the flu. Since no one knew what had happened to Yonnie, they kept going on into Pryor to the emergency center there. If need be, they could helicopter him into Tulsa, though Zeb said a quick prayer that it wouldn't be necessary. He wasn't sure how Ivy would handle such a thing.

"Here." He handed her the steaming coffee and took a sip of his own. It was terrible, but wasn't that part of the hospital waiting experience? Worry and bad coffee?

"*Danki.*" She took the paper cup and blew over the top of it. But she didn't drink it. Her eyes held that listless, dead look. He had only seen it one time before. He hadn't liked it then, and he didn't like it now. "What's taking so long?" she asked.

He wanted to take her hands into his own, tell her that it was going to be okay. But her hands weren't his to hold. Not now. Nor had they ever truly been. And he didn't know if things were going to be okay. He had never lied to her. He wasn't about to start now. "It hasn't been as long as it feels," he replied.

"It's been forever." She took a sip of the coffee, her face impassive. That she could drink it without a grimace proved how preoccupied her thoughts were.

"It's not even been an hour. These things take time."

"These things?" she asked.

"Tests and all that." He waved a hand in the air in front of him. He was doing a bad job in trying to make her feel better, but he hadn't had much experience with that sort of thing.

He needed to keep her mind off worry and onto something else. He glanced around the brightly lit waiting area. The chairs were covered in pastel fabric that he supposed was meant to be soothing. The walls were a gentle white. The overhead lights threw everything into too much relief. It was too bright, too harsh, too real.

"How long do you suppose that Christmas tree has been up?" He nodded to the four-foot tree in the corner. "These *Englisch*. They start Christmas earlier and earlier every year."

"It is December," she countered.

"*Jah.* That's true. And I imagine it would take a while to put up the tree and take it down. Even longer to get it out of storage."

"Or remember where you put it?"

He laughed. "That too."

She smiled, and a little of the worry seeped from her eyes.

"You know, there's a big Christmas celebration in Pinecraft every year. A big parade with all sorts of vehicles. And clowns."

"At Christmas?"

"And Santa."

"I don't believe in Santa." Her words held a ring of finality. Amish children were never taught about such things.

"I've given it a lot of thought since I've been gone."

"Santa?" she asked. Then she took another sip of coffee, allowing herself a small wince as she waited for him to answer. This was good. The coffee was bad and her mind was occupied.

"Of course."

"Why?"

It was a simple enough question. "Why not? I mean, how

can millions of parents pull such a hoax on their children each year and get away with it?"

"And you've figured this out?"

He nodded. "See, Santa is a lot like Jesus."

"I don't understand."

"It's simple, really. He came and brought everyone on earth a gift."

"Jesus or Santa?"

"Both. Jesus." He shook his head. "Just let me finish."

She motioned for him to continue.

"Jesus brought everyone on earth a gift, and all He asked in return was for people to believe in Him."

"What about works?" she asked. "Jesus is important. He's everything, but a person's deeds . . ."

He knew what she was going to say. Amish didn't believe in saved by grace, at least not the ones where they were raised. A person needed to believe in Jesus, follow His word, and work hard every day in order to *hope* they would get into heaven. Nothing was a sure thing.

"The Beachy Amish I was with don't believe in works. I mean, they believe in them, but—" He wasn't able to finish that thought. A middle-aged doctor with graying blond hair and a pristine white lab coat came through the double doors toward them.

"Ivy Weaver?" he asked.

She nodded and stood, hands trembling.

"The best we can figure, your grandfather slipped and fell, hitting his head on the way down."

"No heart attack?"

The doctor gave her a grim smile. "We want to keep him overnight. With a head injury such as this you can't be too careful."

"Overnight?"

"Was he alone when he fell?"

"*Jah.*" Ivy nodded. "I mean, yes."

"Has he fallen before?"

Ivy answered all the doctor's questions no matter how accusing they sounded. Zeb figured it was simply what the hospital did, but it didn't make it sound any less condemning.

"Can I take him home? Please," Ivy pleaded.

"With a head injury . . ."

"Please," she said again.

The doctor seemed to take in her dress and prayer covering for the first time. "He'll need to be awakened every hour or so. All night long."

If he thought that was going to dissuade her, he didn't know Ivy Weaver very well. "I'll wake him."

The doctor looked reluctant, but nodded. "I'll get some instructions for you to take with you."

Ivy nearly wilted with relief. "*Danki.* I mean, thank you," she said.

The doctor shook her hand.

"He's going to be okay," she gushed as she watched the doctor walk away.

"Ivy . . ." Zeb hated to be the one to bring her down from her happy place. "Don't you have to work tomorrow? How are you going to wake him up all night long, then go to work at the bakery?"

"The Super Saver," she corrected.

"What?"

"I work at the Super Saver tomorrow."

"You have two jobs?"

She shrugged.

How bad were things at the Weaver house? "Let him stay here tonight. If all is well, he can come home in the morning."

"I have to stay with him," she said. Poor girl, she had lost so much. After everything, no wonder she was teary-eyed with exhaustion and relief.

"Fine," he agreed. "Stay with him. I'll call Obie's cell phone and have him go by and do your chores."

"The chores!" she exclaimed. "I've been so wrapped up in everything here."

"No worries," he said. "I'll be right back. You tell the doctor you changed your mind, okay?"

She nodded and sat back down in her seat. "Can Obie feed Chester too? I didn't have time to feed her before we left."

"I know he will," Zeb said, then he turned and made his way down the hallway to the small kitchen/snack area where he had gotten the coffee earlier. It was getting late; it was already dark outside. Granted, the day ended a lot quicker in December, but it had been light when they arrived. They had sat through supper waiting on word. Now that it was over and news had come down, he was sure she would be hungry.

He called Obie from the hospital phone and left a message on his voice mail. With any luck, his brother would get it before he went to bed and he could take care of everything first thing in the morning. It wasn't the best-case scenario, but it would have to do.

Then he fed a couple of dollars into the snack machine and got a bag of chips, a candy bar, and two sandwiches of questionable filling for his effort. Then he poured them both a fresh cup of coffee and started back toward the waiting area.

Ivy smiled when she saw him approach. His knees nearly buckled beneath him. How many times had she looked at him that exact same way? More than he could count. But that had been *so* two years ago.

"Here." He held out one of the sandwiches to her.

"A gift?" she asked.

"Just call me Santa."

She smiled.

"I called Obie and left a message. If anything, I can run by there in the morning."

"Could you . . . could you go now?"

He shook his head. "No."

She blinked at him dumbly. "You can't?"

"No," he repeated. "I'm staying right here. We all go home together."

Once her grandfather was settled in a room, Ivy grew antsy. She had too many questions to ask Dawdi, but the doctor had warned them to let him rest well before asking too much. But even as she thought about it, what good would the answers to her questions be? *How did you fall? What happened next? How long were you on the floor?* Did any of it really matter? Or would the knowledge only serve to make her feel worse about his accident?

She pushed out of the darkened room and left her grandfather lightly dozing and Zeb sitting in the room's only chair gazing at the television as if it held all the secrets in the universe.

There was no one up and about this time of night. She wasn't even sure exactly what time it was, only that it was late. The soles of her walking shoes squeaked against the over-waxed floors as she trod along. She thought she would walk down to the kitchen and get a pop. She really didn't want a drink, but it was something to do.

She slowed as she rounded the corner and entered the square kitchen tucked back on the other side of the supply closet. There were drink machines, coffee machines, sandwich machines, an ice machine, and a microwave, along with a refrigerator and a small round table with three chairs. Two women sat at the table, sipping something that looked like hot cocoa. They shifted when they saw her and gave matching nods, almost unnoticeable.

Ivy nodded in return. She was used to having such an effect on people. She always had. She called it the Prayer *Kapp* Complex. Secretly, that was. For when most people saw her prayer *kapp* they immediately changed. Their voices lowered; they ducked their heads and refused to look at her directly. She wasn't sure if they thought she was so godly she would condemn them or they were worried they would catch something from her. Either way, the women shifted, ducked their heads, lowered their voices, and covertly continued on as if she weren't there.

"They're going to put her in a nursing home," the lady in the blue sweater said.

The lady in the orange shirt shook her head and tsked as if it were a shame. "And after all this time."

Ivy moved to the counter and opened one of the top cabinets. She wasn't sure what she was looking for, but for some reason she wanted to hear what they were saying. Maybe she just wanted to be a part of a conversation. Who knew?

"They've done all they can for her," Blue Sweater said.

"But she's their mother."

"Grandmother," Blue Sweater corrected.

Ivy closed the cabinet, then took a cup off the stack and filled it with hot water. She dumped in a packet of cocoa mix and stirred it with one of the little sticks. A nursing home. Weren't those places terrible? Why did she even care? It wasn't like the Amish even used places like that to house their elderly.

Orange Shirt nodded. "I suppose."

"It's a nice place," Blue Sweater continued. "More of a retirement center."

Ivy moved as slowly as she dared. She threw away the little red stir stick and inched toward the door. She knew the women were aware of her. They had been since the moment she had set foot in the door. Stupid Prayer *Kapp* Complex.

"It's still sort of sad, isn't it?"

"Well, yes and no. Her family simply can't take care of her any longer. She's fallen twice, caught the stove on fire, and lost the dog."

"Lost the dog?" Orange Shirt choked.

"Let him out and they never saw him again."

"But—"

"He wasn't an outside dog. She was supposed to put him on a leash and walk him around the block, but she forgot."

"Oh," Orange Shirt murmured.

"I guess there are worse things."

"Is the home here in Pryor, or in Tulsa?"

"That's just the thing," Blue Sweater exclaimed, then hushed her voice once again. "It's over in Wells Landing. Well, between Wells Landing and Taylor Creek."

She could stall no more. She eased out the door and stood there, straining to hear what the women were saying.

"I didn't know there was a home out there."

Blue Sweater nodded. "It's new."

"Nice?" Orange Shirt asked.

"Very."

"Then I'm sure she'll be very happy."

"Happy?" Blue Sweater laughed. "She'll be just fine. That place has everything, and the best of it. She'll be watched over and cared for. I hope someone does that for me when I get old."

"You're too mean to get old," Orange Shirt said.

Blue Sweater laughed. "Thank heavens."

"Bah, all this fuss." Her grandfather crossed his arms and stubbornly refused to get out of the bed. The night had been much easier than she had anticipated. Someone on the hospital staff came in and checked on Dawdi every hour like clockwork. Ivy slept on the sofa, while Zeb somehow managed to sleep sitting up in the armchair. It wasn't the kind that lent itself to sleeping. The back and seat had hard, vinyl cushions, and the rest was made of some sort of wood. But Ivy knew she wouldn't be able to budge Zeb. And if she were to be completely honest with herself, it was something of a comfort to have him near. She would never admit that out loud. Setting the words free would not change one thing between them.

Neither will allowing him to do your chores and stay with you at the hospital.

She pushed that voice away and concentrated on her grandfather. "If you don't get in the wheelchair, they aren't going to let you leave."

"They can't keep me against my will."

"They can if you don't follow the rules."

"Bah," he said again.

He looked at the wheelchair, then at her. "Your jaw's set at that angle like your *mamm*."

"And what would Mamm say?" She folded her arms, hoping the new position was even more intimidating. She was ready to get home. And she still had to get dressed for work.

The hospital orderly shifted in place, his big hands curled around the handles of the wheelchair.

"Dawdi?" she prompted.

"Bah," he said and slid from the bed. With a shake of his head, he settled into the chair and allowed himself to be wheeled down the hallway.

"Where's that boy?" Dawdi asked.

"What boy?" She knew exactly who he was talking about, but she didn't want him to know that.

"Zebadiah."

"He had to go home and take care of his own chores."

Zeb had stayed with her all through the night. This morning, when they had gotten the all's well release from the doctor, he'd told her he needed to be getting home. He had done more than his share to help her grandfather, and Ivy was grateful.

Her grandfather's injury wasn't as bad as it looked. He had lost what appeared to be a lot of blood, but the doctor had assured them that head injuries always bleed more. Once it was cleaned up, a nurse put bandage strips on it to hold both sides together, and now they were on their way. Her grandfather had groused that without stitches he wouldn't have an interesting scar, but Ivy didn't comment. It was better not to engage him any more than necessary. If he'd gotten stitches he would have fussed that they were making the scar worse.

"Where's your car?" the orderly asked as he whisked them through the front door.

Ivy scanned the row of vehicles idling in front of the hospital. "Do you see an Uber driver?"

The orderly looked about, then pointed to a small silver SUV sitting at the front of the line.

Ivy let out a sigh of relief. One of the nurses had arranged for an Uber driver once Ivy had exhausted all her driver contacts. She had never used Uber before, but how different than a regular driver could it be?

If you still had the Mustang, you wouldn't have to be worrying about this.

She pushed that thought aside and led the way to the car. She confirmed it was her driver, helped her *dawdi* into the front seat, and offered the driver instructions on how to get to their house. He smiled indulgently and said he had everything he needed, but would be sure and ask if he had any questions.

Ivy eased into the back and did her best to relax. She glanced at the dash clock. She had just enough time to get home and change for work. But that would mean all her chores would go undone until she got off that evening. She'd thought she had plenty of time. Who knew getting released from the hospital could take so long?

Not being able to complete the chores wouldn't be so bad if Obie had managed to come by the night before and take care of them. She could feed Chester before she left, and everything else could wait until she got home. But if he hadn't . . . she would have to do them. Animals had to eat. Chickens needed water. And she would be late to work. She was certain that this would give them all the reasons they needed to fire her, and there was nothing she could do about it.

She laid her head against the window and watched the land whirl by. If she didn't think about it too hard, the crazy spinning didn't make her dizzy or sick, but she closed her eyes anyway and allowed her thoughts to drift. In the front seat, the driver and Dawdi talked about corn, winter rainfall, and how quickly Christmas had come around once again. Their driver didn't have a smidgen of Prayer *Kapp* Complex, so she supposed that he had picked up a few Amish during his driving days.

So unlike the women in the hospital kitchen. They had shifted and cast their glances to the side. She had to hand it to them though, they did manage to keep up their conversation. Some folks couldn't even do that.

Ivy had no idea what made a person feel intimidated around her. She supposed that was what it was. Intimidation. Perhaps they felt like her life was extremely pious because of her faith. If they only knew.

A nursing home. Someone was going into a nursing home. Someone's grandmother who couldn't take care of herself. Someone who needed someone around all the time. This family loved her and wanted the best for her, so they shipped her off. To a nursing home.

Nursing home.

The words echoed inside her head, and as the miles passed, Ivy fell asleep.

Chapter Five

Her grandfather whistled low and under his breath. "That boy has it bad."

Ivy looked around the barn and scoffed. "He doesn't have anything." Except maybe a way with barns. Hers was the cleanest she had ever seen it. And she knew there was only one person responsible: Zeb Brenneman.

She wandered into the tack room, noting that everything was in its proper place. Some things that had never had a proper place were now neatly hung on the walls where she could easily find them.

And that wasn't the only thing he had done. He had fed and watered all the animals, raked the yard, scooped out the chicken coop, and swept the front porch.

"See?" Dawdi held up a piece of paper like it was a winning lottery ticket. "I told you that boy has a crush on you. Do you believe me now?" He handed the paper to her, and Ivy quickly scanned it.

Zeb had come over and done everything he could to help her. The inside was up to her, but the outside was taken care of. He had signed it with a Z.

He had to have worked for hours cleaning up the place. And until it was this pristine, she hadn't realized how run-down it had become. The farm was really too big for one person to manage. If she could afford it she would hire someone to help out, but as it was, she would have to take care of it.

"He doesn't have a crush on me." She made a noise to show her skepticism, but her grandfather wasn't listening.

"I always thought he liked you."

There had been a time when she thought he had more than liked her and she had more than liked him. But that time had passed.

"It's good to be home," Dawdi said as they headed back to the house.

"I've got to go to work." She would be on time since the animals were fed and the yard cleaned. She could go to work and not worry about all the things she hadn't done before she left and all the things she had to do when she got back home. And all because of Zeb.

"What do you know about nursing homes?"

It was just after the after-work rush. Seven o'clock and the store would be closing soon. The question had been knocking around in her head since the night before. The more she thought about it, the more she realized she wasn't entirely sure what a nursing home was. Or a retirement center, for that matter. She knew that the *Englisch* used them as a place for their elderly. But that was about it.

Sue Ann shrugged. "Not much. Why?"

Ivy sprayed down her conveyor belt and tore off a handful of paper towels to wipe it down. "No reason. Just thinking about them."

"Amish don't use them."

"No," Ivy carefully said. She wanted to know what Sue Ann knew, but she didn't want Sue Ann to know why she wanted to know. "I heard some people talking about them the other day, and I wondered what they were all about."

Sue Ann nodded. "There are all different kinds. Some are for people who can't care for themselves any longer. Some are for people who can care for themselves but don't want to live alone. I guess those are called assisted living."

Didn't Lorie Kauffman work at one of those places in Tulsa?

"Are they good places?"

Sue Ann shrugged again. "I suppose. I mean, some of them are good, and others . . . well, you can't believe everything you hear on the news."

Ivy put away the spray bottle of cleaner and the roll of paper towels.

"Why do you want to know?"

"No reason," she lied. How many of those had she told in the last few weeks? Couple of years? "Did you know they built a new one between here and Taylor Creek?"

"It's supposed to be really nice. They came in the other day and talked to Bill about supplies."

"Oh, *jah*?" She tried not to look too interested.

"I suppose we'll be seeing more of them now they're all settled in and open."

"I suppose," Ivy repeated. Thankfully she was spared having to say any more, as a customer came up with an overflowing handbasket of canned goods and ears of corn.

She shouldn't be here. It had taken a full hour to decide to come and another to decide how she was going to get here, and now that she was actually standing outside the crisp brick building she was doubting herself once again.

This was not something Amish did. They didn't put their elders in homes, locked away. But this didn't look so much like locked away as like living in style with friends around, shrubs outside, and a caring staff. At least everyone she had seen through the large plate glass windows seemed caring.

She sucked in a deep breath and started toward the tinted glass doors.

The place smelled new, like paint and carpet mixed with cleaners and some type of wax air freshener that burned on the front table.

"Can I help you?" The blond-haired woman behind the circular desk smiled as she asked. She didn't seem to have Prayer *Kapp* Complex, and Ivy approached her, returning her smile as she went.

"I wanted to look around."

Her smile froze a bit, but she recovered nicely. "Of course. Were you looking for someone?" Her gaze was steady, almost searching. Yet still friendly. She was heavyset, with deep dimples on either side of her smiling mouth and hoop earrings that glittered when they caught the light. Everything she wore was black, like the women did in some of those stores in the mall. The first time Ivy had seen one of those women, she had thought they were in mourning. Now she knew that *Englisch* women just seemed to like wearing the color. She found it drab and would rather wear red regardless of what the bishop said or how badly her mother claimed it clashed with her hair.

The woman also wore a small white name tag. ANGIE.

Ivy sighed and twisted her hands together. Why was this so hard? "My *dawdi*," she started. "Grandfather. He's been having some problems, and I was hoping . . ."

"You were hoping that we might have the answer?"

She shook her head. "It's dumb. I know." She needed to leave. Get out of there before someone saw her tractor parked out front. Before someone called the bishop or the bishop's wife and told them that she had truly lost her mind. This went beyond extended *rumspringa*. Beyond letting everyone in town think that she was fast and loose, that she really wore jeans when she thought no one was looking, and that she had honestly kissed three boys.

She had only kissed one. Zebadiah Brenneman. But that was long past.

"Are you and your grandfather having problems?"

She stopped, the kindness in the woman's voice almost her undoing. "He forgets things. And I'm afraid—"

She didn't have to finish. The blonde nodded. "I understand. My grandmother was like that. It took years before we had to do something."

"It's just the two of us," Ivy explained. "I can't always be there. It worries me when I go to work."

"*Therefore do not worry about tomorrow, for tomorrow will worry about itself. Each day has enough trouble of its own.*"

"Matthew," Ivy whispered. She couldn't remember the chapter or verse, but her mother quoted it often. Perhaps Ivy had been worrisome all her life.

"Chapter six, verse thirty-four." Angie held up a small desk plaque, the words written there in scrolling letters. "I need to be reminded from time to time." She rocked her head from side to side. "Okay, a lot. So I keep this here." She set the plaque back in its spot.

Ivy could do with a bit of reminding herself. It seemed she worried about everything these days. Everything except what the good folks of Wells Landing thought about her. But that was something beyond her worry. The damage had been done.

"Maybe you can find someone who can come sit with him. There have to be others who need company."

There probably were, but she had managed to push everyone away when Zeb left. How was she supposed to get them back now?

It's not for you. It's for Dawdi. You can do this for him.

"Maybe." Her voice sounded anything but confident.

"You're welcome to stay and look around." The woman obviously felt bad about turning her away. That wasn't her job, after all, keeping people from placing their elderly in their home.

"*Danki*." Ivy nodded, started to turn back to the door, then spun around to face the receptionist woman. "I can look around? Maybe talk to people?"

"Of course." She pointed to a clipboard on the desk and a nearby pen. "Just sign in. We like to know who our visitors are."

Ivy signed her name, the date, and the time.

"If you go down this hallway, you can go to the rec room." She turned and looked at the clock on the wall behind her. "Right now they should be doing some sort of craft. Painting, maybe. The cafeteria is down this other way. You can go down and have dessert with the residents. There's always an extra pudding cup for visitors."

"Thank you." She made her decision quickly, heading toward the rec room and whatever craft the residents were up to.

The hallway was softly lit, creating a homey feel. Framed pictures of the ocean and soft-colored bowls of fruit graced the walls. Ivy didn't understand the connection, but she found them soothing all the same. She was certain the residents did as well.

Residents. It seemed like such a strange word. But she supposed that was what they were.

Double doors with small glass windows waited for her at the end of the hallway. A plaque above the doors declared it to be the "rec room."

Ivy pushed her way inside and stopped immediately. It was unlike anything she had ever seen. Rows of tables held rows of easels, with chairs and residents behind. But the strangest thing of all . . . Lorie Kauffman was leading the class.

She had heard that Lorie was teaching art to senior citizens, but she hadn't known that she went to more than one elderly home. Or maybe she was there as a substitute.

Ivy wanted to slip into the back row and watch, but for some reason she didn't want Lorie to know that she was there.

Too late.

Lorie's eyes widened, then she smiled, but she never once stopped teaching the class. She looked happy, content even, in her *Englisch* clothes with her long blond hair spilling down her back.

Calhoun. The name suddenly came to Ivy. She wasn't Lorie Kauffman any longer. She had married the *Englischer* Zach Calhoun.

Ivy eased down into the back row by an elderly lady who was painting her heart out, but only in shades of purple. That wouldn't have been so bad, except they were supposed to be painting a Christmas scene, complete with fireplace, hearth, and Christmas tree.

"You should have an easel, dear," the lady said.

It took a moment for Ivy to realize that she was talking to her. Not once while she was speaking did the woman look up from her painting.

"Me? Oh, no. I'm just visiting."

"Of course you are. I bet you're Ethel's granddaughter. Please tell me I'm right."

"Sorry." Ivy smiled even though the woman wasn't looking anywhere but her canvas. "I'm not here for Ethel."

The woman tsked. "Shame. She could use a visitor or two."

"She doesn't have many visitors?"

"Well, none of us do, really. I mean, our families come

when they can. Mostly on weekends and such, but when the holidays start coming around, everyone gets too busy."

"That's sad." She looked around. Everyone in the class seemed to be having a good time, and she figured those who were eating dessert on the opposite side of the building were enjoying their pudding cups. They all seemed well cared for. No one was dirty or unkempt. Someone loved these people, and yet they had put them here and forgot them until the weekends. The thought broke her heart.

"Between you and me," she said, leaning in conspiratorially, her gaze firmly fixed on her purple canvas, "Mr. Dallas is the one."

"The one what?" Ivy asked.

"Why, the one you should pray for. Wasn't that what you were thinking? That you were going to pray for us to have visitors?"

"The thought did cross my mind," Ivy admitted, though she didn't understand how this woman knew her thoughts. Just as much as she didn't understand her Christmas painting all in purple.

"He's a nice man. Came here after surgery." She tsked again. "Not sure what for. But I don't think he's had visitor one since he unpacked. So sad."

"Margery, what are you going on about?" Another woman as blue-haired and wrinkled as the one she sat next to came up, cane in one hand, extra-large paintbrush in the other.

"Ethan Dallas," Margery of the purple paint answered. "Have you ever seen him have a visitor, Reva?"

"Not even once. Good-looking man too."

"Good-looking has nothing to do with his family visiting him."

"I'm talking about women," Reva explained. "I could see a hottie or two flitting in."

"Hush yourself." Margery waved her away with one hand, but never quit painting.

"You think he's good-looking too."

"Every woman in here thinks he's handsome. So what?"

Reva nodded and didn't protest. Whoever this Ethan Dallas was, he must be something to see.

Ivy almost wanted to get up and see if she could find him, but she had tarried long enough. If someone were to see her tractor out front . . .

The chances of that might be slim—after all, they would have to be driving by, most likely with a driver, at this particular time. But her luck never seemed to hold out for long. She was pushing her fortune as it was.

Ivy stood and waved to Lorie, a small farewell. Hopefully Lorie wouldn't say anything to her sisters. Maybe Ivy could get out of this without incident.

"Nice meeting you," she said to the two women around her.

"You too, dear," Margery said. "Though I didn't get your name."

Ivy told them.

"Such a pretty name."

"Such a pretty girl."

"We do hope you'll come back."

"The holidays get lonely without the young faces around."

"Merry Christmas," Ivy murmured, unsure of what else she could say. Without another word, she made her way back down the hall to the desk where she had signed in.

Angie was still sitting there with her not-quite-mourning black and deep-dimpled smile. "Did you have a nice visit?"

Ivy took up the pen and added the time to her line on the log. She wasn't sure *nice* was the word to describe her visit. Maybe *confusing*, *enlightening*, or *baffling*. "*Jah*, thank you."

"You know you're welcome to come back any time. The residents love having visitors."

"Strangers?"

"They don't care. Any new face is a joy to them."

Somehow the thought made her even sadder. She only nodded.

"Ivy." Angie stopped her before she could get to the door. "I know this isn't what you came here for, but I know they all loved having you here."

"Thank you," she said again, feeling as if she was somehow stuck on the one phrase.

"I know you're having troubles with your grandfather. But have you considered this? Aside from the cost and him being away from home, have you thought about what life in a place like this might mean to him since he's been on his own most of his life?"

No. She hadn't thought of that. Dawdi would hate this place. There were no horses, no goats, no chickens to fuss about and over. Dawdi loved outside; he loved his freedom. Hadn't that been the one, main reason why she hadn't packed up and gone to Indiana with her *mamm* and Alan Byler? Her grandfather would hate it up north. He wouldn't survive outside of Oklahoma. A retirement home might be part of their state, but it would still be the same to him: a prison. An exile. A place to go and die.

They were struggling, that much was true, but that didn't mean they had to go down without a fight. Somehow, some way.

Yet the whole way home she couldn't stop thinking about Reva, Margery, Ethel, Ethan Dallas, and the visitors they might not get this holiday season.

* * *

If she had thought the yard was cleaned the other day when Zeb came by, she soon learned it could always be cleaner.

"I told you that boy had it bad for you. When are you going to start listening to me, Irene Jane?"

Ivy sighed. "I'm Ivy, Dawdi."

"Of course." He ran his thumbs down his suspenders and rocked back on his heels. "He'll make a good husband for you."

"I'm not marrying Zeb Brenneman."

"You should think about it."

There were so many things wrong with that idea she didn't know where to begin in addressing them. He hadn't asked her, she wasn't a member of the church, she didn't love him, he didn't love her. "Just because a man comes over and cleans up the yard doesn't mean there's romance in the air."

"It's a fine gesture though."

Fine and unwanted. "Where were you when all this happened?"

Couldn't she leave for just a couple of hours without having to worry that everything would fall apart?

"Bah." He waved a vague hand toward the road. "Doing stuff."

If it had been close to her birthday or if her grandfather was the type to go in for parties, she would have thought he was planning some sort of surprise. But as it was she knew that he had already forgotten wherever he had been.

It's not the worst thing for him to forget.

But how long until he started forgetting where he was before he even left?

The thought was sobering.

"Then how do you know Zeb did this?"

"I've seen how he looks at you. That boy's in love, and not afraid to show it."

That "boy" was in guilt. And that was all.

* * *

Saturday's shift at the bakery was more tiring and more satisfying than any other she could remember. She got up early, before light even, and drove her tractor into town. There wasn't a soul on the roads, and the morning air was crisp and fresh. The day promised to be mild for winter, and she enjoyed the feel of the wind on her face. Too bad she would spend most of the day inside.

She helped bake cinnamon rolls, dinner rolls, breakfast rolls, hamburger rolls, every kind of pie and whoopie pie imaginable, and more cookies than she could count. Snickerdoodles, chocolate chip, sugar with icing, sugar without icing, peanut butter, and an *Englisch* recipe called cowboy cookies. She was told they were Andrew Fitch's favorite, and they seemed to be a combination of oatmeal and chocolate chip, with pecans baked in as well.

I should take some home to Zeb. No, Dawdi. That was who she really meant. Zeb wasn't a part of her life, and he wasn't a part of her home. Regardless of what he had said at the hospital.

At the time, she had been so grateful to have him there beside her. But now she realized what a mistake it really was. She had dropped her guard and let him in once again. And that would lead to nothing but heartbreak.

How long before he got antsy and bored and headed off to Florida once more?

Except that he hadn't been antsy or bored when he left in the first place. Like her, he had needed a little space. Some time to heal, clear his head, and figure out the future. But when he hadn't come back, when her letters to him arrived in her mailbox unopened, that was when everything changed.

Ivy pushed those thoughts aside and concentrated on the road before her.

Beside her in the seat was a sack full of cookies. Oatmeal raisin, Dawdi's favorite. As she packaged them up, she realized she didn't know what Zeb's favorite cookie was. Why? Because they had never gone anywhere for the subject to come up. They had kept their relationship hidden, as it was. She wasn't a member of the church and was therefore not allowed to date. They had snuck around, fibbing about where they were going and who they were going to be with. As far as she was aware, only Obie knew about the two of them. That was why she had helped him make Clara Rose jealous last year. She might not be able to have a love of her own, but she did what she could for Zeb's brother.

She turned the tractor down their lane and pulled it to a stop next to the house.

The front door stood open. Several cardboard boxes sat on the porch, peppered with brown paper grocery sacks from the Super Saver.

"Dawdi?" She slid to the ground cautiously, leaving the cookies on the seat until she could figure out what was going on.

With all the filled containers piled on the porch she would suspect some kind of robbery. But what sort of robber left things?

Maybe they were loading up when her grandfather came back home and surprised them. They attacked him and that was why the door was open. He was prone and bleeding on the other side.

Her mouth turned to ash and her heart pounded in her ears. It was more logical than the first scenario and more disturbing by far.

"Dawdi?" she called again, easing toward the house. Surely they were gone now, but she couldn't be too careful. What-ifs kept circling her thoughts like vultures.

"Irene Jane? Is that you?"

She nearly screamed when Dawdi appeared in the doorway.

He shocked her so, she couldn't even correct him calling her by her mother's name.

"What's going on here?" she asked, hand pressed to her heart to hold it in her chest. It was beating so frantically she was afraid it might leave her body.

Dawdi gave a careless shrug. "I don't know. I came home from the auction and found all this stuff out here. I've been trying to get it all in the house ever since."

Ivy crept up the porch steps as if one of the boxes held a live snake. "What is it?"

"Food, mostly. Some Christmas decorations." He chuckled. "There was even one of those *Englisch* Santas in there. Can you believe that? Who would leave something like that on our porch?"

Who indeed?

"Zeb Brenneman," she whispered, her teeth clinched. He had gone and done it again.

"Why would Zeb leave all this out here for us?"

"Why would he do any of the things he's been doing lately?"

"Love will do that to a man. Even make him believe in Santa."

"Dawdi," Ivy admonished. "You don't believe a word of that yourself. Why are you forgiving him already?"

"The Lord tells us to forgive."

"The Lord also tells us to smite our enemies." She marched back to her tractor, her determination and resolve mounting with each step. She grabbed the bag of cookies and tossed them to her grandfather. "I brought these home for you."

He opened the bag and inhaled deeply. "Oatmeal raisin. Yum. I think I'm going to like this new job of yours."

She gave a stern nod and started the tractor.

"Where are you going?"

"I can't let this continue," she said. She adjusted her scarf back over her ears and swung up into the seat.

The wind was chilly as she drove over to the Brenneman place. She barely noticed, she was so angry. How dare he come to her house and leave food and clothing like they were vagrants or something. She had done the best she could to provide for them both and not to pat herself on the back, and all things considered she had done a mighty fine job. Even if she did say so herself.

She fumed the entire time she drove, only the cool air keeping her from catching fire from anger alone.

Wherefore, my beloved brethren, let every man be swift to hear, slow to speak, slow to wrath: For the wrath of man worketh not the righteousness of God.

The words circled slowly in her head, like a buzzing bumblebee on a lazy summer afternoon.

Wherefore, my beloved brethren, let every man be swift to hear, slow to speak, slow to wrath: For the wrath of man worketh not the righteousness of God.

She told herself that over and over as she chugged along the roads leading from her house to the Brennemans'.

She was no less angry by the time she arrived.

Obie came out onto the porch before she even got the tractor parked and the engine killed. "Hi, Ivy."

"Don't 'hi, Ivy' me," she said. "Where is he?"

"Zeb?"

"Of course, Zeb. Who else would I want to see?"

"Uh . . . no one . . . I guess." He turned back into the house, never before having been witness to her redhead's temper. In fact, not many people got a glimpse. She kept it under tight wraps. It was better that way. When she was young, she had gotten into a lot of trouble over her temper and learned early on that if she wanted peace in her family she had to keep her anger buried. But this . . . this was something else entirely.

She sucked in a deep breath and tapped her foot against the hard ground. First she was going to give him a piece of her mind. Then she was going to tell him in no uncertain terms to leave her alone. It was Christmastime. She had a lot of responsibilities. Meeting all the elders at the retirement home and knowing they might not have visitors for the holiday had tossed her over the edge. She could take no more, and that included Zeb Brenneman and his good deeds. He'd have to save his soul on someone else's time.

"Ivy?"

Zeb stepped out onto the porch, and her heart gave a strange jolt. She wrestled it under control and took a lunge toward him.

"I'm not sure what you mean to prove by coming to my house and leaving all that . . . stuff. But we don't need you. We're doing just fine without your help, and it is not appreciated." She whirled on one foot and marched toward her tractor.

"What are you talking about?"

Back she turned. "You know exactly what I'm talking about."

A strange smile quirked the corners of his mouth. Was he trying to make her angrier? Did he want to see how far he could push her before she completely snapped? She was a good, Christian, Amish woman, but everyone had their limitations. "I'm sorry. I don't."

He didn't look sorry.

"You left a Santa Claus in one of the boxes."

He tilted his head to one side. "And that means I did it?"

She threw up her hands. "Of course! Who else?"

"Anyone, I suppose." He gave a casual shrug and loped down the porch steps. He had left his coat in the house, though he acted immune to the cold.

"Anyone? A Santa Claus? You were just talking about him the other day."

"I thought you didn't believe in Santa."

Ivy growled. This conversation was not going according to her plan. She was supposed to come over here, put him in his place, and make him weak with remorse, then she would hop on her tractor and drive back home.

Remorse seemed completely out of the question.

She turned toward her tractor, weary of this verbal battle of wits. "Fine. If you don't want to admit it, I'm not going to make you. But hear me now, Zebadiah Brenneman, if you ever—"

Before she could finish that thought, strong hands clasped her arms and whirled her around. In less than a heartbeat, she was pulled close and his cool lips crashed into hers.

Chapter Six

He had been wanting to do this ever since he had seen her in church. Maybe even before, on the long bus ride from Pinecraft.

Zeb wanted to linger, kiss her until her lips were familiar again. But she was too angry. He would lift his head and she would be spitting mad. Now was not the time to kiss her. Yet he had been unable to stop himself.

Even with her blazing anger, the kiss was all he remembered and more. How he had missed her.

Yet he released her lips, freed her arms, and took a step back.

High color rose into her cheeks, a shade very near the pink peonies his aunt Eileen grew just over the hill. Ivy's blue eyes shimmered with a light he couldn't name. Recognition? More anger? Confusion? Maybe a combination of all three. But the set of her jaw was unmistakable. He was lucky the Amish were a peaceful people. She looked mad enough to haul off and slap him.

He waited for the blow. He deserved it. Not for leaving whatever it was on her porch. He hadn't done that. But for overstepping. He needed her to set things back the way they should be between them. Once upon a time they had thought they would have more. That time had passed and it would never return. They could only be friends. He knew it. She knew it. So why had he kissed her?

Because he wanted to. Because deep down, he had never stopped.

"I didn't leave anything on your porch," he said once it became clear she wasn't going to hit him.

"Then who did?" Her voice sounded far away, distant, as if traveling for miles before it got to him.

"How am I supposed to know?"

She shook her head. "It had to be you."

"Why? Because of a Santa? Maybe the stuff wasn't for you and someone left it at the wrong house."

"That's about as far-fetched as it can be."

"Maybe. But it is possible."

"Maybe," she repeated, though she didn't sound convinced. She crossed her arms. "Why did you kiss me?"

"It calmed you down, didn't it?"

Her eyes narrowed. She couldn't argue with that, though he thought she might. "Don't ever do that again." She marched toward her tractor, started it, and left without so much as a glance back.

"What was that all about?" Clara Rose asked from behind him.

"Ivy thought I left something on her porch."

Clara Rose's mouth twisted into a slant that told him without words she knew it to be more than that. "Uh-huh."

Zeb shrugged.

"What's really going on between the two of you?"

He swallowed hard and shook his head. "Nothing."

"But there was before?" she guessed.

"*Jah.*"

"Before you went to Pinecraft?"

He nodded.

"I see."

She didn't. There wasn't any way she could understand what he didn't get himself.

"I don't know a lot, but I do know this. If you want to win her back, you are going about it the wrong way."

All she wanted to do was go home. And scream. Yelling nothing at the top of her lungs seemed like a beneficial endeavor. Maybe it would bring her a measure of peace. Add some calm to her day. But it wouldn't erase the feel of Zeb's lips on hers.

There had been a time when she would have welcomed his kiss, but no more. That time had passed. The two of them could never be a couple, and there was no sense even thinking about it.

But she couldn't keep it from her mind.

What had he been trying to prove? That he could still get to her? That she wanted to kiss him whether she admitted it or not? Just what?

And there was still the matter of all the things left on her porch. If Zeb hadn't left them—and she still wasn't sure he hadn't—then who did?

It was more of a mystery than she wanted to solve today.

She parked her tractor at the side of the house and headed inside. Her grandfather had a fire going in the fireplace, and the crackling orange flames brought her up short.

What if . . .

She shook her head. She couldn't allow herself to think about such things. He had a couple of off days from time to time, but even then he knew the dangers of fire. She had to get her worry under control or she'd never be able to leave the house.

"Dawdi?" she called. She removed her coat and scarf, then moved to stand closer to the flickering flames.

Her grandfather came out of the kitchen, wiping his hands on a dish towel, his blue eyes sparkling. "What do you think?" He nodded to the mantel behind her.

There among the traditional greenery that her mother had always used to decorate for the holidays sat the plastic Santa from the box on the front porch.

"Get it down." Ivy didn't wait for him to comply and took the idol down herself. That was what it was. An idol. They shouldn't use such things in their decorations for the Lord's birthday. It was wrong. Wrong, wrong, wrong. How had she not seen it up there when she first came in?

Because she had Zeb on her mind. Zeb and Christmas and her new job that she desperately wanted to keep. She was worried about her *dawdi*, worried about his memory and how she was going to keep him safe.

Just the thought made her angrier. The Santa seemed to represent everything that was wrong with the *Englisch* world and all the reasons she had gone to experience it all rolled into one.

She thrust it to her *dawdi*, who looked a bit crestfallen.

"But I—" he stuttered.

"You what?"

He shrugged. "I thought it was kind of funny. I didn't mean it serious-like."

"It was a joke?" Ivy immediately regretted her harsh attitude. Her grandfather was a known trickster. Harmless little pranks, like hiding all her left shoes the night before church or adding green food coloring to the macaroni and cheese to make it look moldy. She thought she had seen them all. In fact, he hadn't pulled a prank on her in quite some time. Maybe that was why today's was so unexpected. Where had his sense of humor been hiding these last few weeks?

Maybe it's not his. Maybe it's yours that's been missing.

He nodded. "I wasn't going to leave it up there." He tucked the offending plastic statue under one arm and sighed.

"I'm sorry," Ivy said. She truly meant it, more than he would ever know. Between his memory loss, her job situation, and Zeb returning, she had turned into a regular grump.

"Supper's on the table." He tossed the towel over one slumped shoulder and made his way back into the kitchen. Chester trotted behind him, hopeful for an early feeding.

Ivy opened her mouth to speak, to say something, anything, to take the hurt look from his eyes, but she closed it again without uttering a word. How had she let herself get this worked up over nothing? A kiss. A really good kiss. But she had been kissed before. By Zeb, even. And she hadn't lost her head then.

Okay, maybe she had, but that didn't mean she had to lose it again this time. Especially not when it meant hurting her grandfather's feelings.

"Dawdi, wait." She hurried after him into the kitchen, a new apology immediately on her lips.

If he wanted to win her back . . .

Zeb scrubbed his hands down his face and stared at his reflection. There was nothing in his expression to give away his inner turmoil, but the words had been snaking through him ever since Clara Rose had uttered them.

If you want to win her back . . .

Did he? Did he want to win Ivy back?

His reflection didn't answer, just stared blandly at him. Same black hair, same green eyes. The same face Zeb saw every time he looked at his brother. So why did he seem like a stranger?

Because he had a question and he couldn't answer it. Didn't even know where to begin to find the answer.

Did he want her back?

Had he ever had her to begin with?

A small knock sounded at the door of his room. Clara Rose. Had to be.

Obie wouldn't have knocked. His brother would have charged in hoping to find Zeb in an embarrassing way. That was just how brothers were.

Zeb checked the buttons on his shirt, tucked it into his pants, and made his way to the door.

"*Jah?*"

"Obie wanted me to tell you that he needs you in the barn."

"His dog?"

Clara Rose nodded, then quickly retreated.

Zeb loped down the stairs, grabbed his hat, and made his way to the barn, thankful to have something other than Ivy Weaver to occupy his thoughts.

Non-church Sundays were among Ivy's favorite days. Or they had been once. She loved waking up a bit later than usual, not having to rush through breakfast, then having the entire day to just be.

She used to get together with her youth group, or even a group of friends. There was no work to be done. Not much, anyway, and they could relax, enjoy each other's company, and . . . simply be.

In the summer months, they would head down to Millers' Pond to swim and enjoy the afternoon. Maybe have a picnic and play a few outdoor games. But in the winter, when the weather turned cold and unpredictable, they pursued indoor entertainment. It seemed like there was always a volleyball game at the rec center. Sometimes they all got together to make Christmas cards for the elderly, comfort patches for the poor, or even strings of paper chains to decorate their house. It was mostly just silly fun, and before Ivy had taken it for granted. Now that she wasn't invited to any of these activities, she keenly felt their absence. Especially on Sundays when there was no church.

She could get dressed and head over to Vernon Treager's district. They had church opposite from Ivy's district, and a lot of the members of her church went there on their off-Sunday. But she would have to go alone if she didn't take Dawdi with her. He would go if she asked, but she knew he needed his every-other-Sunday day of rest. Going alone wasn't an option.

On days like this, when there wasn't anything for her to do outside her home, and even less for her to do inside, she felt the loneliness closing in.

"You got any plans for the day?" Dawdi asked after the breakfast dishes had been washed and put away. It was about the extent of the work they could do on any Sunday. Now the day loomed before her like a chasm.

Ivy looked out the window at the heavy gray sky. It wasn't a day for going out. She had checked the paper, and there was no rain in the forecast, just heavy clouds to block out the sun.

"I thought I might go . . . visit friends." She had almost said *over to the retirement home* but stopped herself just in time. The idea popped into her head so quickly she almost stumbled. She could go visit Margery and Reva. See what they were doing today. But that would mean her grandfather would be home alone.

He'd been having really good days lately, she argued with herself. The cut on his head was almost healed and might indeed leave an impressive scar. Surely he would be all right for an afternoon. She would have to leave him tomorrow to work at the bakery. A couple of hours. Surely he would be okay for that long.

"Friends, eh?" Dawdi smiled. "I was going to tell you that Tassie Weber and her grandson, Karl, were planning to stop by this afternoon."

Ivy's eyes narrowed, and she hid her smile. "Are you matchmaking, Dawdi?"

"Of course not," he blustered, but he glanced away.

"Then how did they come to be visiting today?"

He gave a quick shrug. "I saw them at the auction. Next thing I know, they agreed to come over for pie."

At least he wouldn't be alone all afternoon.

"Do you think you could be home by four? I'm making oatmeal pie," he cajoled.

She found herself nodding. And not just for the pie. She wanted her grandfather to be happy, and she could tell her coming back to see Tassie and Karl would make him happy.

Driving the buggy to the retirement home took longer than she had anticipated, but it was Sunday, and no tractors were allowed. The buggy was slower by far, which only gave her a couple of hours before she had to head back home. No matter. Something in the home called to her, and she felt compelled to visit once again. It wasn't just that so many of them would not have visitors for Christmas. There was more to it than that. Maybe she felt a little guilty for even considering adding her grandfather to the mix, but it only showed how desperate she really was.

There was nowhere to tie her horse, so she hobbled him instead, patted his neck, and promised him a sugar cube when they returned home.

The air in the home was warm and scented with cranberry and peppermint. The aroma was soothing and seemed to calm her nerves. She was here for a purpose. She might not know what it was just yet, but God would reveal it in time. For now she just needed to sign her name on the clipboard and see where Margery and Reva were this afternoon.

Another woman sat behind the desk today. Ivy supposed Angie had weekends off. This woman was younger by far, maybe even a teenager working to pay for her class pictures for the year.

She smiled at Ivy, her curious brown eyes taking in her prayer *kapp* before dropping to her fashion magazine once again. Ivy signed her name on the clipboard, feeling the young girl's gaze returning to her as she did.

Ivy wrote the date and set down the pen. The young woman shifted her attention back to the glossy pages. She wasn't as helpful as Angie had been. But Ivy could find her way. To the cafeteria for pudding or to the rec room for crafts. Pudding, she decided. She started down the hallway in the direction Angie had shown her the last time she visited.

The teenager shifted in her seat, but otherwise did and said nothing.

The hallway to the left was nearly identical to the one on the right. Soft lights, pastel paintings, oceans and fruit.

Hallways branched off, leading down other corridors with other pastel oceans. There were also signs with room numbers like a person sees at a hotel. Ivy supposed they were there to direct the residents and help them find their way.

Then she came to a wall comprised of glass windows half covered with horizontal blinds. Double doors were propped open, and she could just see the rows of tables.

Ivy made her way inside, surprised to only see one person seated at the table closest to the door. Otherwise the room was empty.

"Is this the cafeteria?" she asked.

The man turned and smiled. He had hair the color of snow and twinkling blue eyes. He was as handsome as she had ever seen, and for one small moment, she wondered if he might be the infamous Ethan Dallas. "This is the game room."

Ivy glanced over one shoulder. "I thought the cafeteria was down this way."

"It is. But you have to take the first turn and go all the way down that hall."

She nodded.

"Are you Ethel's granddaughter?"

Ivy cocked one hand on her hip and stared at the man. "Why does everyone keep asking me that?"

He chuckled. "You obviously haven't met Ethel."

"Is she Amish?"

His smile deepened and he shook his head. "We don't get many Amish here."

Something in his smile, maybe it was those dimples of his, drew her in. Pudding forgotten, she sat down across from him. "But you've had Amish here?" She wasn't asking for her grandfather. She had given up that idea. She just wanted to sit with him and talk to him. She couldn't say what it was, only that it was there. The desire to find out the happiness behind the smile, the intelligence behind his eyes, the stories behind the wrinkles that creased his handsome face.

"No. Not that I know of. But I haven't been here long."

"Is your name Ethan?"

He cocked his head to one side. "Have you been talking to Reva or Margery?"

"Both."

"Ethan Dallas." He offered her his hand.

She shook it. "Ivy Weaver."

"What brings you to Whispering Pines, Miss Ivy Weaver?"

She couldn't very well tell him the truth. "I felt the need to do some visiting. You know, bring good cheer and all, since it's the holiday."

He nodded, but she could tell that he didn't quite believe her. Not that she didn't want to bring good tidings, but that wasn't her primary reason for being there. She couldn't very well tell him her reasons. She wasn't sure she understood them herself. But this place, these people, they called to her, and she wanted to know more of them. Plus it gave her something to do when everyone else was out at parties, meetings, and holiday activities. All the events she hadn't been invited to.

"It's good of you to come."

"Well, they told me there was pudding."

"And there is." He stood and offered his hand once again. "Shall we?"

"Of course."

They left the game room and retraced her steps back to the first hallway and on to the cafeteria. Several other residents were seated at the round tables that dotted the large room. Some sat in pairs, while other tables had three or more. They were a mixed lot, all shapes and sizes of grandparents seated around eating pudding and gelatin out of cups and talking about nothing in overloud voices.

Ethan went through the line and got them each a chocolate pudding, then came to sit down next to her.

"So tell me, Ivy Weaver. What brings a nice Amish girl like you to an old folks home on a fine Sunday afternoon?"

Ivy peeled the top off her pudding, taking her time as she unwrapped her plastic spoon. "Who said I was a nice Amish girl?"

He gave a small nod. "Noted."

"That's not what I meant."

"What did you mean, then?"

Ivy stirred her spoon around in the little plastic cup and

thoughtfully stared at the swirls in her pudding. "There are always rumors," she said.

"I see." And from the knowing light in his blue eyes, she had the feeling he knew more than even what she had told him.

"Things happen." It was all she could say. Tears rose into her eyes, and her throat clogged. Yet what was done was done. There was nothing she could do about it now.

"The love of God," Ethan said. "That's the only thing that's forever. Even the mountains shift and change. What is now, doesn't have to always be."

The words lent her hope. Just a small glimmer, but it was there all the same. But she dared not let it take hold. How she wanted to!

"If only that were true," she said. "If only."

After two more pudding cups, Ivy decided it was time to go home. She didn't want to, but she had promised her grandfather that she would be home when Tassie and Karl arrived. She met a lot of the residents there at Whispering Pines, but still not the mysterious Ethel. Three more people asked her if she was there to see Ethel, and she made herself a mental note to seek her out the next time she went.

She nearly pulled back on the reins to stop the horse, but somehow managed to keep going. *The next time she went.* Was there going to be a next time? It seemed the thought was there. But why? And how? She worried so much about leaving her grandfather by himself.

You left him alone today.

Today had been different. He was having a good day. She couldn't count on those good days. But she wanted to go back. No one there looked at her with pity or condemnation. They simply opened their arms, eager to have a new visitor

to share their day with. The welcome was refreshing and
oh-so needed.

She couldn't go back. There wasn't a way. There simply
wasn't time. She wouldn't get to meet Ethel, but it would be
okay. She had much to do for the Christmas season. She had
plenty of hours she could work, and other things . . . Well,
she couldn't think of any right at the time, but they were out
there.

She turned her buggy down the lane, checking the small
solar clock stuck to the dash. Fifteen till four. She had made
it with plenty of time. She'd had a wonderful afternoon,
more fun than she'd had in a long time. Never mind that she
had spent it doing absolutely nothing; it was still fun and
fulfilling.

There was a buggy parked to one side of the yard. The
Webers had arrived early. She sighed, some of that good
feeling leaking out of her.

It was still going to be a good day. Her *dawdi* had made
oatmeal pie.

She stopped the buggy, only then realizing that the buggy
didn't belong to the Webers. It was Paul Brenneman's.

And Zeb was standing on her front porch.

Chapter Seven

"What are you doing here?" She said the words without any sort of greeting. She thought they'd had an agreement. He wasn't going to bother her and she wasn't going to bother him and somehow they would make it through the holiday season without . . . without . . . well, without starting any more rumors in Wells Landing.

"There's a get-together tonight."

Ivy pushed past him and into the house. "That's nice."

"I want to go." He followed her inside, staring off in the direction of the kitchen. "Is that oatmeal pie I smell?"

"Yes. No. Go."

He blinked and faced her. "What?"

"That is oatmeal pie, and you should go to the get-together."

He shook his head and seemed to bring himself back into focus. "I want you to go with me."

"No." The word landed solid and flat between them.

"Ivy . . ."

She brushed past him and over to the fireplace. Her *dawdi* had a fine blaze going. That was good, because it was promising to be a cold night. Chester lounged in front of the hearth as if the warmth were for her and her alone. "Don't do this, Zeb."

"What if I want to?"

"Stop. You don't have the right to want to." Tears pricked at her eyes. She had been so emotional lately, nearly crying at the drop of a hat. That wasn't like her at all. She supposed it had something to do with the holiday season. This would be her first Christmas without her *mamm* there beside her. Surely that was what was making her so emotional. And her tender feelings had nothing to do with Zeb's return and the heartbreak of yet another Christmas on the fringes.

But she hadn't been on the fringes this afternoon. At Whispering Pines she was just a sweet face that had come to visit. She was a novelty and very much appreciated.

"Ivy, is that you?"

She jerked to attention, ceasing her poking and prodding at the already roaring fire. It needed her attention like a mule needed a dress, but she had to do something other than stare at Zeb like a lovesick puppy.

"*Jah*, Dawdi."

He came out of the kitchen, stopping short when he saw Zeb. "Hello, there, Zeb Brenneman. What brings you out here today?"

"I came to see if Ivy wanted to come to an event tonight."

"Oh?" He raised one bushy gray eyebrow, his beard twitching as he leaned a bit closer.

"The youth group is having a get-together at the bishop's house. Well, Emily and Elam's. The wives want to make popcorn balls to take to the hospital for the children."

"And that's what you're doing tonight?"

He nodded.

Dawdi pinned her with his sharp blue stare. "That sounds like fun. Tasty, fun, and helpful too."

Ivy straightened her spine completely and stiffened her resolve. It did sound like fun, and it was a nice thing to do.

But she couldn't go. She wasn't wanted. She wasn't invited. She didn't fit in any longer. There was no sense trying to pretend that she did. Nor did she want to go to perfect Emily-the-bishop's-daughter's house and see her and Elam happily married like the rest of the couples in their youth group. Some match-ups were a bit unexpected and others not so much. She and Zeb could have been one of those, a surprise. Who would have thought? "I was just telling Zeb that we already have plans for this evening."

Her grandfather's brows knit together to form one thick line of confusion. "We do?"

Heaven help her. Of all the times for him to forget. "*Jah.* Remember? With Tassie and Karl?"

"Tassie Weber?" Dawdi asked.

"Do you know anyone else named Tassie?"

"Well, no," he admitted. "But why are they coming over here?"

The one question she hadn't asked him when he told her of his plans. "For pie. You did remember to make the pie, *jah*?"

Dawdi scratched his head. "Let me check." He spun on one heel and headed back into the kitchen.

She could feel Zeb's gaze on her as she stood there. She refused to look at him. Refused to meet those glass-green eyes of his and have him start to ask questions. She had already told him too much.

"Ivy."

She ignored him. Just a few more seconds and . . .

Dawdi pushed back into the living room, a smile on his face. "*Jah.* I baked a pie."

"Are you sure I can't talk you into going to the Riehls' tonight?" Zeb asked.

"I'm sure," she whispered.

He gave an almost melancholy nod, then started for the door. He put his hand on the knob, and a knock sounded.

"That must be them," he said. Then he opened the door and stepped out of sight.

"Hello, Tassie. Karl," he said.

"Zeb Brenneman," Tassie chittered. "What are you doing here?"

"Same as you. Just visiting."

"Good to see you." Karl's voice drifted in to Ivy. She had known Karl her entire life, but he, like the others, had started to avoid her. Her *dawdi*'s attempts at matchmaking would be all for naught, but at least it gave her even more reason not to go with Zeb.

"I was just on my way out."

"Be safe," Tassie chirped.

"I will." Then his footsteps sounded on the porch, and Ivy knew he was gone.

She made her way to the door, telling herself she was going to greet their guests and not to watch Zeb depart, but she knew better.

"Tassie, Karl," she said, trying to appear as gracious as possible. So many things were running through her head, she just wanted to find someplace quiet where she could be alone and try to sort through it all. But there was no time now. Maybe later.

Tassie Weber clasped her hands and squeezed her fingers. "So glad to see you, my dear."

"You as well." It wasn't like she hadn't seen her yesterday at the bakery. Though Ivy wondered how come Tassie never mentioned it at the time. Had it all been another one of her grandfather's matchmaking attempts?

Like that was going to work. Aside from the fact that Karl had gone the same way as the rest of Wells Landing in shunning her, however unofficially, he was not someone she could ever imagine herself marrying. Karl was big. He had to be close to three hundred pounds, though it was solid man. He stood at least six foot six and made Ivy feel like she was eight years old again. Karl was nice enough, but had a tendency to laugh after everyone else had stopped and to scratch his head like he couldn't figure out the answer. Yet a sweeter person she never knew.

Just as she knew in her heart that he didn't have malice in his heart toward her. He was simply following the actions of those around him.

"Let's go to the kitchen. I know Dawdi's been working on a pie all morning."

Tassie smiled and followed Ivy's direction. "I think it's amazing that your grandfather bakes. Not many men do, you know. *Englisch* ones maybe, but not Amish."

Ivy nodded politely and followed them into the kitchen.

The room was filled with the sweet smell of brown sugar and the warm aroma of freshly brewed coffee.

Tassie chatted away about nothing in particular as they settled themselves around the table. Ivy did her best to nod and comment at the appropriate times, but found her mind wandering back to her morning at the retirement home. More specifically, to Ethan Dallas. She wasn't sure what it was about the man, but he intrigued her. Something in his eyes, or maybe it was his smile, drew her in and made her want to know more. About what, she wasn't sure, she just sensed that he had the answers.

Still, the afternoon went by quickly and before she knew it she was walking next to Karl and Tassie out to their buggy.

"*Danki*," Tassie chirped as they made their way. "It's good to get together, *jah*?"

Karl broke away to fetch their horse and hitch her to the buggy.

"*Jah.*"

Tassie looped her arm through Ivy's and pulled her close. "I would like to come back sometime," she said.

"Of course." Ivy smiled. Why in the world would she

want to come back? Unless she was plotting with her matchmaking *dawdi*.

"Maybe this week sometime." Tassie's answering smile appeared innocent, but there was a sparkle in her eyes. "How about Thursday?"

Ivy opened her mouth to tell Tassie that she had to work on Thursday, but she closed it instead. She did have to work. But if she stayed out a bit she could head over to the retirement home and see Ethan Dallas for a bit before heading home. And if Tassie was visiting, then Ivy wouldn't have to worry about her *dawdi* being alone too long. The idea warmed her from the inside. "I'll be at work on Thursday." *Please don't change your mind.*

Tassie patted her hand. "I'll bring Karl, if that's what you're asking about. It might not look good if I came to visit your grandfather all alone. Plus Karl can help him get a few things done around here."

Ivy murmured something she hoped would pass as an agreement and mulled over what Tassie had just said. She was coming, bringing Karl, and it didn't matter that Ivy herself wasn't going to be there.

"Oh, good," Tassie said, her dimples deepening in her wrinkled cheeks.

By now Karl had finished hitching up their mare.

"What's good?" Dawdi asked.

"I'm coming back on Thursday to see you. Would you like that?"

Dawdi propped his hands on his hips and eyed her. "Are you hinting that you want some more pie?"

"Of course. But if I had only come for the pie, I'd be here bright and early tomorrow morning."

Ivy had no idea what Tassie's words really meant, and she wasn't about to look a gift horse in the mouth, as they said.

The week had gone surprisingly well. The sun had been shining, adding another layer to the crisp temperatures. Her grandfather had settled in and his memory seemed as good as ever. So good in fact that she could almost believe that those worrisome days had never happened.

Her job at the bakery was going great, with the exception of the hostile Jodie Miller. But Ivy wasn't letting someone like Jodie get her down. She had been working hard and doing everything in her power to make herself a better person. And she was counting the days till she could see Ethan Dallas again.

Thursday morning started early with cinnamon rolls, biscuits, and a batch of cookies that was to be delivered to the mayor's office. According to Caroline, the mayor always forgot his wife's birthday, then called up the bakery for an emergency batch of peanut butter cookies with mini chocolate chips, her favorite.

By the time Ivy clocked out and headed for Whispering Pines, she was flush with excitement. It was a strange sort of feeling, like a new beginning. Which was a ridiculous thought. She wasn't beginning anything again. She was merely visiting people who needed to see a friendly face. That was all there was to it.

Still, she felt as if a burden had lifted off her when she walked through the doors. She inhaled deeply that mixed scent of pine cleaner, liniment, and Christmas. That was how she had come to describe the scent burning in the little electric pots. Christmas. It could have had something to do with the shiny decorations that layered the home or the soft music that played throughout. She only knew they were Christmas songs because they played over the loudspeakers at the grocery store and she had heard people complain if they started playing too early. But somehow, here in the retirement home, it seemed to all work. She felt warm, welcomed, and wanted.

She would never admit it to anyone, much less someone from the church, but she liked the Christmas decorations. Even the Santa Clauses and glittery tinsel. She wasn't sure why. It wasn't like they truly represented the spirit of the season. They didn't have anything to do with Jesus, Mary, or the three Wise Men. But they made her remember what the season was about. Strange how that worked. She had been so down about the holidays and all the activities. But passing the paintings as she walked into the foyer brought back memories of that first trip to the home. She smiled as she passed Margery's purple painting. She'd have to find out if Lorie was teaching another class soon. Ivy would love to talk to her and see how things were going for her.

Ivy envied Lorie's escape. Not that she wanted to leave, but she wanted that fresh start she had felt when she came into the retirement home.

"Ivy, right?" Angie was seated behind the desk once again.

"That's right."

"I didn't think you'd be back. Are you still thinking about your grandfather?"

Ivy shook her head. "I like visiting the people here." It was a simple answer, but true all the same.

Angie smiled and pushed the clipboard across the desk toward her. "Welcome back."

Ivy signed in and made her way down the hall. She wanted to check in the game room and see if Ethan Dallas was there. If he wasn't, she'd double back to the cafeteria. Pudding was always a good idea.

But after checking those two rooms and the craft room, she headed back to the front desk and Angie.

"Yes?"

"I've been looking for Ethan Dallas," Ivy admitted. "Do you know where he might be?"

Angie thoughtfully tapped the end of her pen against the

desk blotter. "Thursday afternoon?" she queried no one. "I'd say he's probably in his room taking a nap."

Ivy did her best to hide her disappointment. "Oh. I see."

Angie waited as if she expected Ivy to say something. "Aren't you going to ask me what his room number is?"

"You can tell me that?"

"I think he would love to have a visitor. He doesn't get many. Any," she corrected.

"Okay." Ivy nodded. "I would like that too."

Angie checked her list, then told Ivy the number. "It's down the second hallway on the left."

"*Danki*," Ivy said. "Thank you."

She made her way cautiously down the hallway until she came to his room. She knocked and a few moments later, the door opened.

Those twinkling blue eyes widened as he saw who was at his door. "Ivy. Come in. Come in."

"Are you sure it's okay?"

"Of course." He stood back to allow her entrance.

"I just wanted to check on you. See how you are doing today."

He motioned for her to take a seat on the small sofa just inside the room. He left the door open and sat down across from her in the comfortable-looking armchair. "I'm well," he said simply.

Ivy looked around at the plain, tan-painted walls, her gaze landing on the generic furniture and finally the three framed snapshots on top of the television. "Is that your family?" she asked with a quick nod toward the photographs.

"My son, my grandson, and my wife."

"Your wife? I didn't know you were married." If he was married, what was he doing here?

His twinkling eyes dimmed just a bit. "Widowed."

"I'm sorry."

He smiled away her apology. "No need to be. We had a wonderful life together, raised a great family, and now she's gone on to her reward."

Not knowing how else to respond, Ivy nodded. She wanted to ask how he could be so confident in his belief that she had been rewarded in the next life, but the words sounded harsh in her head, and she couldn't imagine them sounding any better once spoken. "You loved her." It wasn't quite a question.

"Very much so." He shifted in his seat, and Ivy remembered that he was recovering from surgery.

"Do you need to walk or anything?" she asked.

"I'm fine. Just trying to figure out what a sweet girl like you is doing in a place like this."

His words held a funny ring and she smiled, hoping her response was appropriate. "Angie, the lady in the front, said a lot of residents didn't have many visitors, so I decided that I might sit with a few people and . . ." She trailed off. *Brighten their day* sounded arrogant. Who was she to brighten someone's day? But she wanted to help, and this was all she knew to do.

"You came to sit with old folks?"

She nodded.

Ethan softly chuckled. "Surely a young girl such as yourself has all kinds of things to do with beaus and friends alike."

Ivy frowned. *Beaus?* "I—uh . . ." She couldn't respond. The truth was too painful, and a lie wouldn't do. She had been telling fibs of one kind or another for so long that they left a bitter taste on her lips. A taste she had grown weary of. "I don't have any beaus." Not even Karl Weber. And especially not Zeb Brenneman. "I don't have any friends either."

Ethan shifted once again, and Ivy bit back the urge to ask

him if everything was all right. "No beaus . . ." he mused. "I might believe that. But no friends?" He tsked.

"It's a long story," she replied. At least that was the truth.

Ethan swept one arm across, indicating his sparse surroundings. "Girl, I have nothing but time."

Ivy met his gaze. She wanted to tell him. She wanted to unburden herself. But that wasn't why she came here. She came here to feel like she had done some good in another person's life. How could she do that if she started blabbering all her secrets? "It's not very interesting." That much wasn't a lie. Her life wasn't interesting, and a man of the world like Ethan Dallas would most likely find her tale utterly boring.

"Why don't you let me be the judge of that?"

How she wanted to! She shook her head, her prayer *kapp* strings barely moving with such a small motion, but they tickled her neck, and she shivered. She let out a small cough.

"Where are my manners?" Ethan stood. "Would you like a drink? I think I have apple juice or water. Or if you want we can head down to the cafeteria and pick up a pudding or two."

Ivy smiled at his flirtatious manner. "Water would be fine."

"Water it is." He ducked into a doorway, and for the first time, Ivy registered that he had a small kitchen area sectioned off by a half wall that had a counter on the living room side of it. A bar, she thought they called it, though there were no drinks and it wasn't round. At any rate, Ethan pulled a pitcher from the fridge and poured them both a glass of water.

"Here we are." He handed her one of the glasses, then returned to his seat. "So you want to come visit and help make our days brighter."

"Something like that."

"What about your days?"

"My days?" She shifted this time. "My days are fine."

"Of course." He said the words, but she could tell that he didn't believe her. Why should he? Her days weren't fine, but she couldn't complain. She had it better than some. Most. "Tell me," he started again. "What's it like being Amish?"

"I . . . I don't know." It wasn't like she knew anything else, just the time she had spent with the *Englisch* in her payback *rumspringa*. A lot of good that had done her.

What was it like being Amish? She had never really thought about it before.

"You don't get asked that all the time?"

She shook her head. "Most people want to know if we really don't have electricity and how we can shun those we love."

"I know about the electricity. Tell me about shunning."

"It's hard to explain to someone who has never been a part of it. But it's not a punishment. It's to bring church members back into the fold."

"I'm afraid I don't understand."

"Say a man is suspected of gambling."

"Gambling?" One snow-white brow rose to an interested angle.

"*Jah.* He would be offered counseling and such, but if he can't stop gambling, then he would be shunned."

"Forever?"

"Until he goes before the church, kneels, and confesses."

"So the shunning is to encourage him to return to his beliefs."

"*Jah.*" She nodded. He surprisingly understood it. But she would admit if asked that there were nuances to some of their *Ordnung* that she couldn't quite fathom herself. Some things just had to be taken on faith.

"Hmm . . ." Ethan thoughtfully rubbed one finger against his chin, just under his lower lip. "That's very interesting."

She had never had anyone ask her about Amish beliefs, and certainly no one had ever declared them interesting. She wasn't entirely sure she was comfortable with the conversation.

"Did you say that middle one is a picture of your grandson?"

Ethan smiled with obvious pride. "Oh, yes, that's Logan." He shook his head with affection. "That boy. Definitely has a mind of his own."

She supposed that was what some had said about her. "How so?" It would be a good change to hear someone else's woes for a while.

"He decided to join a Baptist church down in Texas. They're good people, I suppose. They do these missions in Central and South America. He's gone down there now. I don't even know where. Colombia, maybe. They're building houses for the poor and trying to bring people out of the drug trade."

"Isn't that dangerous?"

"I suppose so, yes. If they upset the wrong people. But he seems very happy with his choices. Regardless of how worried everyone in the family is."

"I would think that you would be proud of him." The Amish went on mission trips. They collected for Haiti and went to places of natural disasters and helped rebuild. Ivy herself had never gone, but she had wanted to. Once upon a time.

"I thought pride was a sin to the Amish." Ethan smiled, taking the sting out of his words.

She shrugged.

"We are very proud of him, except . . . well, he left his church to do this sort of work. And that has his mother pretty upset."

"He had to leave the church to do mission work?" She had no idea.

"No. Not really. That was the choice he made. He was raised Catholic, and his parents were very devout. They managed to stay with their church and do the work of their hearts."

"Catholic?" She knew less about Catholics than she did about Martians.

"He's a good boy though."

"Has he come to see you?"

Ethan shook his head. "He's finishing up down there, then he promised he'd be in, but . . ." His voice cracked a little and he cleared his throat.

"'Were Catholic?' Does that mean his parents left the church as well?" she asked.

"His father died. God rest his soul. His mother still goes when she has the time."

"I'm sorry," Ivy murmured, then something in his voice made her press on. "But your daughter-in-law, she comes to visit you?" She didn't want it to be a question, but it came out that way all the same.

"She's very busy," he explained, which was no explanation at all.

Ivy searched his face for signs of what was going on behind those twinkling blue eyes. She could find nothing. "But you're recovering from surgery."

He frowned. "Who told you that?"

"Margery. Maybe Reva."

"Of course." He pressed his lips together. She couldn't tell if he was angry or trying not to sigh.

"You're not recovering from surgery?"

"No," he said quietly. "I'm dying."

Chapter Eight

He was dying. That sweet old man with the sparkling blue eyes and crinkles of laugh lines that winged to his temples was dying.

Ivy wiped the moisture from her cheeks and blinked away new tears. She had managed not to cry in front of Ethan. He had made his announcement so calmly that she almost believed she had made it all up.

Then he rose and escorted her down to the cafeteria to get a pudding and check up on the other residents of the Whispering Pines Senior Living Center.

"They don't know," she had whispered.

He shook his head. "And I'd like to keep it that way."

"But . . ." She hesitated. "You told me."

"I'm certain you can keep a secret for me. You seem to have a few of your own."

She couldn't argue with that. "Why don't you want them to know?"

Ethan finished up one pudding cup and reached for another. "That's not getting any chocolatier."

She looked down into the creamy brown dessert. It was deceiving. It looked like other things, including black mud, but it was sweet and tasty. Deceiving. Tricky. She took a hesitant bite of the pudding, her appetite and desire for the sweet having gone long before she sat down with the cup.

"You aren't going to tell me." That was something she couldn't wrap her mind around. He would tell her that he was not long for this world, but he wouldn't tell her why she was the only one, staff excluded, who knew his fate.

"I don't want anyone to feel sorry for me," he said. "I've had a good life. I've made my peace with God and this world. Now I'm just waiting."

"To go to heaven?"

"That's right." He finished up his second pudding and eyed her half-eaten first cup. "If you don't get a move on, I'm going to finish that for you."

She pushed it and the unopened one sitting at her elbow across the table toward him. "I don't think I want it." She sat back in her seat and crossed her arms. She needed something to do with them. She needed to walk, swing her arms from side to side, expend some of this energy that coursed through her.

"Eat." He pushed her pudding back. "You need it just as badly as I do."

She smiled and shook her head. "No one needs pudding."

Ethan returned her smile with a grin of his own. "Girl, now there's where you're wrong."

Somehow she managed to finish her opened pudding, but they sneaked the unopened one out of the cafeteria so he could store it in his fridge for later.

"What from?" she had asked him as she was getting ready to leave.

"Cancer," was all he said. He didn't elaborate as she had heard others do. He didn't tell her where in his body it was. How big compared to everyday objects or what stage it was in. He didn't classify it. It was merely cancer. And he was dying. She supposed at this juncture, what did it all matter?

Ivy wiped at her cheeks once more and pulled her tractor

into the lane leading to her house. She needed to get herself together. She had cried more over Ethan Dallas than she remembered ever crying before.

Ethan had seen something inside her, something she had known was there all along, but could never find. Something she had hoped was there. It seemed she had been going around not caring for way too long. She had been putting up a front, telling everyone how tough she was. How she didn't care about the rules, they didn't apply to her, and she wasn't about to follow them. Then this man came along, and now everything was clearer and more confusing all at the same time.

She sniffed and wiped her nose on the back of her gloved hand. It would be much easier to wash her gloves than her winter coat. If what the weatherman on TV said was true, they were in for a cold time the next few days. No snow, which in her opinion would have made all the frigid days worth it, but snow usually didn't fall until January or February.

Who knew what could happen between now and then?

She parked her tractor and got down, rubbing her nose and eyes as she made her way into the house.

"Ivy, is that you?" Tassie called from the kitchen. "I have a new pot of coffee on. Come in here and warm yourself."

She stopped only long enough to give Chester a full-body stroke of greeting, then she did as she was bade. As she stepped into the room, she stripped off her soiled gloves, then held her hands out to the fire-burning stove in the corner of the kitchen. The heat felt good on her fingers, their tingling reminding her that was she alive.

"Have you been crying?"

She shook her head. Another lie. "I rubbed my nose is all. Why? Is it red?"

"Very."

Ivy slid into one of the kitchen chairs and watched as

Tassie ran one bony finger down the open book on the table. "Is that . . . is that my recipe book?"

Tassie nodded. "I believe so. Your *dawdi* gave it to me when I promised to cook for the two of you tonight."

"Gave it to you?"

"Not really gave. *Let borrow*, let's say that."

Ivy had thought her mother had taken the book with her when she left. She stared at it as if it were some unknown creature, then shook herself from her stupor. Her feelings were mixed. She was happy the book was here, jealous that Tassie was cooking from it, and confused as to her grandfather's actions. Hadn't he remembered she was looking for the cookbook? She had gone through everything trying to find it. All the cabinets and drawers. All the little cubby spaces in all the furniture. She had even gotten on a chair and checked the tops of the cabinets. He had watched her, shaking his head the entire time. He had known she was searching for it. So why hadn't he said something?

That was then, she told herself. He might have misunderstood. He might not have realized what she was truly looking for. He might have simply found it later and forgotten that she had been looking for it.

"It was your *grossmammi*'s, *jah*?" Tassie shot her a sideways look that was as unreadable as it was covert.

Ivy nodded. "How did you know?"

Tassie smiled. "I recognized the handwriting."

"You did?"

"Me and Mary Ann, we were good friends once upon a time. We did everything together until . . . well, until we were in our baptism classes." She sighed. "Never mind. It's all in the past now."

Tassie and Mammi were friends? She had never seen them say two words to each other. As a matter of fact, she

had watched her grandmother go out of her way to avoid
the other woman.

"You don't mind me using it. Do you, dear?"

"No," Ivy whispered. And this time it wasn't a lie.

"And I'll take two dozen snickerdoodles and a peanut
butter pie." Gertie Miller smirked at Ivy and waited for her
to comply. "For my Jonah."

Ivy nodded to show she understood and slipped on a fresh
pair of serving gloves.

Buddy Miller shifted beside his mother and eyed the
cupcakes. Ivy had just made them that very morning.
Chocolate with snow-white peppermint frosting sprinkled
with crushed pieces of peppermint candy. The perfect treat
for the holiday season.

He tugged on his mother's arm.

"Honestly, Buddy." She pulled away.

"Can I have one of those? Please." He smiled, and Ivy
wondered how Gertie could tell him no on anything. Buddy
was one of those special children that the Lord sees fit to
give to some families. Born Ivan Dale Miller, Buddy, as
everyone called him, had Down syndrome—at least, that
was what she thought it was called. She had heard others
call him *mongoloid*, but somehow that didn't sound like an
appropriate title. He was a little slower than most, and his
speech wasn't always so clear, but his heart was as big as
she had ever seen.

"May I?" she asked, nodding toward the cupcakes. "On
the bakery."

"Really?" Buddy's eyes glittered with happiness and
excitement.

"If your *mamm* says it's okay."

One good thing about working at the bakery: Even those

people who refused to talk to her at church had to talk to her in order to get their sweets. It was almost a satisfying dilemma.

"I suppose." But Gertie's mouth was pinched into a tight little knot. Ivy wasn't sure if she had planned on buying Buddy the sweet or not, but this way was even better. Who could turn down a free cupcake? And to have to take it from her, Ivy Weaver, the wild child of Wells Landing? Beautiful. Plus, she delighted sweet Buddy. Ivy would ring up the cake later and pay for it out of her own pocket, but it had been worth it, completely and totally worth it.

Buddy danced in place as he waited for his mother to pay for their other goods. He held the cupcake container gently in his hands as though it would shatter if disturbed and followed his mother to the door. "*Danki*, Ivy." He waved and followed her out.

Ivy expelled a heavy breath, only then realizing that she had been holding it. Her shoulders collapsed under the weight of her determination to stand tall and not be intimidated. Her mouth hurt from smiling so much.

"She's exhausting."

Ivy straightened and spun around to find Caroline standing there.

"I scared you. I'm sorry."

"It's okay." Ivy smiled to back up her words. Then she moved to rearrange the showcase to fill the holes where the pie and the cupcake had been.

"You can't let people like that get you down." Caroline's words were quietly spoken but stopped her in her tracks.

"That's easier said than done." What did Caroline Fitch know about such matters? She had everything: a family, a loving husband, three beautiful children, and a horse farm to rival anything else in Green County.

Caroline nodded. She was such a pretty woman, even when she was exhausted, as she was now. She looked thin and wan, but she still pushed through. Esther had cut her hours back to part-time, which left more for Ivy, but Ivy would have rather had Caroline smiling and not so tired.

"Practice," Caroline said. "The more you practice, the easier it will become."

It was on the tip of her tongue for Ivy to ask her how she knew such things, but she refrained. "Why do you work?" she asked instead.

Caroline grabbed a rag and wiped down the top of the showcase, then paused, her expression thoughtful. "I need to have a certain level of independence." She raised a hand as if already anticipating Ivy's response. "I know. I know, but I come from a very conservative district in Tennessee. Andrew understands. I need to know that I can take care of myself and the children if anything were to happen to him."

"I get it." And she did. It was one of the things that kept her up at night. Her mother had sacrificed all to marry a man who would take care of her. She had left Ivy and Dawdi alone in her wake, struggling to find their own way in the only home they had ever known.

"Do you ever go by that retirement home out on 412?"

Caroline paused in her task of rearranging the cookies and thought about it for a minute. "That's the new one, right? I've not been to the new one. But I went with some friends caroling out at the other one. I think they call it assisted living. Whatever that means. Why?"

"Just curious." She didn't want to tell her that was where she was spending all her free time these days. What there was that she got out of it. She wasn't sure how it would be received that she would rather be at a home for the *Englisch* than at her own home. But when she got to Whispering Pines, her own problems seemed to melt away. They were her problems, and she hated them. But they were nothing compared to the issues the seniors faced there.

"It seems like a nice enough place," Caroline added.

"*Jah*," Ivy agreed. "It does, at that."

They spent the remainder of Ivy's shift preparing for the next day's special: a baker's dozen of cookies for the price of twelve. It was only one cookie free, but everyone in Wells Landing preferred a bargain, however small.

Once the cookies were replenished to Caroline's satisfaction, Ivy clocked out. She should go right home, but the retirement center was calling her name. What would it hurt for her to run by there real quick and check on Ethan Dallas?

She buzzed over as quickly as she could, hustled inside and signed her name, then made her way to his room. She knocked on the door and waited impatiently for him to answer.

When he didn't, she knocked again. And once more, her worry starting to rise. The man had no one to worry for him. What had he said? His son was dead, his daughter-in-law too busy, and his grandson somewhere in Central or South America building houses for the poor. She may be all that her grandfather had, but he had her. And she him. Ethan Dallas had no one.

"Ethan!" She pounded on the door, her anxiety mounting. "Ivy?"

She spun about at the sound of her name. "Ethan?"

He was coming down the hallway toward her. Whole and safe. Relief flooded her. "You're okay?"

"Of course I am."

When he got close enough, she rushed toward him and flung her arms around him. "I was so worried about you."

His arms were hesitant, but they came up and settled about her. "Why?"

"You said—" She couldn't even say it now.

Ethan chuckled. "I told you I was dying. I didn't mean today."

She squeezed him a bit tighter, then let him go. It was

completely out of character for her to hug anyone outside her family. Especially an *Englisch* man in the hallway of the retirement home. "Good." She pulled on the waistband of her apron and gathered herself back together.

"What are you doing here?" he asked.

"I can't stay," she said. "I just wanted to make sure that you are all right."

He held his arms out at his sides. "Right as rain," he said. "Fine as frog hair."

"Frogs don't—"

He chuckled. "Just something my granddad used to say."

Ivy laughed and nodded, though she really didn't understand. Ethan was okay, and that was all that mattered. "I'm sorry. I need to go. My grandfather is waiting on me."

He nodded. "Will you come back?"

"Do you want me to?"

"I would love for you to come visit again."

"How about next Thursday?"

"It's a date," he said.

Ivy smiled all the way home. Even the chilly air couldn't dampen her spirits. Ethan was fine. Her grandfather was doing better. She loved her job. Only one part of her life wasn't as she wanted it.

Well, two, she thought as she pulled into the drive.

Zeb was sitting on his tractor as if he had been waiting. His demeanor said he had been there a while.

He was like a thorn in her side. Or perhaps it was a splinter that had festered.

"What do you want, Zeb?" Her good mood disappeared in a heartbeat.

"So good to see you too, Ivy."

She climbed down from her tractor and braced her fists

on her hips. "The weather's been cold, la-la-la. But you didn't come here to talk about that."

"No," he said simply.

"Why are you sitting out here? Where's my grandfather?"

"I don't know. I got here, and there was no answer. So I waited for you to come home."

"He's not here?" Panic reared anew.

"I guess not. I mean, I haven't seen him. Is he supposed to be here?"

"Of course! He lives here." Her voice rose with her panic.

"Calm down," Zeb said soothingly. "We'll look for him."

Ivy swallowed hard and set off toward the barn. Maybe he was in there.

She ducked inside and searched everything, from the tack room to the empty stalls where they stored extra supplies. He wasn't in the barn, or outside the barn. He wasn't in the cellar, the hay barn, or the toolshed. He wasn't on the front porch or the back porch, and with each place she checked off her list, she grew a little more agitated. She had to find him. Had to. And he had to be okay. There was simply no other way for it to be.

"He's not here." Her breath was coming out in ragged, short bursts. Where could he be? Where should she look first?

Zeb grabbed her by the shoulders and forced her to look him in the eyes. "Getting yourself all worked up is not going to help. Let's go in the house and talk through this."

"But—"

"No buts. We're going to sit on the couch and pet the cat like calm and rational people. Then we can think of all the places he could have gone. Okay?"

Reluctantly she nodded. The last thing she wanted to do was say that he was right, but he was.

"Good. Come on." He took her by the hand and led her

up the porch steps, then waited patiently as she got out her key.

She fit it into the lock and it immediately gave way. "Zeb." She did everything in her power to keep the concern from her voice. Now truly was the time to be in control. "The door wasn't locked."

"And he locks it when he leaves?"

She nodded.

"Then he has to be here."

"Or someone else is in there."

"Ivy."

She shrugged. It was Christmastime, and the percentages for home invasions increased the closer they got to the holidays. No one bothered to check for power lines, and many an Amish home had been broken into by someone trying to find gifts under the tree.

"There's no one in there."

She wanted to ask him how he could be so sure, but she stopped herself. "Let's go," she said instead.

They stepped into the house. Ivy looked around, then jabbed Zeb in the ribs. "Don't you think we should have a weapon?"

"A weapon." It wasn't quite a question.

"*Jah.* In case of an attack."

"We're Amish," he pointed out unnecessarily.

"I know that. But they're not."

"What are the two of you carrying on about?"

Ivy slapped one hand over her mouth to keep herself from screaming. "Dawdi! What are you doing here?"

"I live here."

Zeb burst out laughing. "So you do."

"That's more than I can say about you. What are you doing here, boy?" He said the words, then shot Ivy a wink.

Ivy's legs had turned to jelly. She had been so worked up, and for nothing. Her grandfather was fine. Who knew why he hadn't answered the door? It didn't matter. The fact that he was safe was more than enough for her. She drew in a deep breath. Her hands were shaking. Her heart was pounding. She needed a minute to get herself back in order. Apparently, that wasn't to be.

"I came to ask Ivy to go to a Christmas card party with me tomorrow night."

She shook her head. "I can't." She wanted to tell him that she had to work, but it was Sunday. She couldn't use that as an excuse. But that didn't mean she was going.

"Not can't, won't," he corrected.

"All right then, won't."

"Why not?"

She looked at her grandfather, who was watching the two of them as if they were a live play put on for his singular enjoyment. "Dawdi," she said. "Don't you have something to do?"

"Not that I can remember." He smiled innocently.

"Then find something," she said, her teeth gnashed together.

"Fine." He sniffed, feigning hurt, and scooped Chester into his arms. He scratched her behind the ears and spun on his heel. He was mumbling under his breath as he headed off to his bedroom.

She took another, not-so-soothing breath and turned her attention to Zeb. "You know why I can't go to the party with you."

"See? That's where you're wrong. I don't know why you won't go with me. It seems like it will be a lot of fun, and we're making cards for the men and women at the VA hospital in Muskogee."

"Isn't that a conflict of interest?" she asked, hoping to distract him from the original topic.

"We may not fight, but I've long since come to terms with the idea that in today's world it might be necessary for some. And I'm glad those some fight for me. Some of these soldiers have been there for years. Some have no family and need others to support them."

She couldn't protest further lest she look petty and selfish. "I don't want to go to a party where I'm ignored."

"But the soldiers—"

"If it's that important, I can make one here."

"You're missing the point."

Ivy shook her head. "You're missing the point. No one in this town wants anything to do with me. Why should I go where I'm not wanted?"

He stood stock-still, just looking at her. Finally, he spoke. "Do you have another boyfriend?"

A bark of laughter escaped her. The handsome face of Ethan Dallas popped in front of her mind's eye and made her laughter increase. "First off, in order to have another boyfriend, I would need to have a boyfriend. Which I don't. And secondly, why would I have a boyfriend?"

"You're never here when I come over."

"Job. Not boyfriend."

"You never agree to go out with me."

"Nor will I."

"Ivy."

"Zeb." She crossed her arms and waited for his reply.

He shook his head. "You are the most stubborn person I have ever met."

"Ditto."

He looked like he wanted to say more, but he pressed his lips together. "Fine," he said after their stare-down. "Don't come with me. I don't care."

His tone belied his words. If he didn't care, then why was he quickly turning a bright shade of pink? The color made his eyes look even greener.

She stepped aside as he started for the door.

"I retract my invitation," he said, one hand on the knob.

"Noted." She gave a quick nod.

He growled under his breath, rolled his eyes, and let himself out into the cold.

"That's no way to treat a boy with a crush." Her grandfather eased out from his hiding place in the hallway. He still held Chester in his arms, a sure indication that he had never made it to his room and had heard their entire exchange.

"I've never been good with such things," she muttered and headed for her room.

That was the second time Dawdi had mentioned Zeb having a crush on her. Which was ridiculous. So bizarre that the words kept her up most of the night. He didn't have a crush. He just wanted things to go back to the way they were, but that wasn't possible. Not for either one of them.

Consequently, she was exhausted all during work and dragging around while shoppers came in for the weekly cookie deal. Finally, her shift ended and she hauled herself home. Her grandfather had dinner ready and was smiling all the while, like he had a secret no one knew but him. Any other day she might have asked what he was so chipper about, but she didn't have the energy.

To make matters worse, she couldn't sleep. Who had gone to the party? Were they still there or had they gone home? All night long she listened for the sound of tractors chugging down the road. Not that she would have been able to hear them. The weather was cold. Christmas was on the way. The windows were closed tight. But still she listened.

And stayed up.

Which made her late getting up the next morning.

Church Sundays always started early, but there was something comforting about the ritual. Her grandfather would get up and start coffee and breakfast as she went out to feed all the animals. Then they would have their breakfast, get dressed, and drive the buggy to the home of whoever was hosting this service. This morning, however, the ritual was thrown out the window as she scrambled to get ready. She rushed around, wishing she had time to iron her white church apron, but today that just wasn't possible.

She skipped down the stairs, making a quick note that her grandfather wasn't awake either. Which meant no coffee, and no breakfast, at least not a hot one. And the animals would have to wait until after the service to be fed. She just wouldn't stay for the meal. She'd make some excuse, like anyone would care when she left, and head home to feed them as soon as possible.

She pinned up her hair, set her covering in place, and snatched up a leftover piece of corn bread from last night's supper. It wasn't a good breakfast by far, but it was better than nothing. And it could be eaten on the way. She wrapped it in a paper towel, then started up the stairs. "Dawdi," she called as she went. "Dawdi!"

Her grandfather was a sound sleeper, but he was also an early riser. What a day for both of them to oversleep.

She tucked a wayward strand of hair under her *kapp* and prayed that it stayed there. She didn't have time to redo the whole thing.

"Dawdi." She stood outside his bedroom door. He was usually up by now, and she only had to call once or twice when she got up before he did. She knocked on the door. "Dawdi! We're late. Come on!"

No response.

"Dawdi!" She knocked again, as a sinking feeling hit her stomach. He wasn't in his room. She knew it. She wasn't sure how she knew, but he was gone. She knocked one more time for courtesy's sake and wrenched open the door.

Her instincts were correct. He wasn't inside. The bed was perfectly made, leaving her to wonder if he had been gone all night or gotten up this morning.

Frantically she looked around the room. His shoes were by the bed. He had probably left this morning. But where had he gone?

Chapter Nine

Where could he be?

Ivy grabbed her coat and scarf from the peg by the front door and put them on as she hurried from the house. He couldn't be far. He didn't have on shoes or a coat. She had seen the last still hanging next to hers this morning.

Maybe he was in the barn. Just because he wasn't in his room didn't mean he had gone far. He might have been trying to be kind in letting her sleep in. He could have gone out to the barn, fed all the animals, and lost track of time.

But he wasn't in the barn. Or the toolshed. He wasn't in the hay barn, the loft, or the cellar. She even checked the old outhouse that sat at the back side of the garden but was never used anymore. Ivy thought it was charming in an old-fashioned sort of way and was loath to tear it down.

She bit her lip and scanned the horizon. He wasn't in the empty fields. Or the small orchard that sat between the house and the road. And that left . . . the road.

The tractor sat in its usual place, under the awning that jutted from the side of the hay barn. At least she knew he was on foot. *Bare feet,* she corrected. With transportation on her side, she might be able to catch up with him, but church was out of the question.

She gave the tractor one last longing look, then whistled for her horse. She would have rather taken the tractor. It would be much faster, but tractors weren't allowed on Sundays. She hitched up the gelding and said a quick prayer. She had to find him. She simply had to. But even as she prayed, worse-case scenarios ran through her head. Unconscious in a ditch, hit by a car, hit by a truck, lost in the woods, and even more terrifying outcomes.

She would find him. She would.

She stopped at the edge of the road, looking first one way and then the other. Which direction? She had no idea. Left would take her toward the bishop's house and would eventually lead to the Millers', where church was to be held today. Right would go toward town. She would pass by the general store and several *Englisch* churches. Why would he have gone that way? No reason, she deducted, and turned toward the Ebersols'.

Going was slow. She was doing her best to look at both sides of the road, which wasn't easy through the small buggy windows. At least not while trying to keep Harvey, their gelding, on the right side of the road. At the rate she was going, she would never find him before church started. Yet at this point she was truly concerned with finding him at all.

Each road that branched off from theirs created even more possibilities and more confusion. Would he have turned? Why? Was there any logic to this at all?

Her head began to throb as up ahead another buggy came into sight. Seemed she wasn't the only one running late this morning.

Even better, maybe they had seen her *dawdi*. Maybe they had even picked him up! The thought sent her heart pounding a little harder in her chest.

She flicked the reins over Harvey's back and sent the horse into a faster clop.

In no time at all she could pull even with the buggy.

"Zeb?" she called in surprise. Of all the people.

"Ivy." Somehow, he sensed her need and pulled his buggy to the side of the road.

"What are you doing?" he asked.

Her voice was frantic. "I can't find Dawdi." She bit back her tears. "I got up late, and he wasn't in his bed. I checked all over the property. I don't know where he is." She didn't need to add that she was worried sick.

Zeb turned back to his brother and Clara Rose. Ivy had been so wrapped up in her own problems that she hadn't seen the two of them sitting in the buggy. Obie was in the front and Clara Rose in the back, with the baby next to her on the small bench. "Y'all go on without me."

Obie nodded and slid into the driver's spot without asking question one.

"I'll pray you find him quickly," Clara Rose offered. Then Obie set the horse in motion and they were gone.

"Let's go." Zeb took her by the elbow and led her back to her buggy. She swung up inside, and he took over driving. She was glad to have him. Even after all the times she had declared—sometimes loudly—that she didn't want his help, or need it, she was so thankful to have him with her now.

"Where all have you checked?" he asked.

Ivy ticked all the places off one by one, starting with his room and ending with the very road they were traveling.

"Has he mentioned someplace recently? Anyplace? Another church? Someone's house?"

"No." She didn't recall him saying anything that would give her any clues. He was the same as always: a little flighty, a little forgetful, and completely lovable.

"Well, then, he has to be around here someplace. He can't have just disappeared. And I'm pretty sure there haven't been any alien abductions in the area for quite some time."

Ivy blinked. "What?"

"I'm teasing. You look like you could use a laugh or two to release the tension."

She moved her head in a half-nodding, half-shaking motion that said nothing at all.

"We'll find him." Zeb's demeanor turned serious, his eyes determined. Then he reached behind the seat and grabbed the blanket. With one hand, he laid it across her lap. "Cover up. You look cold."

She was. So cold she was shaking. Or was that caused by nerves? She felt like she was about to come apart. What if he had forgotten who he was this time? It was one thing to think it a different month or year. But if he couldn't remember his own name, how would anyone be able to help him? The police wouldn't be able to, or the firemen, or medics; none of the first responders. Not unless they were Amish volunteers. And they wouldn't be called out today. Not on Sunday.

Please let someone find him, she prayed. *And please let that someone be Amish.* It was perhaps the most heartfelt and silly prayer she had ever uttered. But she needed him to be okay. Nothing else would do.

"We'll find him," Zeb promised again.

And she believed him.

It couldn't be any other way.

Ivy shivered next to him. He wasn't sure how much of her trembling was caused by the cold and how much of it was the shock of losing her grandfather.

Zeb liked the man. He was a little goofy, but it made him charming all the same. Yonnie's hair never seemed to be combed, his suspenders were always a little crooked, but if a person needed something, Yonnie could always be counted on to come through.

And then there was Ivy. Zeb couldn't stand the thought of her worrying herself so. But if he put himself in her shoes, he knew he would have been beside himself.

They drove halfway to the Millers', asking anyone they encountered if they had seen Yonnie. It was a challenge, seeing as how Ivy hadn't seen him before he left and didn't know what he was wearing. She told them what he'd had on last, but to the *Englisch* people, Zeb knew all the Amish looked alike.

"Let's go back toward town," he suggested.

She shrugged and huddled a little deeper into the blanket. "Whatever you think is best."

He reached out and clasped one of her hands. He squeezed her fingers, praying that the action would comfort her. "It can't hurt," he said.

She nodded, and he turned the buggy around. Just how far could an Amish man go on a winter day with no shoes and no coat? Far enough, he supposed, that he could freeze. Well, maybe not literally. He didn't know much about such things. After all, he never planned on going out without shoes or a coat on a day when the temp dropped to or below freezing. He had read the weather report in the newspaper, and it was supposed to warm up nicely by the afternoon. But for now, it was fairly cold. Forty degrees at the most. Could a man freeze or get frostbite from forty-degree weather?

They rode along in silence. Zeb searched for something to say. Something that would give her peace and comfort, but there were no words.

He and Ivy had agreed to watch opposite sides of the road, but he couldn't stop his gaze from straying to her side. He didn't want to miss anything. The Lamberts' farm, the old Yoder place. It was empty. Could her grandfather have gone in there to rest out of the cold?

It was on the tip of his tongue to ask if she wanted to stop and look when another sign caught his attention: *Mayfield Cemetery.*

It was an *Englisch* cemetery, not as fancy as some, but better than most. And it gave him an idea.

"Ivy?"

"Hmm?"

"Is your grandmother buried here in Mayes County?"

"*Jah.*"

"Do you think maybe your grandfather could be there?"

She pushed herself up in her seat, the sparkle returning to her blue, blue eyes. "Maybe."

"Let's go see." He turned the buggy around and circled back to the side road and headed across to the Amish cemetery. It wasn't far from her house, and Yonnie could have walked there this morning without any problems. Well, Zeb supposed he would be cold. But it wouldn't have taken him long.

Half a mile later, Zeb turned again, then a quarter mile and a turn once more. It seemed to take forever, but he could see the thin wire fence that surrounded the final resting place for most of the Amish residents of Wells Landing.

"Is that—?" He thought he saw a flash of blue.

"*Jah.*" Ivy sat up in her seat, her blanket pooling around her feet. "Dawdi," she called. "Daw-di!"

The old man was sitting on the ground in the second row toward the back side of the cemetery. Just as Ivy had said, he was wearing no coat and no shoes. But he had stopped long enough to don his hat before wandering off.

Yonnie looked up as Ivy called his name. There was no recognition in his actions or posture. He was too far away for Zeb to read his expression.

"Dawdi!" Ivy was up and out of the buggy before Zeb had

even stopped all the way. He should have expected it. But he hadn't, and he was thankful that he hadn't accidentally run over her feet.

She called his name again as she ran toward him.

Zeb crawled down from the buggy a little slower, using the time to take in the situation. Her grandfather appeared to be unharmed. From what Zeb could see, there was no blood on him. He didn't appear to be injured in any way. In fact, he seemed as fine as fine could be.

So why had he run off this morning?

Zeb followed behind as Ivy launched herself at her grandfather, hugging him close before pulling away to assess any damage.

"What are you doing out here?" she asked, hugging him close once again.

"I wanted to see your grandmother." He said the words as if they were the most logical ones on earth. Where else would he be?

"Dawdi, we were supposed to be at church this morning. Did you forget?"

Zeb stopped next to them as Yonnie pushed back his hat and scratched his bald spot underneath.

"We were?"

"I'd take that as a yes," Zeb said.

Ivy glared at Zeb, then reached for Yonnie's arm. "Are you hurt?"

"Why would you ask something like that?" He pulled away from her. This time he was the one with a sharp look.

"You've been gone for hours." Ivy's voice cracked. What little composure she had managed to pull together slipped.

"I'm fine, I tell you."

"Your feet are freezing. We'll be lucky if you don't get pneumonia."

"Quit your fussin' and help me up."

Zeb stepped forward and offered the old man his hand.

Yonnie took it, and Zeb helped him stand, but not before he noticed the smears of blood on his feet. The man had walked at least three miles this morning. It wasn't feasible to think he could march around town for so long without a scratch. "Come on," Zeb said. "Let's get you home."

Dawdi acted as if nothing was wrong the entire trip back to their house. Ivy was torn between wanting to hug him or lock him in his room for the rest of his life.

"Next time," she said, "next time you have to tell me before you leave the house."

"Bah." Dawdi brushed away her concern as if it were for nothing. But it was something to her.

"Do you realize that we missed church?" She tried to keep her voice calm, but her anxiety was rising. Missing church was frowned upon. The bishop would most likely be at their house first thing in the morning to make sure they were fine, not ill, and didn't need anything. She needed a very good reason for missing the service, and *My* dawdi *forgot what day it was and I overslept* wouldn't exactly cut it.

No one missed church unless they were in the hospital. Or dead. She and Dawdi were neither. But Cephas Ebersol was a fair bishop. That didn't mean she wanted him coming over, worrying about them, or worse . . . calling her mother in Indiana.

"I did when you told me." He slid down from the buggy and landed softly on the ground. He winced as his cut feet touched the dirt.

Ivy's anger and frustration melted away. He couldn't help that his mind didn't always stay on track. She had no idea where to turn. They were simply making do. She just hoped the bishop would understand.

"Come on," she said, looping her arm through his and

helping him toward the house. "Let's soak your feet in Epsom salts."

Behind her, Zeb cleared his throat. Then she heard his footfalls following them. She didn't say anything. It wasn't that she wanted him to come in; she was just tired. Tired of worrying, tired of pretending, tired of a lot of things.

They entered the house one behind the other. Zeb helped Dawdi settle in on the sofa. Chester hopped up next to him, marking him with a loud purr. Ivy made her way into the kitchen and ran the tap water until it was warm. She had no idea how bad the cuts on his feet were. Bad enough that they had been bleeding. This would help. Then she would find them all something to eat, and after that . . . well, they would just have to wait and see.

Two hours later, Ivy was calmer by far, but exhausted from the day. She carried their pie plates and milk glasses into the kitchen.

She quickly filled the sink with warm, soapy water and dropped the dishes into it. She wanted to crawl into bed and forget that today had ever happened. Except it was barely two o'clock in the afternoon and she couldn't go to bed. Maybe she could talk her grandfather into dozing with her.

Then what are you going to do? Tie a bell to one of his toes?

His feet weren't as bad as they looked. Mostly small cuts and a lot of blood. She had patched them up as well as she could and called it done.

"When are you going to tell me what's going on?"

Ivy jumped, splashing suds as Zeb came into the kitchen behind her. Her first instinct was to send him back into the other room to sit with Dawdi, but that seemed a bit excessive even to her. She let out a small laugh. It was meant to sound carefree. Instead it came out strangled. "There's nothing going on." But her words rang as the lie they were.

"Uh-huh." Zeb turned and leaned his backside against the counter next to where she stood. He crossed his arms and watched her.

"Nothing, really."

"Try again."

She stared out the window over the sink to the backyard and beyond. She could feel his gaze upon her, searching, watching as she stared at nothing. Typical for Oklahoma, the sun was shining, but the wind held a vicious bite. It must feel extra cold to Zeb. "How are you adjusting to the weather since you came back?"

"Not what I want to talk about."

"Hmm?" She looked at him then, tearing her gaze from the landscape to settle on him. If she was being completely honest with herself, he was even more handsome now than he had been when he left. The last two years had taken some of the wild from his gaze. He was steady and true, the kind of man a girl could depend on for always. She hadn't seen that in him before he left.

"How long has he been getting lost?"

Ivy sighed. She should have known he would go for the direct approach. "A couple of weeks."

"Try again."

She heaved another breath in and then out. "Since this summer. It started off small. I would lose him in Walmart or the Super Saver, then he started losing his way coming home, losing track of the time." She shrugged. "Things like that."

"Ivy." He shifted as if he wanted to take her into his arms. She moved a couple of steps away from him just in case. There would not be a repeat of the other day.

"I appreciate your concern, Zeb. But this is something I have to deal with myself."

"Says who?"

"I do." Her mother was gone. She alone was responsible for her grandfather's well-being. If Zeb couldn't see that, how could she explain it?

"This is a family problem."

"Do you see any family around here?" It might be a family concern, but she was all the family her *dawdi* had left in these parts. His last living sister had up and moved to Ohio just last year.

"And how are you handling this on your own?"

She bit back a sigh. No sense in letting him see how tired and worried she was. What good would it do to spread her troubles to others? "Just fine."

"Uh-huh. I suppose that was why you were running all over the county today looking for him. That was why you had to miss church, because you are handling it so fine."

Church. She had practically pushed the thought from her mind. She had enough trouble today, no sense borrowing some from tomorrow. But tomorrow would come, and with it the deacon. Maybe the bishop. Possibly both. And they would want to talk about Dawdi missing church. Why he wasn't there and how she needed to make sure that she got him there every week. It was her responsibility, and if she couldn't handle it, she would have to arrange something so he didn't miss. Or move to Indiana. That was one thing she couldn't bear to think about. Indiana. Moving was a little too much like giving up. She'd had enough troubles in the last two years. She didn't need to add "being a quitter" to the list.

"So he has a couple of setbacks. It's not all the time."

Zeb shot her a grim smile. "You just keep telling yourself that. You say it enough times and maybe it might be the truth."

* * *

The knock sounded on the door just after nine. Just like Cephas to be early. He was one of the hardest working men she knew, their bishop. He was fair and caring. He had concern for his members, more than any other bishop she had ever met. But with that concern came knowledge and knowing and finding out all of Ivy's secrets. That was something she couldn't allow to happen. Not yet anyway.

"Cephas," she greeted him as she pulled open the door.

She had already sent her grandfather over to Bacon Dan's to pick up some eggs. He would be home shortly. It wasn't that far, after all, but if she knew her *dawdi* and the talkative Bacon Dan, they might linger for hours.

Or he might leave right away and forget himself on the way home.

She pushed that thought out of her mind and smiled at the bishop. "Come in. Come in."

The bishop stepped into the warm house, bringing with him some of the cold winter air. Ivy shut the door behind him. "Would you like a cup of coffee?"

"That would be good, *danki*."

"Have a seat," she invited him, then headed for the kitchen.

Her hands were shaking as she poured the coffee. She could do this. It was as easy as pie. As soon as she sent Cephas on his way, she had to get ready for work. She had the late shift at the bakery. Not her favorite, but still good. She preferred to be there in the mornings so she could help Esther bake the day's goods. But that meant being up and out of the house no later than four thirty.

She placed the mugs of steaming brew onto a tray, then added a plate with a few leftover peanut butter and Christmas sprinkle cookies. She had been experimenting, trying to come up with new recipes and win Esther's favor. She wanted to keep her job past the holiday season, and she needed all the good points she could get to combat all the negative she was sure Jodie Miller was feeding Caroline and Esther.

"Here we are." She smiled, but her lips trembled as she set the tray on the coffee table. She handed Cephas his mug and motioned toward the cookies.

He accepted the cup, then shook his head at the cookies. "I missed your grandfather yesterday at church. Is he here?"

"As a matter of fact, no."

"He's not sick?"

She shook her head.

"I know he doesn't drive much these days, but he does still get out in the buggy from time to time, *jah*?"

She nodded. He drove all over on the tractor and in the buggy. But she wasn't going to point that out to the bishop.

"If he's not going to drive, I need you to make sure he gets to church on time. Can you do that?"

"*Jah*." The word was barely above a whisper.

"Why did he miss yesterday?"

The one question she hadn't wanted him to ask.

"He wasn't feeling quite himself." It was the closest she could come to the truth without revealing too much. Now if Cephas would accept it as the answer.

"Not himself? But he wasn't sick?"

"No."

"Ivy." His voice was kind, gentle, and she felt tears prick at the backs of her eyes. She blinked them away. She was not going to cry. "Is caring for your grandfather too much for you?"

She dropped her gaze to her cup of coffee. She could just see her reflection in the liquid depths. "No."

"I know your mother left suddenly. I can contact her if you wish. She should know if her father's having problems."

Ivy pulled at her composure, securing it around her like a turtle's shell. "That won't be necessary. It was a one-time thing. It won't happen again."

Chapter Ten

"What did the bishop say?" Zeb asked that afternoon. Once again he had come to help her with her chores. This time she didn't protest. She needed the help, and there had been a time when she considered Zeb a friend. Friends helped friends. That was just how it worked.

"He asked me if I wanted him to talk to my mother." She straightened from smoothing out the new hay in the horse stall and propped her arm on the top of her yard broom.

"Do you?"

"No." Somehow she managed to hold back her unlady-like snort.

Zeb seemed to sense her scorn and stopped his own work. "You have a problem with your mother?"

Ivy shook her head. She did not want to get into this today. "Of course not."

He grinned at her. "If you don't want to tell me, all you have to say is you don't want to tell me."

"I don't want to tell you."

"Which means yes."

She propped one hand on her hip and narrowed her eyes at him. "You are trying to trick me."

"And doing a great job of it, as a matter of fact."

She shook her head and hung the yard broom back in its place on the far wall. He followed suit with the pitchfork, and together they left the barn. There was a biting cold to the wind, a chilly dampness that hadn't been there before.

"Is it supposed to rain?" she asked, looking at the sky. It was gray, but that was normal for this time of year. Still, she would be happy with blue skies all year round.

"They are calling for sleet tonight and into the morning."

Sleet. Ivy made a face. "Why couldn't we just once have a white Christmas?"

"It happens now and again," he said as they made their way to the house.

"Name one time."

"The Christmas of 2000."

She rolled her eyes playfully at him. "And you honestly remember that?"

"Vaguely."

"Tell the truth." She opened the screen door and held it for him.

"Mostly I remember the old folks talking about it. There was a lot of snow that year. And then again on New Year's."

"I don't care about New Year's. I just want it to snow on Christmas."

"I wouldn't count on it," he said. "The almanac's calling for a lot of ice, but not much snow."

Just then the sky opened up and the sleet began to fall.

"Come on," she said. "I'll make you a cup of coffee to take on the road. You don't want to be out in this any longer than necessary."

Zeb took a sip of the coffee from its to-go mug and let its warmth trickle down his throat. He had wanted to stay a little longer, talk with Ivy a little more, but he knew it was better this way. No matter how hard it was for him to walk away. Today she had almost been the same as the Ivy he had known before. He couldn't say that he didn't know why the changes had occurred in her, and that made him hate them even more. They had both been through so much, but today it was like having the old Ivy back. He wanted to see more of that girl.

After they had gone into the house, she had started a pot of coffee and given him time to warm up by the fire. He wanted to stay, talk, just be, but with the turn in the weather, he knew he needed to get home before the roads turned slick. In Oklahoma, sleet could easily turn into snow, which was bad enough, or freezing rain, which was worse.

"Are you going back to Florida?" She spun to face him, the surprise on her face clearly telling him that she hadn't planned on asking that question, at least not right then. But once it was out, there it was.

"I'm thinking about it."

"Thinking about it," she repeated. "What does that mean?"

"I guess it's a fancy way of saying I don't know."

"Do you want to?"

He thought about it a moment. Thought about lying, telling the truth, or telling part of it, and then decided. "Sometimes." It was the closest to the truth he would come. He did think about it. There were times when he longed for Pinecraft. Not the beaches and the perfect weather, but the people, their faith, and the laid-back lifestyle they lived.

"Why?"

He shook his head. No one would understand. He had all but turned against his upbringing. He hadn't jumped the fence, but he had done something almost just as bad. He had taken up with some Beachy Amish. And if his father ever found out . . . He shuddered and took another drink of his coffee.

He should be brave enough to stand up and tell his father that he was beginning to think about God and Jesus in a different light. Not that he thought his father was wrong for what he had raised him up to believe, but maybe, just maybe there was something else out there. Something more. That was what he'd found with the Beachys.

He should have told Ivy right then, about saved by grace and knowing that God's love was always with you. It was about more than always doing the right thing. It was about a love so pure and true that nothing in this world could tear it down. That was powerful love, and he wanted Ivy—he wanted *everybody*—to experience the joys of that love. He didn't wonder if he would make it to heaven. He didn't worry about his loved ones. He knew. God had promised him as much. The thought was liberating and binding all at the same time. It freed him from unnecessary fears and bound him forever to God.

But he didn't say any of those things. He turned to Ivy and said, "It's beautiful there. The people are always nice, and the weather is always perfect."

She nodded toward the window, where the sleet was still coming down. "I can't say much for the weather, but the people are pretty nice here too."

He resisted the urge to reach out and touch her cheek. He had given up that right a long time ago. If it had ever really been his. Instead he had stepped back, moved away, and wrapped his scarf around his ears. "I guess I should be going."

But he didn't want to leave. He could have stayed there all night, watching the fire flicker shadows across her face. He wanted another chance to see the girl he had once known. Once loved. But he didn't have the right.

Especially not if he truly planned on returning to Florida. He couldn't connect with Ivy, then walk away when it suited him.

That's exactly what you did last time.
And look where it had landed him.

He took another sip of coffee and wished that he could push the tractor to a faster pace. Thankfully the roads weren't slick. Yet. Once the sun went down completely, they would be, and it was sinking fast.

Or maybe it felt like he was moving so slowly because Ivy had filled his thoughts once again. Sweet, beautiful Ivy. There had been a time when he had thought they would be the next big couple in Wells Landing. The next Caroline and Andrew, the next Emily and Elam. But it seemed that wasn't in God's plans for them. He'd headed off to Florida, and she had . . . well, if the rumors were true, she had turned a little wild.

He'd heard all sorts of things, but the ones he heard the most were that she wore jeans, drove a car, and had kissed three boys. He wasn't sure he believed any of them. Or perhaps he simply didn't want to. She was better than that. She was good and wholesome. She was godly. Plus he couldn't see her mother allowing her to drive around in a car. Lots of girls wore jeans under their dresses. Well, mostly the Mennonites over in Taylor Creek. But then she told him that her mother had moved away. She had gotten married and headed for Indiana.

Zeb shook his head. She had met a man, fallen in love, married him, and moved in less than two years. The thought made his head spin. Maybe that was the problem. Ivy's was spinning too.

Finally his drive came into view. Zeb said a quick prayer of thanks and pulled the tractor into its spot next to the hay barn. Now that he was home, he had his own chores to do, but he'd rather be over with Ivy. He wanted to be there to make sure her grandfather got back home safely, that she had a warm supper, a nice bath, everything she needed.

He shook his head at himself and headed for the barn.

"Hey." Obie nodded and shot him a smile. "About time you got here. Clara Rose was beginning to worry."

"The roads aren't bad yet."

"But they're going to be?"

Zeb nodded and picked up the pitchfork. He headed toward the hay barn.

They worked side by side in silence. Half an hour? An hour? He wasn't sure. Then Obie spoke, breaking the quiet. "You've got something on your mind, brother."

That was the problem with having a twin. They might be two separate people, but they had a connection that others would never be able to understand.

"Do you believe all that stuff everyone's saying about Ivy?"

Obie thought about it for a moment. "I haven't given it much concern."

"Would it matter to you if it were true?"

"Everyone deserves a second chance."

Maybe even a third and a fourth.

But for some reason he felt like Ivy didn't deserve the rumors. She hadn't done anything to make him believe that she was guilty. She may not have joined the church, but he had never seen her in jeans, there was no sign of a car, and, well, he didn't want to think about her kissing other guys. Which was ridiculous. They had made their choices, and he didn't have the right to question who she kissed or how many she kissed.

"You spent some time with her last year. You said yourself you were trying to make Clara Rose jealous."

Obie grinned. "And it worked too."

"Are you one of the three?" The question was quietly spoken.

"No." Obie's smile turned into a frown. "I know that you two had a thing."

"It wasn't a thing."

"What do you want to call it then?"

There were several names, but *thing* wasn't one of them. "We had a relationship." Now they had an understanding.

"How can you call it a relationship? You never got to go out in public together. And it was going to be a while before she could join the church and date. How does sneaking around make a relationship?"

"I loved her!" The words were more of a roar than simply spoken.

"Loved? As in not any longer?"

Did he? He wasn't certain. Leaving her had been the hardest thing he had ever done. But they had both needed space and time to heal. He had gone to Florida and discovered that being that far away was good for him. He wasn't constantly reminded of her everywhere he went. Those first few months, he thought of her every day. But as time went on, she came to mind less and less. Until he hardly thought of her at all. Her memory had faded to a fuzzy warmth that he examined every so often, but not too closely. This way was more comfortable. Did he love her? He had no idea.

"Tassie!" Ivy smiled and stepped back to allow the petite widow to enter the house. The sleet from the day before had already disappeared, and with any luck tonight wouldn't fall below freezing and they wouldn't have to worry about any ice on the roads. "We weren't expecting you today." Were they? Dawdi hadn't mentioned it if he had known.

"It was kind of a surprise to me too." Tassie's brown eyes twinkled merrily in her sweet, wrinkled face. She stepped in from the porch and raised the brown paper grocery sack she carried. "I baked some bread this morning, and I guess my recipe got away from me. Before I knew it, I had two extra loaves."

"*Jah?*" Just how did a bread recipe get away from someone?

"So I thought to myself that you and your *dawdi* might be able to use it."

"Of course. *Danki*." Ivy took the sack and carried it into the kitchen. She left it on the table and turned back to face Tassie. "That's very kind of you. Would you like a cup of coffee?'

"*Jah*, please." Tassie took off her gloves and glanced around the kitchen. "Where's Yonnie?"

Ivy filled the pot and waved toward the backyard. "He's out hanging laundry."

"Oh?" Tassie's eyebrows shot up nearly to her hairline. "I don't believe I've ever seen a man hanging laundry."

"We have sort of an unusual arrangement," Ivy confessed. "He does all the inside chores and I do all the outside ones."

"And he's really hanging laundry?"

"Honest."

"This I got to see."

Tassie rushed to the back door. She peeked out the window, shaking her head and letting out a small chuckle. "Beats all I have ever seen."

Ivy smiled to herself. She supposed that it was something to see. Most Amish men didn't touch the laundry, except to put their soiled clothes with the rest of it.

"He's a hard worker, your *dawdi*."

"*Jah*." He used to be. Before his shoulders slumped and his eyesight turned bad. These days he was content to cook, clean, and attend the occasional auction. "Where's Karl?" The question surprised even her. She hadn't noticed his absence until now. But she had thought her *dawdi* and the widow were trying to set her up with Karl. If he wasn't here and the widow was . . .

Nah.

"He had some work to finish at home. I came over just for a bit, you understand."

"Of course." She studied the widow's face. But she was giving nothing away.

Outside the window, her grandfather picked up the laundry basket. He propped it on his hip as he hobbled toward the house. But he stopped short when he saw Tassie standing there.

"Hello, Yonnie."

Dawdi nodded. "Tassie."

"I brought you by some bread. Made it this morning, I did."

"*Danki.*" Dawdi took off his hat, then unbuttoned his coat. He hung it on the peg next to his hat, then turned to Ivy. "Is that fresh coffee I smell?"

"*Jah.* Would you like a cup?"

"Very much so."

A few moments later, they were seated around the table, steaming cups of coffee in front of them and a plate of iced sugar cookies for them to share.

"I've got an idea," Tassie chirped.

"*Jah?*" Ivy said.

"We could play Uno. Wouldn't that be fun?"

Ivy wasn't sure how much fun Uno with three would be, but Tassie seemed so captured with the idea, all she could do was nod.

"I'll get the cards." Dawdi stood and made his way over to the cabinet drawer where they kept such things.

"Are you planning on decorating for the holidays, dear?" Tassie shifted in her seat and watched as Dawdi retrieved a pad of paper and a pencil for them to keep score and headed back to the table.

Ivy glanced around the room. She hadn't given much thought to Christmas decorations in her own home. She had noticed all the ones at the retirement home, but the *Englisch* ones and the Amish ones were as different as east and west. Amish Christmas decorations usually included a nativity scene, candles, and greenery. Some of the fancier folks even used the battery-operated lights to offer up a sparkle for the season, but she had never bought any of those.

Why hadn't she put up any decorations this year? Because she had been busy. Sort of. Maybe *preoccupied* would be a better word. She had definitely been that. But after her trips to the retirement center, putting up pinecones and cedar boughs seemed sort of . . . bland.

What would happen if I bought some of that Englisch *tinsel and strung it about?* As far as she knew there was nothing against it in the *Ordnung.* A Santa Claus or even a snowman might be pushing it, but tinsel was just shiny fluff. What could be the harm in that?

Maybe she could get some for her house and Ethan Dallas's room at the home. That way if someone saw her buying it, she could say it was for him. Then she could add some sparkle to the holiday season. Maybe that was what it needed. That and nothing more.

"It's your turn, dear." Tassie touched her arm, and Ivy resisted the impulse to pull away. She had been so deep in her own thoughts she hadn't been paying good attention to the game. She studied the cards in her hand and the discard pile before her. Both her *dawdi* and Tassie were down to three cards each. Why did she still have such a handful? She threw down a green seven and play resumed.

"I know it's not a big place, but after a while . . ." Tassie shook her head. Ivy silently vowed to pay better attention. She had missed the first half of whatever Tassie had been saying. "I feel like I rattle around." Tassie sighed and played her discard. A blue seven. "It just gets lonely."

Ivy tried hard to understand. How could Tassie feel lonely? She was in the *dawdihaus,* mere feet from the rest of the family. She had her son, his wife, and all their children, including Karl. So many people around all the time. How could she be lonely?

She supposed it was because she was newly widowed. It

had only been six months or so, and Tassie was still wearing her mourning black.

Her grandfather played a blue draw two and Ivy automatically palmed the cards and looked for one to play. How ironic was it that her grandfather could keep his mind on the game, play the appropriate cards, but there were times when he couldn't remember what year it was? Or the day. How did she explain that?

"I've been thinking," Tassie said. "How about I come over on Thursday and we can do this again?"

"I'm not sure . . ." Ivy started. She didn't want to make any promises. Thursday would make a week since she had been to the retirement home, and for some reason she was anxious to go back. It was almost as if God was whispering in her ear that the home was where she would find the answers she needed.

"That would be fine, *jah*," Dawdi said.

"I might have to work," Ivy warned. With any luck, she would be able to swing by Whispering Pines before she had to come home.

"That's all right. I'll be here."

"Good." Tassie shifted in her seat. "So we're all set, then?"

Dawdi nodded, and Ivy followed suit.

"All set," he said.

And that was when she realized it. Her *dawdi* had a better social life than she did.

"What do you think about the widow Tassie Weber?" Ivy asked Zeb the next day. Once again he had come over to help her with her chores. It wasn't as cold out as it had been the last couple of days, but she craved the company more than the actual help.

"I think she's a nice woman." He poured the fresh water into the pan she had put out for the chickens and tried not to smile as they tumbled over one another to get to the metal bowl.

"No. What do you *think* of her?"

Zeb frowned and turned his attention away from the hens. "I'm not sure I understand what you want to know."

"She's been coming over to visit. With Dawdi." Ivy cast a sidelong look at him. Was he shocked? He didn't appear to be so. Was she the only one surprised by Tassie's interest in her grandfather?

"Oh, *jah*?"

Ivy nodded. "I thought perhaps . . . well, she brought Karl with her the first couple of times, but yesterday . . ."

"Karl? Her grandson Karl?"

"*Jah.*"

Zeb's handsome face split into a grin. "Really?"

"Don't laugh."

Chickens fed and watered, the two started back to the barn, side by side.

"I'm not laughing." But he was.

"I think she's interested in Dawdi."

Zeb sobered a bit and seemed to think about it. "Why not? Your *dawdi* is still handsome enough. He's having a little bit of trouble getting around, but not as bad as some."

Once inside the barn he returned the bucket to its place on the wall with the other tools, then settled down on one small stack of hay.

"Would you be serious?" She grabbed his arm and shook him a bit.

"I am being serious. What's the problem with her liking your *dawdi*?"

What was the problem? Well, it was . . . and . . . there were times when . . . okay, so she couldn't find the words for the problem, but it was there all the same. Ivy settled down near him. Not on the same bale, but close enough.

"She says she's lonely. She lives in a house with all these people. How can she be lonely?"

This time Zeb's expression definitely turned serious. "It's possible," he said.

Ivy studied him, wondering where the dark clouds that shadowed his features had come from. Or maybe that was just the changing lights inside the barn. "Something happened in Florida."

He shook his head, and just like that the sun shone on his face and the darkness disappeared. "Nah," he said. "Just life."

"And Florida?"

"What about it?"

"You never answered me. Do you mean to go back?"

"What difference does it make?"

"I'm sure it makes one to your family." She stood to put some distance between them. She wanted to touch him, to see if he felt the same as he had back then, the same as the other day when he had kissed her. It was an impulse, she understood that, and he had promised it wouldn't happen again. But there were times . . .

"What about you?" he asked. "Does it make a difference to you?"

She stopped, searched for an answer, then shook her head. "Nice try, Zeb. You're not going to put this on me. Not this time. Leave if you want to leave, or stay if you want to stay, but make that decision on your own and leave me out of it."

Chapter Eleven

Ivy knocked on the door and waited for Ethan to answer. She'd heard talk this morning at the bakery about a Christmas present exchange tonight. Everyone in her youth group had been invited. Everyone but her.

She tossed her head and told herself it didn't matter. Because it didn't. They could do whatever they wanted. She had her own plans.

She shifted the book she held under one arm and knocked again.

This time the door opened and Ethan stood there. One look at her and he grinned. Some people wanted her around, even if the youth group didn't.

"Ivy." He stepped back so she could enter his room. "What brings you by today?"

"I thought I might read to you." She held up the book, then lowered it back to her side. "Is that weird? I know you can read. But I thought you might enjoy—"

"It's not weird. And I would love for you to read to me. I don't see as well as I used to."

She settled down in the chair opposite him and began to read. An hour later they took a break, got something to drink, and sat back down. She opened the book to the page where they had left off and trailed one finger down the words to find her place.

"Tell me again, Ivy. Why's a girl like you at a senior home instead of out with friends?"

A girl like me? She looked up and met Ethan's gaze. "It's a long story."

"I have time if you want to share."

But she knew better. He didn't have time. He was dying, and she wanted to spend all the time she could with him. Knowing him was a blessing. God had put him in her path for a reason. She knew it as sure as she knew her own name. She just had to be around until she figured out the reason for herself.

"It's—" She stopped. How wonderful it would be to unburden herself. She could tell Ethan all her problems—well, most of them anyway. That way she wouldn't have to carry them around by herself.

She stuck her finger between the pages of the book and set it in her lap. "What do you know about sin?"

Ethan gave a casual shrug. "I believe the Bible speaks clearly on the matter. There are the seven deadly sins."

Not exactly what she wanted. "Forgiveness?"

"The Lord forgives, if only you ask."

Asking. That was the problem. How could she stand in front of the church, in front of God, and confess all that she had done?

She wasn't a member of the church, but she couldn't see a way around it in order to clear her conscience. If she went to the bishop now and asked about joining the church, about taking the following year's baptism classes, she wouldn't feel right doing so without coming clean about all she had done.

Maybe his church was different.

"What about . . . well, say a girl and a boy . . . you know . . . before they are married."

Ethan's eyes narrowed only slightly, but she knew he was thinking. He was taking her words and fitting them with everything he knew about her, about church, about God.

"Sin is sin," he said simply.

She knew that. What had she hoped—that she could leave her church and go to one where the rules for such things would suit her better?

"But the Lord forgives."

The Lord forgives.

"Tell me about him."

She lifted her gaze to Ethan's. She was surprised by his request. "I—"

"Please don't tell me you were asking for a friend." He gave her a sad little smile. "We both know that's not the truth."

Ivy shifted in her seat, turned the book over in her lap, her finger still keeping her place between the pages.

She examined his expression, did her best to read the emotions in his eyes. She could trust him, that much she knew. Instinctively. She could tell this man anything and it would go no further. Even still, she was scared. She liked Ethan, admired him even. If she told him about her and Zeb, would that change how he felt about her? She wasn't sure she could handle damaging herself in his eyes.

There was only one way to find out.

"Do you know much about the Amish religion?" she finally asked.

"No. Quite the opposite, in fact."

"It's the church. It's all about the church."

"That's not always a bad thing," he said.

"*Jah.*" But there was still more. "If a young person hasn't joined the church, they aren't allowed to date until they do."

His eyebrows shot skyward, but he didn't comment.

"But sometimes, a boy and a girl can start liking each other, but if they haven't joined the church . . ."

He nodded. "I get it. So what happened between you and this boy who hasn't joined the church?"

"It's me," she said. "I'm the one who hasn't joined the church."

"I see."

She believed he did. "Zeb joined long ago."

"This is the boy you liked."

"Loved," she corrected. Might as well get everything out if she was dragging things onto the table.

"Tell me about Zeb."

"He's great. He'll be a great provider, a strong husband, a loving father."

"But?"

"Just not for me." The thought sent tears pricking behind her lids. Not now. Not anymore.

"What happened?"

Ivy trained her gaze on the book still in her lap. She stared until the words on the back blurred to a smear against the cream-colored background. "Since we couldn't date, we started sneaking around. Little things at first: going down to Millers' Pond, taking a walk through the woods. But soon that wasn't enough, and we wanted to spend more and more time together. Or maybe it was the fact that we were always alone together."

She took a deep breath, then let it out slowly. "We . . . uh . . . well . . ." She shifted in her seat, unable to say the words out loud. At the time it had seemed so natural and right, but now she was embarrassed to admit how stupid and naive she had been.

But it was more than lack of sophistication and brains. She had truly thought they could have more without following the rules. What an utter fool she had been.

Ethan held up one hand. "I think I can figure it out for myself."

She couldn't help it; she nearly wept with relief. "I wanted it to make us closer, but in the end, it drove us apart." It was a bit more complicated than that, but it would do for now.

"Sin is sin," he said again. "And forgiveness is forgiveness."

But how could she ask for forgiveness when she couldn't even name her sins aloud? "I suppose." But even to her own ears her words sounded downtrodden.

"Do you believe that all you have to do is ask for the Lord to pardon you?"

She nodded.

"Then that is what you must do."

She stared at the book again, this time her eyes tearing in frustration and confusion. "I'm not sure I can ask Him for that." She wasn't sure it would be granted. Why embarrass herself and Zeb by stating their sins for their entire district to hear if God might deny her request?

"Why would God deny you? I've always been taught 'ask and you will be forgiven.'"

"I can't get up in front of everyone and confess." It wouldn't be expected of her, since she wasn't a church member, but how could she accept forgiveness if she didn't? It just wasn't possible. And she surely couldn't join the church and then do it. The truth would weigh her down even more than it did at the moment.

"Is that what you would have to do? Get up in front of the church and declare your sin?"

Not technically, but she didn't think she could feel absolved any other way. And if she thought her peers and other members of the district despised her now . . . "*Jah*. I mean, yes." But something in his tone made her continue. "What do they do in your church?"

"We go to confession." He shifted at her frown of confusion and tried to explain. "It's like a closet with a screen divider in the center. You go in one side and the priest goes in the other."

"Then what happens?"

"You say, 'Bless me, Father, for I have sinned.' And then you tell him how long it's been since your last confession. And then all that you have done since your last confession."

She mulled this over. "Everything?"

"Just the things that you know are sinful."

It was better than announcing her transgressions to the whole church. "And that's it?"

"That's the most of it. Then the Father gives you penance to say."

"I don't understand."

"They're a little like poems. You say them with your rosary."

Now she was really confused, but she didn't want to tell him that. She simply nodded like she understood and vowed she'd go by the library and look it up. After all, Ethan Dallas had an interesting religion.

"And that's it?" she finally asked.

"In a nutshell."

Two thoughts occurred to her at the same time. How could a God forgive on that alone? And what would it take for her to be a part of such a belief?

But just as quickly as they had come, she shoved them aside. She couldn't change her religion as if she were changing shoes. And her problems with forgiveness were her own. Until she could forgive herself, she couldn't ask God to forgive her. And if she couldn't stand in front of the church the way her beliefs and her heart dictated, then forgiving herself would not be possible.

She was chasing her tail like a silly mutt. Round and round in a circle, ever tightening.

Ethan looked out his window. "It's time for you to get home."

She followed his gaze, noting the darkening sky. "*Jah.*"

Though she didn't want to leave. She wanted to stay, to learn more about Ethan Dallas and his interesting religion.

Ivy marked their place in the book with a slip of paper and stood. "Thank you for listening to me."

He smiled, and she was filled with the need to hug him. She refrained. "Will you come back?" he asked.

"If you'll have me."

"I would love nothing more." His smile expanded until the tiny creases at the corners of his eyes became actual wrinkles and his dimples looked deep enough to fall into. "Next time I'll tell you all about Mary."

She said her farewells and made her way down the hall. If it weren't getting dark, she would go back in there and have him tell her all about Mary. She stopped and wondered who Mary really was. His wife? His sister? Maybe he was speaking of Mary, mother of Jesus, or even Mary Magdalene, the prostitute. Whoever she was, Ivy was anxious to hear about her. Or maybe she was excited to visit with Ethan again. Ethan who knew her secrets and neither condemned her nor ridiculed her. He had simply told her that she would be forgiven as soon as she asked. Except he didn't know all her secrets. Only one other person knew them all. Zebadiah Brenneman.

As if she had somehow made him appear with her thoughts alone, she turned the corner to leave the home and there he was.

And not just Zeb, but a great many others from their youth group. There were Clara Rose, Obie, Thomas Lapp— even Sarah Miller, who used to be Sarah Yoder.

She had only a moment to wonder what to do, but then it was too late. He had already seen her.

"Ivy?" Zeb's voice was full of astonishment. His eyes as well. He rushed toward her, even as she wished she could duck out of sight. "What are you doing here?"

"I—I—I—" was all she managed to say as he grabbed her arm and led her back down the hall.

He opened one of the first doors and gently pushed her inside. The door closed behind them with an ominous click, then he flipped on the light.

They were in some kind of closet filled with mops, buckets on wheels, and jugs of cleaner. The place smelled of lemon scent and bleach, with an underlying musty hint of dirt.

"What are you doing here?" he asked.

Ivy crossed her arms. "I could ask you the same thing."

"We came to sing Christmas carols to the people who live here."

Of course. Every year they did the same at the other home in town. Why would this home be any different? They came to the home, walked down the halls, and sang to people. It was a fun and joyous endeavor, and she had looked forward to it . . . then.

"Ivy?"

"I—" She shifted and tried to come up with a good reason for her being here. *These people understand me* didn't seem to be what he wanted to hear. "I came to visit with the residents." She saw no need to mention anyone in particular.

"You could have come with us."

She shook her head. "I'm tired of being ignored." She didn't say *by my own people*, but it somehow remained there, suspended in the air between them. Just as it had always been.

Zeb was still reeling with shock. He had invited Ivy to this very event and she had turned him down flat, stating that she was busy. It seemed "busy" was hanging around with old people and whatever else it was she did here.

"Why didn't you come here with me?" he asked. "I won't ignore you."

"Everyone else would."

"Ivy," he started, but she shook her head.

"They don't mean to. I understand. I'm that girl. The one who nobody wants their sister to be friends with or their brother to be interested in. I've kissed three boys, you know."

He didn't believe it for a second. He had been her first. Her first kiss, her first everything. "That's not true."

"Everyone says it is. Everyone but the people here."

"So that's why you come here, because these people don't talk about you?"

"No," she said simply. "They don't. And they certainly don't talk about my kissing three boys."

"Look at me and tell me it's true."

She looked at him, but the words didn't come. "No," she finally whispered.

"I want to know who started that rumor." The hate in his voice was alarming. If he had been *Englisch* he would have followed that up with *I'll rip him apart*, but he closed his mouth instead. "Who did this?"

She whirled on him. "I did."

No other words could have sent him reeling like those did. "Why?" His question was little more than a whisper.

"I wanted to keep them at a distance."

"Did it work?"

"On everyone but Obie."

He knew about that. About how Obie and Ivy had worked together to get Clara Rose's attention. He could find no fault with it.

"I didn't mind helping him," she said. "I wanted to help him."

He believed her. "I guess that worked too."

She smiled, and his heart felt a little lighter. He felt like he hadn't seen that smile in a long, long time.

"You're supposed to be singing."

He looked toward the closed door. From somewhere close he could hear the others caroling. Yes, he came here to sing. But those plans had changed the moment he saw Ivy.

"What are you really doing here?" he asked.

She shook her head. "I already told you."

"The truth?"

"As much as I want to tell you."

He wanted to press her. Make her tell him all that she was holding back. All the reasons why she was here. All the reasons why she had spread vicious rumors about herself. But there were some he knew and wasn't sure could stand up to repeating. The others would have to wait until she was ready.

Just make sure you're around when she is.

But he could only hope she wouldn't shut him out forever.

He took a step toward her, hesitant to get too close, needing to be next to her. He had missed her so much when he was gone. He'd thought he'd gotten over it, over her, but all he had to do to change that was see her again. "Let me take you home," he said, hazarding another step. He needed to be just a bit closer.

"You came here with the others."

He nodded. "*Jah.*"

"Didn't you bring a bus?"

"*Jah.*"

"I drove my tractor."

"Then you give me a ride home."

She hesitated, and he was certain she would tell him no. Finally she gave a quick nod. "*Jah,*" she said. "Let's go."

She should have told him no. That she couldn't take him home. And then made up a reason—any reason—why she couldn't. And in the end she had given in to those clear green eyes and that slightly crooked grin. She had been a fool for Zeb Brenneman since the first time she had laid eyes on him. But bad timing had plagued them. Before she knew it, he had joined the church and she wanted to be with him more than she ever thought was possible.

She peered up at him from her place in the seat to where he stood behind her on the tractor. He had his head ducked against the wind and a dark blue scarf covering the lower half of his face.

It would be mean-spirited to smile at his discomfort, but she almost couldn't stop herself. Instead she concentrated on the road ahead and the *Englisch* Christmas lights as they passed. If she were allowed electricity, that would be the very first thing she bought. Miles and miles of pretty, twinkling lights in every color imaginable. She wouldn't have to have a Christmas tree in order to enjoy them. She would string them up all over and maybe not take them down, even after the New Year. There was something about the little pricks of light piercing through the dark. Every night they gently proclaimed the birth of the Savior like miniature fireworks. Or perhaps she was being overly romantic. It wasn't like she would ever have electricity, but sometimes it was fun to dream.

"Are you cold?" she called up to him.

"Fine," came his muffled reply.

She stifled a laugh. "Did Florida make you soft?"

He pulled the scarf down below his mouth. "Places without a cold winter are actually pretty fun."

"In the wintertime," she volleyed.

He laughed. "You'd be surprised."

She might be at that. She had never been much of anywhere, not even to Clarita for the annual school auction. Her biggest trip had been to the mall in Tulsa, shopping for shoes. At the time it had seemed like a grand adventure. But Florida . . . Suddenly she longed to travel as Zeb had. See some of the country. Even riding the bus across all those states and seeing the different places. That alone would be enough. She could buy a round-trip ticket, ride the bus to the ocean then back without even staying for lunch.

Like that was going to happen. She had her grandfather to worry about. She had responsibilities, as they were. He needed her and she needed him. And that was all there was to it.

She remained in her thoughts the rest of the way to the Brenneman place. It was safer there than wondering about everything Zeb had seen on his trips. That just made her want to go more. The biggest problem of all was that she wasn't sure if it was really traveling that she wanted or to just get away from herself for a while.

She left the tractor idling as he stepped down. He was still staring at her, his hat pushed back now that he was out of the wind. "I would like to say that I had a fun time tonight."

"That's what you're supposed to say at the end of a date. And this is not a date."

"It could have been." His words were quietly spoken and almost carried away on the cool night breeze.

"No." She shook her head. "It can't, and it can't ever be."

She could see it on his face. He wanted to protest, tell her they could start over, but there were no second chances. They'd had their opportunity, and they had blown it.

Then his expression changed. It became one of serenity. "We'll see," he said, then turned and made his way into the house, leaving Ivy staring after him.

"Is she still out there?" he asked some fifteen minutes later.

"She's pulling away now," Clara Rose said. She moved away from the window and took her seat back by the fire. She picked up her yarn and hook and after a short count began to work her magic once again. How anyone could take a string and make it into something useful was beyond him.

He sat down on the couch and tried to relax. But seeing Ivy by surprise had him all wound up. He took a deep breath and forced himself to relax.

He had come into the house feeling her stare on him the entire way. It had taken everything he had, but he hadn't looked back. He wanted her to wonder about what he said, wonder about what he meant. He wanted her to stay awake all night trying to figure it out. And he wanted more. So much more.

When he had first come home to Wells Landing, he'd believed that he wanted to return to Florida. He'd only come home for a time. To see his brother, to let his family know he was okay. And if he was truly being honest, he wanted to see Ivy one more time, if only to prove to himself that he was over her.

How could one man be so wrong?

Chapter Twelve

Somehow she managed to avoid Zeb for the rest of the week. He didn't come into the bakery. Or by the house. At least if he did, he was gone by the time she got home.

Tassie and Karl seemed to drop by every day, and Ivy never knew if it was Zeb or Karl who kept up her chores. One thing was certain: Tassie Weber wasn't trying to set Ivy up with Karl, she was trying to set Dawdi up with herself.

The thought made Ivy want to laugh and cry at the same time. She was glad her grandfather had someone interested in him, though she wouldn't know what to do if he married Tassie Weber and moved into her *dawdihaus*.

He would have plenty of people around all the time to help make sure that he didn't forget himself or start a fire. All the things that Ivy constantly worried about. And Ivy would be . . . alone.

She shifted uncomfortably on the church bench and did her best to direct her attention to the bishop. Cephas was delivering the main sermon today, and she usually enjoyed his message, but her mind kept wandering.

What-ifs plagued her. *What if this* and *what if that* . . . all useless thoughts that only kept her from focusing on the now. That went double for speculating about the future.

That too kept her mind on things best not dwelt on. She didn't know what the future held. No one did. One thing she did know for certain: what it didn't hold. And that was Zeb Brenneman.

Somehow she kept herself from cutting her eyes in his direction to see if he was watching her. Because if he was looking at her, then he had to be thinking about her like she was thinking about him. And . . .

And nothing. Thinking, watching, looking, none of those amounted to anything when it came down to love in the real world. That was what they had been given two years ago. A dose of real-world love. It didn't last forever. It didn't always survive tragedy. And no matter how much two people felt they cared for each other, there was a limit to it all. She and Zeb had reached that limit.

She managed to keep her gaze centered on the bishop for the remainder of the service. Once church was dismissed, everyone worked together to set up the tables in the barn, which kept them out of the wind and the cold.

It was less than two weeks until Christmas. Ivy was still hoping for a white Christmas, even though she knew better than to get her hopes up. She could dream and pray all she wanted, but that didn't mean the stubborn Oklahoma weather would cooperate. It could just as well be sixty-five degrees and sunny as cold and snowy.

Once everyone had filed out of the house, Ivy felt her feet taking her across the yard to where Zeb stood talking to his brothers.

She walked straight to him. Not pausing to answer any greetings. Not that there were any. The crowd simply parted and allowed her through.

"What about the blizzard of 2009?" she said without preamble. She stopped just short of being toe-to-toe with him.

"Pardon?" Zeb asked.

"You were talking about a white Christmas, and you said the last one we had was the Christmas of 2000."

He nodded. "I'd forgotten about 2009. That was some snowstorm."

And it was. Wet fat snowflakes had fallen from the sky at such a rate that before anyone knew what happened there were feet on the ground, not inches. The storm took everyone in the area by surprise.

"*Jah.*" She nodded dumbly, not knowing what else to say. She had beelined over to him to tell him about historical weather, and now that the deed was done, she was searching for something to say.

Because you don't want to look stupid? Or because you don't want to leave him?

She didn't have an answer to that.

"That's all I wanted to tell you." She gave a quick nod, which was really more of a jerk of her chin, then started to turn away.

"Can I come over this afternoon?"

"There are no chores to be done today." The words fairly jumped from her lips. It was neither a yes or a no, simply a statement that if he came over he couldn't work since it was Sunday.

"Maybe I want to come and just be with you for a while."

She searched her mind for some excuse, any excuse, and told him the only one she could find. "I'm sure Tassie will be coming over." She had taken to coming over alone these last few days. Ivy wasn't sure if Karl had refused to be a part of her plan any longer or if she had merely given up the pretense of having him along for Ivy.

"I don't mind."

I do! she wanted to shout. She wanted Zeb all to herself. She wanted him as far from her as possible. And she wanted him forever.

But he wasn't hers.

"Are you up for a few hands of Uno?" she asked.

Zeb blinked as if trying to clear his mind enough to decipher her words. "Uh, sure," he finally said, followed by, "Uno?"

Ivy smiled. "Tassie loves it."

Zeb shook his head. "Of course she does."

"So?" She waited for his answer.

"I'm looking forward to it," he finally said.

Ivy walked away, laughter threatening her solemn exit.

Uno.

The one word dogged him all the way to Ivy's house. *Uno?*

Why couldn't they play Scrabble or even Rook? They had enough players.

Unless Ivy was teasing him and there would be no one involved in their afternoon. That was something he could accept. But somehow, no matter how hard he wanted to hang on to the idea, it slipped away. *Jah*, Uno was definitely part of his immediate future. He just knew it.

But then again, so was Ivy. Spending the afternoon with her would be wonderful, amazing whether they actually played cards or not. Truth be known, he didn't care what they did as long as they were together.

There. He had finally admitted it to himself. He liked spending time with Ivy. He always had. And if they didn't dwell too much in the past, couldn't it be possible for the two of them to have a future?

He reined in that thought as he pulled the buggy into her drive.

A future with Ivy wasn't something he could hang his hat on. They had tried, had even planned for a future only to have it cruelly snatched away from them. Some would call it divine intervention, others God's will, but he knew

what it was . . . a second chance for them both. They had
agreed to use that chance for themselves and not look back.

So why had Ivy "gone wild" once her mother remarried?

It was one question she had not answered. Maybe she
never would. But how could she have a second chance if
she was starting rumors about herself and keeping the entire
community at a distance?

The thought slammed into him like a runaway horse.
Unless she didn't want that second chance.

He couldn't get his mind wrapped around the thought as
he climbed down from the carriage and unhitched his horse.
He turned the beast out into the pasture and made sure there
was water in the trough before heading into the house.

The question knocked around in his mind, bouncing off
the sides of his brain until his head was nearly throbbing.

He reached out to knock on the door, but it was jerked
open before his knuckles met the wood.

"Zeb!" Ivy's tone and smile were overbright. "So good
to see you." She grabbed him by one arm and dragged him
into the warm house.

He barely had time to take a breath and get his bearings
back before she continued. "Can I take your coat? I mean,
you can hang it up there by the door. We were just about to
start a game of Uno."

Yikes! She was serious.

He removed his coat and hat and hung them on the peg
hooks next to the front door, then turned toward the small
table by the kitchen. True to her word, a deck of Uno cards
was sitting in the middle of the table, waiting for play to
begin. Yonnie was there, patiently waiting, as was the promised Tassie Weber, and . . . Karl.

Zeb glanced back to Ivy, the cause for her trouble dawning
on him. Tassie was trying to set her up with Karl. The thought
was unimaginable. Karl was large but as mild-mannered

as they came. He seemed a little slow on the uptake, and though Zeb had no problems with him personally, he imagined that Ivy would run all over the man before the ink dried on their marriage petition.

"Come." There was that overbright smile again. Ivy's tone was pitched so high, Zeb wondered if only dogs could hear it. "Come sit down. Dawdi, deal Zeb in this hand."

Zeb dug in his heels even as Ivy urged him toward the table. "Oh, no. I wouldn't want to intrude. I had no idea you had guests already. Perhaps I should go."

Ivy leaned in close. "Not on your life." Then she straightened and trilled in that too-high voice, "We would love to have you join us. The more the merrier, isn't that what they say?"

"Of course, my dear." But Tassie's eyes held a resigned edge.

Karl frowned, and as far as Zeb could tell, Yonnie was oblivious of the entire interaction.

"If you're certain," Zeb said, stalling. He loved watching Ivy squirm. He supposed it was terrible of him, but watching her flit around unable to manipulate the situation to what she desired was somehow amusing to him.

Because he had spent so much of his time unable to get her from his thoughts? Or perhaps because he enjoyed the pink flush that stole into her cheeks and made her freckles stand out in stark relief.

Definitely the freckles.

"There." She sat back down with a thud, looking somewhat exhausted for her efforts.

Karl continued to glare in a hurt sort of way, and Tassie herself seemed to wear a forced smile.

"Are we ready?" Yonnie looked around the table.

Everyone nodded except for Zeb.

"I don't have a seat," he said mildly. There were only four chairs situated around the table.

Ivy was on her feet in an instant. "You can have mine." She gestured grandly to it.

"Where are you going to sit?" he asked.

She smiled, a little like a crazy person might smile. "I'll just go . . . into the kitchen . . . and get us . . . some pie." She was gone in an instant.

"What are you waiting for?" Yonnie asked. "Sit down, boy."

Zeb looked from the frozen smile of Tassie, to Karl's hurt, calflike gaze, to the kitchen door where Ivy had gone. "Maybe I'll go help Ivy," he said.

Yonnie shrugged. "Suit yourself." He started dealing the cards.

For a moment, Zeb thought Karl might offer to go with him, but the time passed and the other man picked up the cards as Yonnie slid them to him.

Tassie frowned at her hand, and Zeb figured it had nothing to do with her cards. He pushed into the kitchen after Ivy.

"What are you doing?" Zeb asked. She hadn't been in the kitchen more than a couple of minutes, and yet half a bag of flour had been dumped into a bowl and the milk was sitting opened on the countertop.

She didn't bother to turn around. "I'm making a pie."

"Now?"

"It's not going to bake itself." She opened the bottom cabinet and pulled out her saucepan. She plunked it down on the stove top, lit the burner, then started for the larder.

"I thought you meant you were going to *get* us some pie."

She nodded. "Yes, but we don't have any pie. So I'm going to make one."

He started forward, then stopped, unsure it was wholly safe. "You don't have to do that, you know."

"Oh, yes, I do. Have you seen them?"

That was it. He was going in. Braving the storm that was Ivy Weaver and whatever it was that had her so riled.

He was directly behind her in a second. He spun her around, and grabbed her arms just to be on the safe side. "What is wrong with you?"

For a moment he thought she was going to twist out of his grasp, then she seemed to wilt before his eyes.

"She keeps pushing him at me, and he keeps resisting. I don't need a reminder of what everyone says about me. I know the rumors. I *started* the rumors."

"So why is it bothering you at all?" he quietly asked.

Why had she told him any of this? Why had she told him anything at all?

She gathered her strength and twisted away from him. Not that his grip was tight, but she needed some kind of fortitude to pull herself away from him. It had always been that way between them. It didn't matter that her head knew that they could only be friends, that everything between them had run its course; her heart hadn't gotten the message.

"It was all right at first," she said. She hadn't wanted to tell him this either, but somehow the words had a mind of their own. They needed telling whether she wanted them told or not. "Then it sort of snowballed and got out of control."

"Will you tell me why you want to keep them at bay?" he asked quietly.

How could she? She shook her head. "It doesn't matter now. The damage is done."

He nodded and looked to the counter, where all her ingredients were scattered about. "What kind of pie are you making?"

She sighed. "Vinegar."

"I love vinegar pie. Can I give you a hand?"

"You like making pies?" she asked.

He grinned. "No. But I hate playing Uno."

Ivy ran the brush through her hair, smoothing it down when the crackle of static electricity reached her ears. Brush. Smooth. Brush. Smooth. While over and over in her head, the events of the afternoon played.

She had never been so happy to see anyone in her life as she had been to see Zeb Brenneman that afternoon. Maybe she had been wrong about Tassie's intentions. Once Ivy had thought the woman meant to pair her with Karl, then Ivy had suspected that Tassie herself had her eyes set on Dawdi. But after today, she was beginning to wonder if both might be on Tassie Weber's agenda.

A soft knock sounded at her door.

"Come in."

The door creaked open and her grandfather stood on the other side. "Getting ready for bed?"

She nodded.

He paused there in her doorway, then leaned against the jamb. "About this afternoon . . ."

She stopped brushing her hair and held up one hand to stop the rest of his words. "You don't have to say anything. If you enjoy Tassie's company . . ." Did he enjoy Tassie's company?

She had never really thought about her grandfather with another wife. He had been married to her *mammi* for fifty years or better before Mammi died. And he had never acted as if he might ever get remarried. Now she wondered if there was more to it than merely true love.

"Why are people saying all these horrible things about you?" Dawdi asked.

Her heart sank. It was one part of her plan that she hadn't

thought through. She hadn't wondered what would happen if the rumors got back to him.

"You know how it can be," she said, but she couldn't meet his gaze.

"I'm not even going to ask if they are true."

She turned and looked at him then. "You're not?"

He shook his head. "I know they can't be. You were raised better than that."

"But you . . . you saw the car."

"Bah." He waved a hand as if dismissing her words. "That's just a car. And jeans are just clothing."

But the three boys she had allegedly kissed . . .

"And the other," he said, pinning her with clear blue eyes. Tonight it seemed as if all of his memory was intact. "I don't believe that for a moment. What I want to know is what happened between you and Zeb Brenneman?"

Ivy sputtered, recovered, and started brushing her hair once again. "What makes you think there's something between me and Zeb?"

"I've got eyes."

She should have outright denied it. What was wrong with her? She had been lying about her relationship with Zeb for as long as . . . well, as long as there had been a relationship with Zeb. But she couldn't lie to her grandfather. Not now. No matter how badly she wanted to. "There's nothing between us." And that was the truth. As painful as it was.

"I would say that's not the truth."

"It is." Whatever had been between them had died long ago. They had agreed to go their separate ways. Was it her fault that Zeb had decided to break their agreement and come back to Wells Landing? Was it fair of her to think he could stay away from his home forever? "Listen, Dawdi—"

He shook his head. "You don't have to tell me," he said. "But one day you're going to have to acknowledge it to yourself."

* * *

Long after her grandfather had kissed her cheek, told her good night, and hobbled off to his own bedroom, his words stayed with her.

One day you're going to have to acknowledge it to yourself.

Was that what he thought she was doing? Hiding from the truth? Was it what she was doing? She had been telling herself lies for so long that she had come to believe them as the truth. That she didn't need Zeb. She didn't love him. She didn't want him. That she didn't miss him with each breath.

But nothing had changed since he'd come back into town. She still didn't want to need him, want him, miss him, love him.

She got up the next morning and went through her normal Monday routine, headed for the bakery, then back home again. It was perhaps the first day that she hadn't truly enjoyed her job. Her *dawdi*'s advice haunted her. And she found less satisfaction in making the good folks of Wells Landing talk to her. She burned her arm on the large oven and broke one fingernail down to the quick. Thankfully, neither bled, but she drove home with a throbbing arm and a bandage over the end of her thumb.

"Of course," she muttered as she pulled onto the short lane leading to the house. A tractor was parked off to one side. A machine that didn't belong to her or her *dawdi*.

Visitors. Just what she needed.

She searched her memory for the owner of the tractor, but she couldn't place the machine with anyone in their church district. Not that she knew every tractor that belonged to every family. She was more familiar with everyone's horse and buggy than the many rusty tractors that chugged down the Mayes County roads daily.

She continued to assess the tractor, but couldn't remember

who it belonged to. The bishop? Tassie Weber? One of the other Brennemans?

Ivy parked her own tractor in its usual spot, then climbed down. There was no one hanging out in the cool December air, and she pulled her coat a little tighter around her and headed for the house. With any luck her *dawdi* was home and their visitor had been offered some of last night's pie and a fresh cup of coffee.

She took off her coat, bonnet, and gloves, then followed the delicious aroma of coffee straight into the kitchen, surprised to see Clara Rose Brenneman sitting across from Dawdi. She was perhaps the last person Ivy would have expected.

"Clara Rose, so good of you to come by," she greeted, wondering what had the woman visiting. Did she come to talk to Dawdi about hay, or was she there for Ivy?

Ivy remembered the scathing looks that Clara Rose had sent her way last year during the fall hayride. Not that Ivy could blame her, given all the rumors that were circulating at the time, but she had hoped that at least one person would give her the benefit of the doubt. Well, one person other than Obie. But that was in the past.

Now the rumors had grown. The censure had doubled. Yet Clara Rose sat at her table, her chin set at a determined angle.

"I need to talk to you about something." Clara Rose pushed herself to her feet, her half-eaten pie still on the table in front of her.

"*Jah.* Sure." Ivy nodded dumbly. She wasn't sure she wanted to talk to Clara Rose, not with the fire burning in her sky-blue eyes, but she might as well get it over with.

Dawdi's chair scraped loudly against the floor as he pushed it out behind him. "Y'all go ahead and sit here. I've got some things to tend to in the barn."

Ivy couldn't imagine what, since she did all the outside

chores, but she wasn't about to call her grandfather out in front of company, such as it were.

Clara Rose settled back into her seat as Ivy poured herself a cup of coffee. She took it over to the table and eased down into her grandfather's vacated seat.

"I'll get right to the point. What are your intentions toward Zeb?"

Ivy nearly choked on her mouthful of coffee. "My what?"

"Your intentions. Zeb is back, and I know that the two of you had something a few years ago. Now he's home but moping around the house. He's over here more than he's at home. Just what do you want from him?"

"How do you know there was something between us?" She could have simply denied it, but she wanted to hear this answer.

"Last year after the hayride. Obie told me."

"Told you what?" Just how much did Clara Rose know?

"He told me that he used you to make me jealous."

And that worked? Maybe she wasn't such a pariah after all. "He did?"

"I jumped all over him for . . . contributing to your reputation." She stopped, using her fork to pick at the edge of the pie still sitting on the saucer in front of her. "But he wasn't really contributing, was he?"

Ivy shook her head.

"Zeb is a good man. I've known him almost my whole life. He knows what's right and what's wrong. He's good and godly and has made his vows to the church."

"*Jah.*"

"So how do you figure into all this?"

How indeed? "I don't."

"I don't believe that. I've seen the way he looks at you. The way he watches you when he thinks no one will notice."

Oh, how she wanted to unburden herself, tell her entire story to Clara Rose, put it out on the table and examine it.

Maybe if she did it would appear smaller, maybe even manageable. Or it could grow to out-of-control proportions.

"Zeb wants something that's gone, something that we can never get back." She swallowed the lump that had formed in her throat. It had nearly choked out her last couple of words.

"Have you tried?"

"It's not as easy as that."

Clara Rose nodded sagely. "Never is."

Chapter Thirteen

They finished their pie and talked for a little more, sticking to safe topics like how the baby was doing and how happy the Brennemans were to have Zeb home.

"I don't think he'll stay," Clara Rose said, her voice full of lament.

Ivy shook her head. "Probably not." Like Chris Flaud, Zeb had a wandering soul. Unlike Chris, Zeb didn't have a paralyzed brother who was bedridden and needed constant care. Zeb would stay as long as he could, then he would head out again. They'd all be lucky if he stayed past the New Year.

Clara Rose nodded slowly. "If anyone could get him to stay, it would be you."

Two things occurred to Ivy in that moment. The first was that it was true what they said: when people were in love they tended to see love all around them whether it was there or not. Why else would Ivy be able to get Zeb to stay? And the other was that Clara Rose could be the friend she had needed all along. Ivy wanted to unburden herself, explain to Clara Rose why it looked as if she and Zeb were in love. Perhaps there had been a time when they really were in love, but the time had passed. They couldn't go back. And she had to believe that their unfurled relationship was just proof that sometimes God's will prevailed. Well, it did all the time, she supposed, but in cases like theirs when each had prayed for a different outcome, it was more obvious than others. She might not know where she was supposed to be in life, who she might marry, if at all, and where Zeb would finally end up. But she knew the answer was not with her.

Clara Rose waited expectantly, as if she could sense Ivy's inner turmoil. But she couldn't do it. Ivy couldn't tell Clara Rose everything that had happened between her and Zeb. Wells Landing was tiny. What would happen if she did tell? What kind of judgment would she face in their close-knit community? Would she lose her job? Would she be able to hold her head up and walk down the street? Amish were forgiving, but that didn't mean they would forget. And if everyone in town knew what had happened . . .

"I guess I should get back home." Clara Rose stood. "It's going to be time to feed Paul Daniel soon."

"Of course." Ivy pushed herself to her feet. "You'll have to bring him next time." Like there would be a next time. Surely not if Ivy told Clara Rose the truth.

"*Jah.* I will. I wanted Daddy and baby to have a little alone time." She winked. "Makes them appreciate the *mamm* all the more."

Clara Rose slipped back into her coat, tied her bonnet under her chin, and pulled on her gloves. With a flourish, she wrapped the scarf around her neck and started for the door.

Ivy stood on the porch and waved as she backed out of her drive.

Not so very long ago, Clara Rose was engaged to marry Thomas Lapp. Ivy wasn't sure what had happened, but she'd heard that at the wedding, Thomas had announced that he and Clara Rose weren't getting married after all.

Ivy wished she had been there to see that. Things like that didn't happen all the time in a small community like theirs. Clara Rose had started off that day believing she was marrying one man and ended up a few months later marrying another. Some things just didn't work out the way a person suspected.

They both figured that Zeb would return to Florida, or at least that he wouldn't stay in Wells Landing. But anything was possible. If he did stay, he would eventually get married, maybe raise a family. The thought sent her heart plummeting to her toes. How would she be able to go to church, to the store, even to the bakery knowing that she might run into Zeb and the family they would never have? The thought was almost more than she could bear.

If that time came, maybe she would move to Indiana, but she knew she wouldn't. Watching Zeb be happy with another would be just another part of God's punishment for actions past. She would have to learn to live with it.

With one final wave at Clara Rose, Ivy pulled the ends of her sweater around her a bit tighter and made her way back into the house.

The rest of the week fell into a comfortable pattern. Ivy would drive home from work each day to find her grandfather playing some sort of game with Tassie Weber. Thankfully Karl had "other plans" this week and chose not to visit. That was just fine with Ivy. It was one thing to be forced to go places where she knew she would be shunned and another to have it in her very own house. Karl held censure against her, and it was best if the two of them stayed as far apart as possible. There was no need for them to be obliged to visit just because his grandmother wanted to come see her grandfather. But it wouldn't do to try to tell Tassie that.

Ivy sent up a small prayer of thanks for the "other plans" Karl had. She was grateful to them, whatever they were.

When she got home each day, her grandfather and Tassie were in the kitchen and her chores in the barn were all taken care of—and it seemed that Tassie had taken over the cooking duties from her grandfather. She didn't notice much change in the food, since Tassie was using her grandmother's own recipe book to pick meals from. Tassie kept the ingredients the same and rarely deviated from the original. It occurred to Ivy that maybe her grandfather couldn't tell that Tassie seemed to be after herself a new husband, but Ivy figured she shouldn't interfere. Every time she came in, the pair was laughing and having a great time, eating pie, and sharing stories about when they were in school together. He seemed happy, and if he was happy, Ivy was happy for him.

It was also a relief not to have to worry about him when she was at work. His memory had seemed to be holding these days, but it could be that he stayed in the here and now because he was grounded there by Tassie's presence. Ivy didn't know a lot about such things, but she decided she would go the following day and look it up on the computers at the library.

Whatever had caused it, she was grateful. But today was Thursday and she had been waiting all week to visit with the residents at the Whispering Pines Senior Living Center.

She was getting to be a common sight there, and no one paused as she came in and signed her name to the guest book. A few people greeted her—a couple of the residents, one nurse, and a couple of other employees that she had seen before. She smiled a little to herself as she made her way to Ethan's room.

"Tell me about forgiveness," she asked after they had greeted one another and settled down into his small living area where she read to him.

He looked at her, his eyes bright, if not a little droopy at the corners. He looked tired, and she worried that he wasn't getting enough rest. She would have to talk to Angie about it on her way out. "What do you want to know?" he asked. "Forgiveness is forgiveness."

"You've said that before," Ivy commented. "What does it mean?"

"It means that there are a great many ways to ask for forgiveness, but God's forgiveness is the same no matter what."

She nodded slowly, thoughtfully. "Then why are there different ways to ask?"

Ethan gave an elegant shrug, and she couldn't help but notice that his hands trembled. Had they always done that? Maybe she should talk to the nurse . . . "Just different beliefs, is all."

Different beliefs. But those beliefs were what separated them all. Yet not from God. The thought was like a whirlwind in her mind.

"I thought that one day we would get married, you know?"

He nodded, but didn't comment.

"We only have baptism classes once every two years. So when I waited too long, Zeb and I knew that we would have to wait even longer."

"But you didn't want to."

"We just wanted to be together, you know? Spend time together like all our friends who had found boyfriends or girlfriends. But because I wasn't a member of the church, we couldn't officially date. So we snuck around." She had already told him all this, but he didn't bother to point that out to her. Ethan was kind that way, as if he knew she needed to say the words again, even if to the same person who had heard them before.

"There's a reason why spending so much time alone is frowned upon." She shook her head. "That's not entirely true. Amish parents trust their children. They have raised them up in the way and have faith that they will not deviate from their righteous path."

"But?" he quietly asked.

Ivy centered her gaze on the paper chain of green and red they had made on her last visit there. It was a crude decoration, hardly worth the time they had spent making it. But they had laughed, and had talked other residents into helping them cut all the paper strips, and she had listened to all their stories about life in the 1950s and what it meant to be a part of a war that hardly anyone supported. She had listened enthralled. It was easy sometimes to forget that these sorts of things happened outside her beloved, quiet Wells Landing.

"But it's different when you are always alone. We never sat on my parents' sofa in the middle of the night, knowing full well anyone could come down the stairs at any minute."

"So you were alone, but not *alone*."

She nodded. "Except we were *alone*. Always."

"And temptation got the better of you."

She nodded. "But there's more." She drew in a deep breath, not sure that she could continue, but if she was to have this forgiveness that Ethan talked about with such conviction, she would have to tell someone.

"I found out I was going to have a baby." The shame and joy of it almost choked her. She had been so happy, so remorseful, so many things that warred with each other inside her heart.

She had found out early and on a fluke. She had barely been late with her period before she had the opportunity to buy a pregnancy test and give it a try. Maybe it was something of intuition, but somehow she knew before she even opened that slim pink-and-white box what it would reveal.

But she didn't know what the two of them would do, her and Zeb. Would he be happy? Sad? Regretful? What would they tell their families?

But they didn't tell them anything. She miscarried before they got the chance.

The pain of that time was still so sharp and real, nearly tangible. She knew in her heart it was for the best. God had given them a second chance, a chance to start again, to forget it ever happened. They didn't have to confess. They didn't have to let everyone know their transgressions. But along with that freedom came an acute sense of guilt. Had they cheated? Or been cheated?

"What happened?" Ethan asked, bringing her out of her memories.

"I lost the baby. Zeb went to Florida, and I started a wild *rumspringa*." The kind they made movies out of on public television. Or so she had heard someone say.

Ethan took a deep breath. "We are the same all around."

She nodded. It could have happened to anyone, but it had happened to her.

"All you have to do is ask," he said quietly.

"No." There had to be more than that. How could asking relieve the thud in her heartbeats, the pain in her stomach, the mourning in her soul?

"Last time you came, I told you I was going to tell you about Mary."

"*Jah.*"

"Mary was persecuted. Frowned upon by her neighbors and those she once called friend. She endured it all because she knew she was to give birth to the Savior."

How many times had she heard the Christmas story? She had read it straight from the Bible herself. She knew of Mary and Joseph and their trip to Bethlehem. She had heard it every year of her life.

But persecuted?

It wasn't anything she had ever given much thought. Mary knew she was going to have the son of God. Wasn't that comfort alone enough?

"Mary endured months of doubts, but still she pressed on. She had to tell her intended that she was going to have a baby. A baby that was not his. And she swore that no man had ever touched her. Who would believe such a thing?"

"No one," Ivy whispered. And yet she had done the exact opposite as Mary. She had told everyone lies in hopes they would stay away, so she wouldn't have to answer the hard questions. So she wouldn't have to confess her sins. And yet those sins were eating away at her from the inside out. "What did she do?" Ivy asked.

Ethan smiled. "There's a reason why the Catholics hold Mary in such high esteem. She did more than have our Savior. She lived for him, raised him, suffered for him. Would have died for him had he let her. A mother's love."

A mother's love. Was it so simple? She would have done anything for the child she had carried. And in the end she could do nothing. It occurred to her then that she had more remorse for being thankful that God had taken the burden from her than she had for the sin itself. What kind of person did that make her?

"A human one," Ethan replied.

Had she said those words aloud? "I didn't want to lose the baby," she said, feeling the trickle of tears on her cheeks. She wiped them away with the back of one hand. "I thought I was coming here to make your day better. How is it that you turned that around on me?"

"That's why we're here," Ethan said. "To help each other every way we can."

She gave her tears one last swipe, feeling lighter than she had in the last two years. She had lifted part of the burden, just by telling someone about the baby, her and Zeb, and the feelings she had held in for so long.

"What now?" she asked.

"You have to find it within you to forgive yourself. You have to forgive yourself for the transgressions, real and imagined. And you have to forgive God. Only then can you allow Him to forgive you."

How? That had been the next question she had asked him, but Ethan had merely smiled and offered her a pudding. They walked down to the cafeteria together, and despite all the other things racing around in her head, she couldn't help but notice that his steps were a little heavier, the trip a little longer than it had been before.

"I'm fine," he said with a smile. "I'm going home soon."

She frowned, unsure of this meaning. "Your grandson is coming to get you?"

His smile deepened, became even more indulgent. "To heaven."

She took a deep breath, unsure of whether she should ask the question on her mind.

"Yes," he said before she could utter a word. "I know I have a home in heaven. Last rites and all aside, when I die, I will go to be with Jesus. And Mary."

Tears filled her eyes once again, but this time she managed to blink them away. She didn't want to think about him dying. She only wanted to think about him like he was right then, eating pudding, smiling, and talking to her about Mary.

But she had known he was not long for this world when she first met him. Now she prayed that his grandson would get back to the States in time to see Ethan before he died.

She couldn't imagine her grandfather dying and her not being able to see him before.

Ethan's wrinkled hand covered hers where it lay on the table. "'Now is not the time for tears, for I have been . . . I have joined with my fellow man, and I pray leave this world better than I found it.'"

"Wh-what?" she stuttered, and her breath caught in her throat.

"It's a poem I read once."

"It's beautiful."

"There's more, but I don't know it all."

She smiled and shook her head. "What you recited is fantastic."

"Don't be sad, Ivy. Learn to forgive yourself. The sooner the better, okay?"

"Okay."

He squeezed her fingers. "Promise me."

"I promise."

He held up one hand, pinky up in the air. "Pinky swear?"

She laughed. "Are you serious?"

"Very. You can't break a pinky swear."

She hooked her pinky with his. "Pinky swear." She started to pull away, but he held tight to her little finger.

"Repeat after me. 'I, Ivy Weaver, do hereby pinky swear that I will learn to forgive myself and allow myself to be happy.'"

Between incredulous laughs, she managed to repeat the vow. They ate one more pudding cup, and she headed home, his last words to her still playing over and over in her head. *Start with Zeb.*

She wanted to ask Ethan what he meant, but someone had come up and the question had gotten lost in the good-byes and Merry Christmases.

There were only three days until Christmas. She only had one more gift to get for her grandfather, and she wanted to wait until Christmas Eve. She wanted his favorite oatmeal raisin cookies to be fresh.

She wondered what kind of cookies Ethan would like. He seemed like a sugar cookie kind of man to her, but one could never be sure. But who didn't like decorated Christmas cookies with icing and sprinkles? That was what she would do. Oatmeal raisin for her *dawdi* and holiday cookies for Ethan Dallas.

She smiled to herself as she turned down the lane that led to her house. It would be dark soon, and though the days were mild for this time of year, once the sun went down, the wind turned cold.

There was no smoke puffing out of the chimney. Her grandfather should have started a fire this afternoon. Maybe even kept the morning fire going.

The thought sent a shaft of panic slicing through her. She took a deep breath and pressed it down. She couldn't let herself get all bent out of shape because he had forgotten to keep the fire burning. She couldn't let herself get that far out of control.

She parked the tractor in its usual spot and made her way to the house. She kept each step slow and measured, even though she wanted to run into the house and search for her grandfather. Somehow she knew he wasn't there.

"Dawdi," she called as she walked through the house. She had to be sure he hadn't simply fallen asleep and forgotten to relight the fire. But she didn't bother to take off her coat or bonnet. "Dawdi!"

She checked all the rooms, but she knew it was a waste of time. There were only a few places he could logically be. The graveyard, an auction he had forgotten to tell her about, or maybe over visiting with Tassie. The last one seemed to be the least likely. She couldn't imagine her father going to Tassie's house. Tassie had been content to visit his home all this time. Or maybe that was further proof that was where he was.

With a sigh, Ivy shut the door behind her and started back to her tractor.

* * *

An hour later and she was beyond worried. Tassie claimed that she hadn't seen him all day. She and Karl had gone to a doctor's appointment in Pryor and only then had returned to Wells Landing. The cemetery was empty of visitors, and the auctions had all closed hours ago. Her grandfather was missing.

She stopped at every house along the road back home, but no one had seen her *dawdi*. She passed by the Brenneman place and nearly drove past before changing her mind and pulling down the lane. It was dark. The lights on her tractor were meant for plowing, not a long trip down winter roads.

"What's wrong?" Zeb asked as he opened the door for her. Behind him she could see Clara Rose rocking baby Paul Daniel while Obie watched. She had heard them before she knocked. Obie had been reading from the Bible, the story of the first Christmas. The perfect Amish family. A far cry from what she had.

"Dawdi's missing." She hated the tears that sprang into her eyes. She had cried so much this day, she didn't have patience for any more tears.

Zeb grabbed his hat and crammed it onto his head before pulling on his coat and scarf.

"Can I help?" Obie was on his feet in a second.

But Ivy shook her head. "You stay here with your family."

Obie glanced adoringly at his family, then turned back to Ivy. "Two is better than one."

"But—"

"You could wait at the house while we go around. That way if he comes back . . ." Zeb didn't finish the statement. There was no need. If Dawdi came back to the house, Obie wasn't to let him leave again.

Obie kissed Clara Rose and the baby, then grabbed his own coat and hat and followed them outside. "You take the tractor over to Ivy's. She and I will take hers around to see if we can find him."

Obie nodded, and Zeb took her arm and led her back to her tractor.

"Do you want me to drive?' he asked.

She wanted to say no, that she had this, but she had been strong for so many months, years. She wasn't sure she could keep it up much longer. How wonderful to be able to lean on Zeb and not have to shoulder all the worry herself.

"That's fine," she said. She almost convinced herself that by letting him drive she would be the one searching the fields and ditches in order to find her *dawdi*. Almost.

They drove around for what seemed like hours, but could only have been about forty-five minutes. Still, it was long enough that her nose was near frozen and her teeth were chattering, and yet they hadn't seen even the first sign of her grandfather.

"Do you think he's returned back to the house?" Her voice was filled with both hope and despair, lending it a husky tone.

"We can check," he replied. His mouth was set in a firm line, and she knew that he was as worried as she.

Her heart was heavy as he turned the tractor around and headed back toward her house.

He didn't speak all the way back. It wasn't a great distance, but it was long enough, and Ivy was grateful for the silence. The rest of the world kept going. She pretended she could hear music and television shows coming from the *Englisch* houses. Christmas lights twinkled merrily. And the creatures of the night who were brave enough to face the cold were creating their very own special music.

When he pulled into the lane that led to the house, Ivy spied the plumes of smoke rising up from the chimney. Her hopes raised until she realized that it was most likely a fire built by Obie to ward off the chill inside the house.

Zeb parked the tractor in front of the house. Ivy thought about telling him to put it up for the night, but decided against it. At this point, she really didn't care. She had to find her grandfather, and that was all there was to it.

"Any word?" Zeb asked as he pushed into the house.

"I was going to ask you the same thing."

They stood side by side, handsome matching bookends, and Ivy simply stood there and stared. Her ears started to buzz as the feeling returned to her cold face. Her grandfather was lost. Lost! They had been all over the county. Unless he had holed up in an *Englisch* house. They hadn't checked any of those. It was a slim hope, but the only one she had.

She touched Zeb's arm, feeling the warmth of him soak through the material of his shirt through to her. When had he taken off his coat? When had she taken off her gloves? She shook her head, trying to put her rambling thoughts in some kind of order. "Let's go check the *Englisch* houses."

He stared at her for a long while, then finally spoke. "It's too dangerous being out there on a tractor. Dangerous and cold."

"But—" She wanted to protest further, but she couldn't find the words. Stress and activity had exhausted her.

"No buts," he said. He tilted her chin back to where he could look into her eyes, then said the words that she had been dreading all along. "I think it's time we take this to the police."

Chapter Fourteen

The Wells Landing Police Department was small and brightly lit. Almost too bright, after searching in the dark for her grandfather. Someone had strung a blue and silver garland twisted together with yellow police *CAUTION* tape around the front desk and all the other desks she could see. Blue-colored Christmas balls hung from the tinsel every couple of feet, though a few were missing. Ivy counted them, then went back over them in reverse order. She needed something to occupy her mind as they waited.

Zeb had driven her into town and now sat beside her in the front waiting area of the police station. The receptionist looked to be a uniformed officer, but was busy manning the phones. She had told them to wait, and that was what they were doing. Waiting.

Ivy bounced one leg and tried to gather her patience. She needed her grandfather to be found. She needed him to be okay. She needed him to be safe.

Zeb placed one hand on her knee. She stopped bouncing, her gaze flying to his. "He's going to be okay," he said.

"You don't know that," she whispered in return.

"No. I don't, but I have faith that everything will turn out fine."

Faith. That had been in short supply these days. At least for her. Zeb had faith. Ethan Dallas had faith. Why couldn't she muster up enough faith that she could calmly sit and wait for the officer who was going to work her case?

Because you're a sinner. And you can't ask for forgiveness. If you could, then maybe you would have faith. But you don't have enough faith to trust God to forgive you.

The words flooded her mind. They were bold, sharp, and, heaven help her, true. She hadn't had much faith these last couple of years, so why did she think she would have it now?

"Miss Weaver?"

She turned at the sound of her name.

"I'm Officer Downy. I hear you're missing someone important to you."

She nodded and stood. "*Jah.* My grandfather."

"Come right this way," he said. "Let's see what we can do."

An hour later they were no closer to finding her grandfather, but at least they had expanded their search. Officer Downy had issued a "silver alert," which meant a senior citizen had gone missing and everyone needed to keep an eye out for him. He contacted the Mayes County Sheriff's Office in Pryor in case they heard anything. They would also cover the farms outside the Wells Landing city limits.

"Come on." Zeb clasped her arm and helped her to her feet.

"We'll let you know the minute we find out anything." He looked at the papers that she had filled out. "Do you have a cell number?"

She shook her head. "That's the phone shanty down from the house."

He nodded, obviously accustomed to working around the limitations of the Amish community.

"My brother has one," Zeb said. "A cell phone." He rattled off the number for the officer to jot down.

They had done all they could do. It was time to leave.

"But—" Ivy wanted to protest, yet she couldn't find it in her. She wanted to stay there until her grandfather found his way home. She wanted to walk every street and road in the area until she located him. She wanted to *find* him.

"Let's go, Ivy." Zeb tugged on her arm.

"We'll let you know as soon as we have something for you."

She nodded and allowed Zeb to lead her away.

"I can't just . . . go home," she said. That was a little too much like giving up. And she could never do that.

"It's dark, Ivy. The roads are getting dangerous. We need to go home and wait for an officer to contact us."

"On your brother's cell phone?"

He shook his head in resignation and helped her onto the back of the tractor. "Obie's at your house. We'll have him leave the phone, then we wait for your grandfather."

Or news of him.

"You'll stay with me?" she asked. She couldn't be by herself right now. There would be talk about the two of them when word got out that he had stayed with her tonight. But she didn't care. She didn't want to be alone. Not now.

He hesitated for a brief moment, then nodded. She supposed he had come to the same conclusion she had: there wasn't much more damage that could be done to her reputation now. "Of course."

When there was no news about her grandfather and ten o'clock came and went, Zeb convinced Ivy to try to get some sleep. He could only do that by promising to keep the phone in his hand at all times.

He lay down on the couch, but could hear the restless squeak of her bedsprings as she tried to get comfortable. Obie's phone was stubbornly silent. Zeb wanted to will the thing to ring, but he only wanted good news. In the end, he settled for prayer. He asked the Lord to take care of Yonnie, wherever he might be. To keep him safe and warm. Thankfully it wasn't raining, but that was about the only plus he could find with the situation.

He had just drifted off to sleep, his dreams only partly fantasy. A creak of the floorboards roused him fully. It took him a moment to realize he wasn't at home. He wasn't in Florida. He was in Wells Landing. In Ivy's home. And she was . . .

"Ivy?" He didn't see her, but somehow he knew she was there.

"Did I wake you?" she asked into the darkness. Then she came into view, stepping into the shaft of moonlight that filtered in from the living room windows.

"Why are you up?"

She shrugged, just a quick rise and drop of her shoulders. She looked something like an angel standing there in her soft white nightgown, moonlight spilling over her. But he knew she would say she was unworthy of the title. She had seen to that herself with hateful and false rumors.

"I couldn't sleep."

He pushed himself up on the couch, leaning his back against the armrest. "Staying up all night will not make finding him come any quicker."

She sighed. "You're right, but . . ." She perched on the end of the couch, gently moving his feet to make room. "I can't sleep not knowing if he's okay or hurt or—"

"Hey," he said, leaning closer to clasp one of her hands in his own. "We are praying and thinking positively."

"I know." She pulled in another breath to let it out on a shudder. Her composure was paper-thin. No wonder she couldn't sleep. But it was too late for her to do anything but rest.

He shifted until he was sitting right on the couch. "Come here." He pulled her down next to him and she went willingly, settling in the crook of his arm much like she had long ago.

It was both joy and torment having her so close. He wanted to ask her if they could go back. Why couldn't they go back? But now was not the time. And he knew the answer without even asking. There was no going back.

She rested her head on his shoulder. He kissed the top of her head and closed his eyes. Now was also not the time to over-worry about propriety. Once upon a time they may have shared more, but this was about human contact. Not being completely and utterly alone in a time of need.

The question became who needed who more?

Sunlight blazed in from the window, shining directly onto Ivy's face. It warmed her and at the same time made her blink in annoyance. She'd never had this happen before. She had slept in the same room since she was a child, and she never awoke with sun glaring directly into her face.

Ivy blinked again, then reluctantly opened her eyes. Only a force higher than she kept her from jumping to her feet. She wasn't in her room. She was in the living room, on the couch, and Zeb was next to her.

She couldn't help herself. She needed to get up, move away from the circle of his embrace, but she couldn't make herself. She took the intimate moment to watch him, look at him like she hadn't been able to since he had returned. He was asleep still, his head back, mouth slightly open. His inky hair was excessively messy, and she could clearly make out the scar underneath his right eye. It was the only difference between him and Obie. That tiny crescent line that was the result of a scooter accident when they were younger. Second grade, if she remembered correctly.

And in that moment she couldn't lie to herself any longer. She still loved Zeb Brenneman. For a lot of good it would do her. Too much had happened. Too many unhappy things for them to get past. Too much that stood against them.

He hadn't been in his *rumspringa* when they'd had their indiscretion. She might be excused from confessing all before the church, but he wouldn't be. He had knelt before them all and God. And he would have to do it again if she confessed her own sins. She couldn't ask him to bear that embarrassment for her.

She sighed, then reluctantly moved away from him. She felt immediately cold. She needed to get the fire going again.

"What?" he mumbled, then pushed himself upright.

"It's morning." She moved toward the hearth, grabbing the poker and stirring the coals. She added another log to the top of the grate, thankful to see the flames growing and licking at the wood.

Zeb yawned and stretched, then stopped. "Your grandfather?"

She shook her head, unable to say the words. There had been no word, and the longer they went without news, the more worried she became. Did that mean the chances that the news wouldn't be favorable grew? She wished she knew. No. She didn't.

"Coffee?" she asked, starting for the kitchen.

"*Jah*. That'd be good." He padded off toward the bathroom while Ivy put the water on to boil.

This morning was entirely too intimate. How had they found themselves here? Together? Almost as if they were married. They almost had been. But she couldn't look back on the time that was lost. But it was hard not to. Waking up side by side, drinking coffee. How long would they be able to pretend that it meant nothing? Then again, maybe she was the only one who felt the connection.

Zeb came out of the bathroom just in time for her to pour the coffee.

"Should I make some breakfast?" She needed to do something. She needed to keep busy. Otherwise she might explode.

"That's okay. I thought I would call the police station." He held up Obie's cell phone.

She nodded, but moved to the propane-powered refrigerator and started pulling out food. Bacon, eggs, cheese.

She lit the stove and tried to not pay attention as Zeb pulled the policeman's card from his pocket, then growled with aggravation. "The phone's dead."

She hid her disappointment, instead concentrating on her task of keeping busy. Maybe they would hop on the tractor and head back into town today. She couldn't sit home and just do . . . nothing.

He stopped. "Do you hear that?" He cocked his head to one side.

She turned off the gas and walked toward the door. From outside she thought she could hear the sound of a car engine. Then a thump that could have been someone getting out of a car. Then a second one.

Ivy turned to Zeb. He set the phone down on the side table, and together they walked toward the front window.

Part of her wanted to run to see if her strongest wish had come true. Had her grandfather returned home? But what if the news was bad? What if he was hurt? Or worse? And the police had come to deliver the horrible truth? Her heart pounded in her chest, and her mouth went instantly dry.

"Ivy?"

She shook her head. She couldn't speculate. She couldn't look at Zeb. She took a deep breath and peeked out the window.

Her grandfather was walking between two uniformed officers. His head was down, but he was walking on his own. He didn't appear to be confined in any way; he was simply flanked by the two men escorting him to the house. One was tall, broad through the shoulder and possibly bald. She couldn't tell, since his knit cap covered most of his head. But no hair stuck out from under the edge. The second officer was smaller, thinner, and had a full head of blond hair. They both wore thick blue jackets with badge-shaped patches sewn onto the left breast.

Her grandfather wasn't wearing a coat, but someone had wrapped a blanket around his shoulders. This time, he had remembered to put on his shoes and hat before he left. Had he been out all night without proper covering? She couldn't imagine. Last night had gotten down to freezing. He was lucky he was still alive.

"Dawdi," she breathed. She rushed to the front door, wrenched it open, and stepped out onto the porch. "Dawdi," she called, louder this time.

He lifted his head, his eyes shining with both recognition and confusion.

"Is this your grandfather?"

"*Jah.* Yes." Ivy nodded, tears of relief threatening.

"We tried to call, but the number went straight to voice mail."

"The phone battery died." Zeb's voice sounded from behind her.

"Where was he?" Ivy asked. She had been worried sick

all night, unable to sleep until she was sitting beside Zeb's warmth. And yet something kept her from flinging her arms around her grandfather and never letting go. Maybe it was that weird look in his eyes, wary and suspicious, but not afraid.

"We found him at the high school this morning. He was asleep on the bleachers."

"Actually, the football coach found him," the second officer said. "He had morning detention."

It took a moment for his words to make sense. The football coach had morning detention. Her grandfather had been asleep in the seats around the football field.

Football? What had he been doing at the high school? And on the football field?

"Dawdi?" she cautiously asked.

He raised his head, and there was that missing look once again. It wasn't that he didn't know things; he just didn't know all things he had known before.

"Sir, is this your granddaughter?"

"That's Irene."

Tears pricked in Ivy's eyes. "That's right. I'm Irene. Won't you come inside, Dat?"

He grunted.

"It's warmer by far," she said invitingly.

"*Jah.*"

"Come." Zeb went down the porch steps and clasped her grandfather by the elbow. "I'll walk you inside." He shot a pointed look at Ivy, telling her without words that she could stay out there and clear things up with the officers.

She nodded, but felt strangely bereft when the door closed behind the two men she loved most in the world.

"Miss Weaver?"

"*Jah?*"

"We're glad he's home safe, but in the future—"

"In the future," the second officer broke in, "you might

consider having someone stay with him when you're going to be out. Everything turned out okay this time. But we might not be so lucky the next."

"*Jah*. I will," she whispered, not trusting her voice any louder. If she spoke up, she might start yelling and never stop, just a loud steady sound to relieve the pressure of responsibility building inside her.

They tipped their heads toward her, then started back toward their car. There was a Christmas wreath wired to the front grille and a small plush Santa in the corner of the front window. For a moment she had forgotten that it was so close to Christmas.

She waved as they backed up their patrol car and drove away. Then she took a bracing breath and let herself back into the house.

She had no idea how to handle the situation. Should she chastise him? Try to discover his reasoning? Make him promise not to set foot outside the house without telling her first?

What good would any of that do?

If he couldn't remember how to get home and that she was Ivy, not Irene, how would he remember instructions that were supposed to keep him safe?

"Dawdi." She stepped into the house and shut the door behind her. It was warm inside, but she was still shivering. Partially from the cold. But mostly with fear. This was getting worse, and she had no idea what to do about it.

He was sitting on the couch, cradling a steaming coffee mug in both hands. He was on the side closest to the fireplace, no doubt to ward off the chill. The orange flames danced and crackled, creating both a real and a false warmth in the room.

Zeb was standing at the end of the hearth, sipping coffee and merely waiting.

"I know what you're going to say, and I'm sorry, Irene. I lost track of time and stayed with a friend."

"Oh, Dawdi." She went to him, knelt in front of him, and threw her arms around his neck. "You don't need to apologize, but we do need to talk."

She wasn't sure how much of her talk actually penetrated the barrier of confusion that seemed to surround her grandfather. Zeb sat close, but not touching; supportive, but not talking. Him just being there lent her strength. But it was something she couldn't rely on. Hadn't he said he would be returning to Florida soon?

"What time do you have to be at work today?" Zeb asked after her grandfather had gone to lie down.

Work? She had forgotten all about having to work! She mentally traced her schedule. "Ten."

Zeb nodded.

"How am I supposed to go to work and leave him here alone?" It just wasn't possible. The job she had been dreaming about, waiting for, was about to slip through her fingers.

"I'll stay here."

His words were so plain and solid that she almost didn't hear them. At least she wasn't sure she had heard them correctly.

"You can't stay here."

"Why can't I?"

Why? A hundred reasons. A *thousand* reasons. Though right then, she couldn't think of a single one.

"I can't ask you to do that." She didn't want to be beholden, but more than that, she didn't want to take advantage of the tenuous relationship they had forged the night before. They had almost been back like they had been. Almost. Perhaps the closest they would ever be again—and she didn't want to do anything that would jeopardize it.

"You didn't ask. I offered."

She shook her head. "I can't—"

He took her hands, squeezing her fingers to focus her attention on him. "Yes," he said sternly. "You can."

Somehow she managed to do exactly as Zeb said. He promised to stay with her grandfather until she got home from work. She wanted to tell him no, but she knew that wasn't a good idea.

It is also a blessing to receive, her grandmother had continually said. For if no one was receiving, then how could others give? It made perfect sense to Ivy, maybe because she had been hearing it her entire life.

Work was as expected. They had several orders to fill for the holidays. Rolls, bagels, breakfast buns, pies, cookies, and cakes. Ivy was thankful they were so busy. It kept her hands and mind occupied as she went through her day. There wasn't much time left to worry about what her *dawdi* and Zeb were doing. Or, heaven forbid, what they were talking about.

At the end of her shift, she gathered up some of their best cookies and wrapped them in wax paper. The stack went into a small paper sack. She wanted to give some to Ethan Dallas, as well, but she had already cleared it with Esther to bake those the Saturday before Christmas. By then all the orders would be complete and picked up. On that day, most were rushing around to get the last-minute things they had forgotten.

She hopped on her tractor and headed for the house, belatedly wondering about supper. She had grown accustomed to her grandfather preparing something each day. But she had no idea if he had been up to the task today. Maybe she should have picked up some chicken from Kauffmans', or even a pizza from the place off Main. But it was too late now. She was already halfway home, and darkness was quickly approaching.

She was also a bit worried about what she would find when she returned to the house. Zeb had promised to stay, but she had no idea how his day had gone. Her grandfather had seemed docile that morning. Had his demeanor remained the same throughout, or had he resented having a grown-up babysitter? Had he even noticed?

A healthy stream of smoke puffed up from the chimney. That was a sight better than the day before. But what was inside remained to be seen. She parked her tractor in its usual spot, pulled her scarf a little closer to her ears, and headed for the house. The temperature had definitely dropped during the day. She could only say a prayer of thanks to the good Lord for holding that change until today, after her grandfather was safe at home.

She skipped up the porch steps and let herself into the house. If the weather kept this up for the next couple of days, they might end up with the elusive white Christmas. But she wasn't wasting a prayer on that.

"Ivy, is that you?" Zeb.

Those few words shouldn't have made her heart skip a beat, but they did. And another prayer of thanks went up toward heaven.

"*Jah.*" She pulled off her coat and slipped the scarf from her head. She hung them both on the hooks near the front door and headed for the kitchen and the sound of Zeb's voice.

Her grandfather and Zeb were seated at the table playing Uno. The sight brought a quick smile to her lips. Zeb hated Uno. He had told her so himself. Yet he was playing it with Dawdi.

"Having fun?" she asked.

Neither one looked up from their game.

"*Jah,*" Dawdi said.

"Yep," Zeb added.

"I thought Uno wasn't fun with only two people."

"We're playing two each."

That explained a lot. Neither one took their attention from the game. Each held two hands of cards, literally, one in each hand.

"Are you going to play or not?" Zeb asked.

"I'm getting there," her grandfather groused back.

Had she missed something here? She turned and looked back to the door where she had entered. She had come in, but that was all. She looked back at these two men, both so important in her life. "I have cookies," she said, holding up her brown paper sack.

"Uh-huh," they said at the same time. Still neither one looked at her.

Her grandfather closed one of his hands, stacking the cards in front of him and freeing his fingers to pluck a card from the other hand. He laid it down on the pile, then snatched up his opposite hand.

"I was hoping that was what you would do." Zeb grinned. He slapped down a card.

Her grandfather's grin matched Zeb's, then widened to a playfully sinister width. "And that's what I was hoping *you* would do." He slapped down another card with pleased aplomb.

"Ugh!" Zeb groaned, then centered his attention on his cards once again.

Ivy was at a loss. The game looked the same as any she had ever seen. So why the intensity?

"I guess it's sandwiches for supper." As cold as it was outside, she could have used a big piping bowl of soup. Or chili. Maybe even chicken and dumplings. But her grandfather had never been good at dumplings. Not that he had remembered to cook anything. Apparently he had been too busy playing with Zeb. And there was no time to start them from scratch.

She set the cookies on the table and marched over to the fridge. She didn't want to feel jealous, but she was. She had gone to work, kept herself exhaustingly busy in order not to worry about the two of them, and they had been here playing cards for how long she might not ever know. She was jealous that her grandfather got to spend the entire day with Zeb and that Zeb had kept her grandfather out of trouble. Wasn't that her job? And now her job was to get them all supper? It didn't seem quite fair.

She wrenched open the icebox and peered into its depths. She needed sandwich stuff. That was the best they were getting from her tonight.

"What are you doing?" Zeb asked.

"Looking for something for supper," she muttered in return. Where had all the sandwich stuff gone? Lunch meat? Cheese? Even the hothouse tomato she had picked up at the Super Saver.

"Truce?" she heard Zeb say.

"Bah," her grandfather replied.

"We said until Ivy got home."

"Eh," her grandfather grunted.

"She brought cookies," Zeb reminded him.

"Fine," Dawdi grumbled. "Truce."

She turned around slowly, trying to keep her composure. "What happened to all the food?" she asked. She managed to keep her voice from rising. She wasn't about to show them how juvenile and jealous over their friendship she had become.

"It's on the stove." Zeb reached for the paper sack of cookies and peered inside. "Are there any peanut butter?"

"Get me an oatmeal raisin."

Of course they expected her to bring home their individual favorites. Well, she had, but that they expected it rubbed her all wrong. She lifted the lid off the only pot sitting on the stove. The warm, savory smell of chicken and dumplings wafted up from the pot. Yummy chunks of chicken and perfect strips of dumplings in a thick, creamy broth. One thing was certain: these weren't from her grandfather's hand. "Where did these come from?"

"Clara Rose made them for us," Zeb mumbled around the bite of cookie in his mouth. "Good, *jah*?"

Her grandfather shoved his entire cookie into his mouth and reached into the bag for another.

Zeb snatched the bag away and shook his head. "Only one until after supper."

Her grandfather scowled. "Bah," he muttered, but he sat back in his seat.

"We may have to warm them up a bit," Zeb said.

"How did they get here?" she asked.

Zeb grinned, obviously pleased with himself. "When we went over to take Obie back his phone, Clara Rose asked after you, and one thing led to another. She brought them over about an hour ago."

Ridiculous tears pricked at the back of her eyelids. In a community that seemed to turn its back on her regularly, there were still a few who cared. Christmas spirit was not dead. It was still alive and well.

Chapter Fifteen

"I just don't think it's a good idea," Ivy protested. Falling asleep next to Zeb last night and waking up next to him this morning was one thing. But what he was proposing now . . .

"There's nothing wrong with it," Zeb protested. "I spent the night here last night. And I'm going to do it again. That way there will be two of us here to keep an eye on your grandfather."

"But he's fine now," she said.

Zeb shook his head. "Don't make me say it."

Okay. If she was being truly honest with herself, her grandfather was not up to his usual stuff. He couldn't remember half of what had happened last night, though she was beginning to wonder if he just didn't want to confess. After everything they had been through, Ivy couldn't say that she blamed him. "He's better," she finally said.

"And he could have a relapse and walk right back out the door."

It was the one thing she didn't want to think about. And yet she knew it to be a fact as sure as the sun set in the west.

"What will everyone say?" she asked.

Zeb propped his hands on his hips and eyed her skeptically. "Really? That's what's worrying you? You haven't cared about what everyone thinks of you in the last two years. Why all the sudden are you bringing it up now?"

Why indeed?

"I have cared," she finally admitted.

He frowned at her. "Then why did you spread all those rumors about yourself?"

"I told you. To keep people away."

He looked around her small house. "It seems to have worked."

So why wasn't he half the town away with his family instead of standing there in her living room arguing with her? "It's not a good idea," she sternly repeated.

"*Jah?* Neither is leaving the two of you alone." He kicked off his shoes and grabbed the blanket from the end of the couch. It was the same one he had used to cover up with the night before. Was this going to become a habit? Did she want it to? What would the town say about that?

She threw up her hands in a show of frustrated surrender. "Fine. Whatever makes you happy." Though as long as she was admitting things she should note that him sleeping on her couch made her happy, if nothing else.

For two days, their pattern remained the same. The three of them got up every morning and ate a breakfast prepared by her grandfather, who was closely monitored by Zeb. Not that he knew anything about cooking. But he could sure enough tell if Yonnie had left anything turned on.

After breakfast, Ivy headed off to work, while Yonnie and Zeb were left to entertain themselves in her absence. They further increased their customized Uno game, which now included a second deck and a whole new set of rules. Yonnie might not be able to remember things from time to time, but there was nothing wrong with his reasoning. He was as sharp as a tack when it came to games and other endeavors, but anything beyond that seemed to confuse him. He could feed the chickens just fine, muck out a few stalls, and take care of all the animals, but Zeb didn't feel he could trust him to be alone in the barn.

Zeb had no idea what was wrong with Yonnie's memory beyond what Ivy had told him. He wasn't sure how much Ivy understood of the deficit. But Zeb did know that it was getting worse. From what Ivy had said, the times were getting closer together and lasting longer. What was she going to do when they blended completely together?

It didn't bear thinking about.

"Come on," he said to Yonnie just after midday. "Get your coat. Let's replace these pine boughs before Ivy gets home."

"All righty." Yonnie was on his feet in a second, eager to be moving around. The man was more active than most, and Zeb knew this confinement was trying for him. "Maybe we can find some ivy to dig up and mix with the greens. Get it? Ivy?"

Zeb shook his head. "I get it. It was just a very poor joke."

"But it would be pretty, vines of ivy around the pine boughs and poinsettias."

One of them had taken silk poinsettias and placed them throughout the greenery on the mantelpiece. The mixture of red and green was beautiful.

"Maybe we should get Ivy a real flower. As part of her Christmas present."

"A poinsettia?" Yonnie shook his head. "They're poisonous to cats, and Chester wouldn't leave it alone. She eats all the plants we bring in. Bad kitty."

As if she knew her name, Chester sauntered in, swishing her tail back and forth, daring them to say any more about her.

"What about the pine boughs?" Zeb asked, starting to gather the drying limbs so they could replace them.

"Only the good Lord's grace keeps her off the mantel.

Well, that and the water pistol Ivy keeps by the kitchen sink."

Zeb laughed. He had wondered what that was for. Leave it to Ivy to use a water pistol to keep her headstrong cat in line. Then again, what had they expected from a calico named Chester?

"Okay," he said. "No real poinsettias. But new pine boughs, *jah*?"

Yonnie nodded. "*Jah*."

Ivy was near exhausted by the time she turned her tractor down the lane that led to her house. So tired that she only wanted to go in, take off her shoes, and prop her feet on the coffee table. What they had thought would be an easy day turned into a rush as word of her chocolate peppermint cupcakes spread throughout Wells Landing. Amish and *Englisch* alike came for a dozen, half dozen, and in one case three dozen cupcakes to round out their holiday desserts.

Not that it was a bad thing. It was just what she needed to help Esther realize that Ivy needed to become a permanent fixture at the bakery. She just wished they'd had a little warning. But with Christmas Eve falling on Sunday, that left one less day to buy things before Christmas. The result was aching feet and exhaustion, but they'd had a successful day, of that she was certain.

But she knew she wouldn't be able to sit down the minute she got home. She'd had Ethan on her mind all day. She did as her grandmother always said and sent up a prayer every time he popped into her thoughts, but it had happened with such regularity that she felt compelled to go see him. It was so close to Christmas, after all. Others would have visitors. Some would even be staying with close family for the next couple of days so they could be there for Christmas morning. But not Ethan. Not unless his grandson had made it back from wherever he was.

And that was what drove her. That and the two dozen sugar cookies she had baked him that afternoon. Somehow between waiting on all the customers and restocking the chocolate peppermint goodies, she had whipped him up a few cookies for the holiday. Crosses with gold-colored icing, snowflakes with shimmering sugar crystals, and Christmas trees in all sorts of colors. She wanted him to have them, wanted him to know that someone was thinking about him and wishing him the best Christmas ever.

She parked her tractor out front and made her way into the house. She couldn't just leave Zeb and Dawdi alone with so much left to do. Maybe they would want to go too.

She let herself into the house, the scent of fresh pine tickling her nose.

"Dawdi?" she called. "Zeb?" She shouldn't get used to calling his name when she got home. Christmas Eve was tomorrow. How long before he had enough and headed back to Florida?

She pulled off her coat, scarf, and gloves, then walked to the fire to warm her nose. The weather was definitely showing that it was Christmas. But she had heard people talking as they came into the bakery all day. Zero chance of a white Christmas this year. But they were due for snow soon.

She smiled as she caught sight of the mantel. That was why the pine smelled so strong when she entered. Someone had placed fresh boughs on the mantelpiece, along with strings of ivy. It was beautiful and somehow poignant. The red silk poinsettias dotted the row, intermixed with white candles that had been lit a while ago, if the dripping wax was any sort of indicator.

"Dawdi?" she called again. They couldn't have gone far if they had left lit candles in the living room.

"Meow?" Chester sashayed into the room in that slinky

way of hers, then jumped up onto the couch so Ivy could better reach her to scratch between her ears. Her loud purr joined the crackle of the fire. But where were Dawdi and Zeb?

"Ivy?"

She relaxed in an instant as Dawdi came through the door from the kitchen, Zeb right behind. Why was she so wound up? Maybe it was just the holiday getting to her. It was the first Christmas without her *mamm*.

"We didn't hear you come in," Zeb explained.

"We were cooking," Dawdi added.

"Cooking?"

They nodded.

"Well, more like warming up," Zeb added.

"Clara Rose again?" she asked.

They nodded each in time with the other again and Ivy wondered if they might be spending too much time together.

"Is it almost ready?" she asked.

"In a bit," Dawdi answered. "What do you think of the mantel?"

"It's beautiful." She kissed his cheek, then stood on her tiptoes and kissed Zeb as well. She inhaled the familiar scent of him. That mix of outdoors, soap, and sandalwood.

The men led the way into the kitchen, where the table was already set and more candles burned.

"If y'all keep this up, you won't have anything special for tomorrow."

Zeb grinned. "I wouldn't be so sure."

"Are you ready to eat?"

She bit her lip and looked at the beautiful table they had created for her. How could she tell them that she wanted to go back into town and check on a man she barely knew?

Zeb shifted in place, cocking one hip like she had seen him do countless times. "What's going on?"

Could he read her mind? Or was her expression giving her away? "Nothing. Just—"

"Spill it," Zeb demanded in that no-nonsense way of his.

"There's a man, at the retirement home. I wanted to go by and see him today. He won't have any visitors for Christmas. Not unless a miracle happens."

Dawdi grinned. "I got an idea. Let's go be a Christmas miracle."

They put their supper on hold, blew out all the candles, and hitched up the buggy. It would be faster to take the tractor, but easier by far to fit three people in a carriage. It might be the Saturday before Christmas, but the sheriff wasn't above handing out tickets if he felt there were shenanigans about.

Ivy's heart lifted as they drove to the home. She had been worried about Ethan Dallas all day, and now she would see him. Wish him a Merry Christmas, give him the cookies she had made for him, introduce him to her family. And Zeb.

Zeb parked the buggy and hobbled the horse, and together they went inside.

The home seemed almost deserted this time of day. Or maybe it was the day itself. She had known that some residents would go home with their families to spend Christmas, but she hadn't expected so many to be gone. Poor Ethan. Left all alone.

Angie's eyes widened as she saw her.

Ivy smiled. "Hi, Angie. This is my grandfather, Yonnie, and my friend, Zeb."

"Nice to meet you," Angie said, but the sentiment didn't reach her eyes. She looked . . . preoccupied. No, that wasn't the word. She looked worried, concerned, maybe even regretful.

"We're going to go visit with Ethan for a bit," Ivy said as she signed the book. She added Dawdi and Zeb's names next to hers.

"Ivy." Angie spoke her name so softly Ivy was surprised she had heard the woman at all. But something in her tone had Ivy raising her gaze to that of the receptionist.

"What happened?" Ivy asked, her own tone beyond hushed. Suddenly the Christmas music seemed too loud, the lights too bright, the decorations too garish.

Tears filled Angie's eyes. "I'm sorry. So sorry." She pulled a tissue from the box on her desk and daintily dabbed at her eyes.

She was sorry? There was only one thing for her to be sorry about, and there was no way that—

She couldn't even think the words, but even as she refused to let them cross her mind, they stabbed at her heart.

"What?" Dawdi asked, clearly confused.

Zeb shot her a sympathetic look, then leaned in close and whispered into her grandfather's ear.

Dawdi gave her an identical look, but at least now he wasn't asking questions she couldn't answer.

Like *How?* Or maybe that wasn't a good one. She knew how. They had talked about it before. But she didn't know when. Or if his grandson made it up in time to see his grandfather one last time.

"—couldn't call you," Angie was saying. "But he left you this." She pushed an envelope across to Ivy. She noted her name was scrawled across the front in bold black letters, then she shoved it into her coat pocket.

"Can I see him?" she asked. She needed to see him to realize, to know, that he was truly gone.

Dead, deceased. How could this have happened?

"I'm sorry," Angie said once again. But Ivy missed the first part of what she was saying. She really needed to pay more attention, but right now she couldn't focus. She could only pick up the last half of what people were saying, and that was being generous. She couldn't concentrate. She didn't want to. She just wanted to see Ethan one last time. But now she never would.

She wanted to go to his room, look at his things, touch his clothes, something, anything to keep a connection with him. She had been raised to believe that death was all a part of God's will. But this . . . this was beyond her understanding.

She wanted to find a way to stay, but she couldn't. Her good friend was gone. Her *dawdi* and her friend had come to town with her to see a man they wouldn't be able to see ever again.

"Ivy," Angie called, bringing her out of her stupor. "It's time to go home."

She nodded. "*Jah.*" Going home was the last thing she wanted to do, but it was the only choice offered to her.

"Come on." Zeb gently took her arm and turned her toward the door. Ethan was gone.

Ivy tried to get a handle on her emotions on the ride home. They weren't out of control, but all over the place. She was happy for him and sad for herself. She just wished . . .

She let that thought go before completing it. Wishes would do no good other than to make her even more miserable. *It is what it is.* Wasn't that what people said? Wasn't that a little like God's will? Whatever may be, may be. Was that part of a song? If it was, she had no idea where she had heard it. She wondered if Ethan knew it.

Christmas lights twinkled merrily on the houses set on both sides of the road. They seemed joyous and bright. No one had told them that a sweet man had died that day.

"How can the world continue like nothing happened?" she murmured to no one and anyone who might answer.

Maybe if his grandson had made it in, or his daughter-in-law had taken the time to come and visit. That would have made Ivy feel much better, but as it was, Ethan Dallas died alone. The thought was beyond heartbreaking. She should have been there for him. But she hadn't known he was that near his time.

"He knows you cared about him." Zeb leaned close as he said the words.

"How do you know that?" she whispered in return.

In the back of the buggy, her grandfather snored softly. Nothing like a swaying ride back from town to put the man to sleep.

"Because that's how you are," Zeb replied simply. "When you love someone, they know it. You're the most giving person I know. You're always baking things for other people, making things, doing things."

"I didn't get to give him these." She lifted the paper sack she held in one hand.

"And today was the only time you brought him cookies?"

She shook her head.

"And I bet the two of you had something special you would do each time you came for a visit."

She scoffed. "If you call eating pudding cups special, then *jah*."

He took his attention from the road and centered that intense gaze on her. "Eating pudding cups is special, if you're with someone you care about."

She shivered, not from the cold. Something more. An understanding that sent chills down her spine.

"I wanted you to meet him." She hadn't realized until that moment that she had truly wanted them to meet.

"I saw him. When we came to sing to the residents."

"But you didn't get to talk to him." There was something special about Ethan Dallas. She had been raised her entire life to accept God's judgment, but this was beyond her acceptance. She wanted to know why. Why had God taken such a special man before he could spread more of his joy and acceptance? *Why, Lord, why?*

"Then you'll have to tell me all about him."

That was exactly what Ivy wanted to do, but she could tell her grief was putting a damper on the evening these two men had planned. She smiled maybe a little stiffly when they got home and went into the kitchen to warm up their supper. Like she wanted to eat. Food was the last thing she wanted. But she needed to feed the men.

In no time at all, they were all seated around the table. Someone had gathered more pine boughs and tied them with jute to make a circle. In the center sat a fat white candle that flickered and smelled like sugar cookies.

"The table looks nice," she told them as she started setting the food there.

"Thanks." Zeb smiled at her compliment.

Wait. He had been the one? Her grandfather she could have believed, but he was a romantic like that. She had never known that Zeb could be as well. *Because you never gave him the chance to be.*

They had always been running around, hiding their relationship, hiding their feelings. There wasn't any time to decorate tables and light candles. Just another part of the beauty of together that they had missed. She was certain it would be impossible to get it back. She would have to wait until someone else came along and wanted to show her such things.

Like that was ever going to happen. She had done so much damage to her reputation, she was lucky the good citizens of Wells Landing didn't run screaming for the hills whenever she came near.

They gathered around the table and bowed their heads to

pray. Ivy's prayer was a jumble of words, but she knew God understood. She wanted Him to watch over Ethan and take him in the way Ethan so firmly believed. She asked for peace in her own heart to allow the man she had barely known to be a part of her memories, but not a painful one. She needed her grandfather and Zeb to be safe. She even managed to get in a couple of lines for her mother and Alan before Dawdi raised his head.

She went through all the motions. Scoop food up onto her fork, lift it to her mouth, chew, swallow. She even managed to smile occasionally and utter a few of those phrases of polite supper chitchat.

And for a time she thought she had even fooled them into believing that everything was normal. But by the time she got the kitchen cleaned up and kissed her grandfather good night, she knew that she had fooled no one.

"Come sit down," Zeb invited, patting the couch seat next to him. The fire crackled warmly, casting shadows and flickering lights over the room. The candles on the mantel had been relit and added to the cozy feel. Christmas. It was almost Christmas.

She eased down next to Zeb, doing her best not to sit too close. Her grandfather had already gone to bed. Tomorrow was a church Sunday, and he always liked to get up early. Well, when he wasn't oversleeping.

But even as she kept a respectable distance between her and Zeb, she wanted to scoot in close, tuck her head under his chin, and absorb his warmth into her own. She wanted to lay her cheek just below where his heart beat in his chest. And she wanted to stay that way all night long.

"Tell me about him," he coaxed.

"What?"

"This Ethan Davids."

"Dallas," she corrected, then paused to collect her thoughts.

"I don't know a lot," she admitted. "Only that he had cancer, not much family, and he was kind."

Why was it that simple kindness seemed so rare in the world?

Kindness was free, like smiles and hope. So why wasn't there more of it?

"He sounds wonderful."

And he was, but she didn't have to tell Zeb that. "I just wish I could have done more," she lamented.

"I'm sure to him it was more than plenty."

She murmured something she hoped would pass as a response, then settled back into the couch cushions. She was a better person from having known Ethan Dallas. She could only hope that sometime in her life someone would say the same thing about her.

Sunday morning dawned reluctantly, as if the gray sky had been asked to stay for an extended visit. Heavy clouds kept the day from being beautiful. But they did match her mood. She hadn't wanted to wake up so . . . sad. It was Sunday. She loved Sundays. She loved going to church. Sure, no one said much of anything to her, but that wasn't what was important. At church, she could forget for a bit that she was all alone. That no one loved her. That her chance at happiness had long ago slipped through her fingers. And it gave her plenty of time to pray for what was to come next.

God had a plan. That was what her grandmother had always said. God had a plan, and when the time was right He would reveal it to her.

She added Ethan to her prayers. Along with his grandson and daughter-in-law. He hadn't mentioned anyone else, so she added family in order to cover anyone she might have missed. Prayer always made her feel better, and this time was no exception.

She cast a quick look toward Zeb. He was sitting on the bench next to his father and brothers. Clara Rose was sitting a few rows ahead of Ivy next to the women in her own family, Paul Daniel asleep in her arms. Ivy's attention strayed back to Zeb. He was looking particularly handsome today. Maybe because he was well-rested. Or maybe it was the ironing that she had given his church clothes.

Ivy did her best to keep her attention on the preachers' words for the rest of the service. It was Christmas Eve, and she needed to receive God's word. She needed to have the reassurance that worship usually gave her. When all else was wrong, the church was always there. But today something was different, and she hated it. There was no comfort. Only questions.

She needed that comfort. She needed to know that everything would go back to the way it was before last week, before yesterday. But could it really? And did she want it to? No. Not really. She wanted it to go back to the way it was two years ago and have a do-over, as they say. A second chance. But it was too much to ask, even at Christmastime.

Once the last prayer was said and the members dismissed, Ivy grabbed her grandfather by the arm and directed him away from the tables.

"I want to go home," she said.

"We will," he promised.

She shook her head. "I want to go now."

Church was at the Tommy Lee Detweilers'. They lived only a few houses away from the Weavers, but Ivy had insisted on taking the buggy this morning. Now she wished she hadn't. She wanted to go home, but she didn't want her grandfather walking by himself.

"Ivy," Dawdi started.

"I'm going to walk home." The day was cold, but she needed the chilly wind on her face to remind her of where she was. The here and the now. It was Christmas Eve. There would be no Christmas miracle for Ethan, or her for that matter, but it was a beautiful time to be alive, and she needed to remember that.

"It's too cold."

She wrapped her scarf around her head and pulled on her gloves. "You tell Zeb where I've gone. Maybe he can drive you home. Then I'll take him on home later."

"Take him home? Whatever for?"

"It's Christmas Eve, Dawdi," she explained. "He needs to be with his family."

Dawdi nodded thoughtfully. "Christmas."

Had he forgotten? From the look in his eyes, she supposed he had. But it was something anyone could have let slip their mind. Right? Yet she knew that wasn't true. It might be easy to forget what day of the week it was, but Christmas was another matter entirely.

"I'll see you at home, okay?" She had to get away. She might be standing in the middle of the yard, but she felt as if everything was closing in on her.

"Okay."

"What are you supposed to do?" she queried.

"Tell Zeb you had to go and he needs to bring the buggy home."

"Right." Ivy smiled. Her grandfather was going to be okay. For a while yet, anyway.

She nodded her head and started toward the road. It wasn't a far walk, and she really needed the cold, fresh air to clear her mind. Her thoughts had been running around in circles since the day before. She hadn't managed to come to terms with Ethan's death. She couldn't believe he was gone. Maybe if she saw his room, or even talked to his family she could believe it. But there was a disconnect that kept her from moving on.

She couldn't go back to the senior home today. It was Sunday and Christmas Eve. But soon she would, maybe the day after Christmas. Second Christmas, they called it. It was a day for visiting friends and loved ones. The perfect day to visit again, talk to some of the others, and get her mind straight.

"Ivy!" She was halfway home when she heard him call her name. She didn't need to turn around to see who had followed her. She would know that voice anywhere.

"Zeb." She wanted to keep walking, but she knew he could overtake her in seconds. Running away wasn't the answer.

He ran down the road until he reached her side. "Where are you going?"

"Didn't Dawdi tell you?"

"He said you were going home. Why?"

She shook her head. "I need some time to myself."

His mouth pulled into a frown. "Being alone is the last thing you need. It's Christmas. You've lost a friend."

She had lost so much more than that.

"Let me walk with you," he said.

"What about Dawdi?" Weren't he and Zeb driving home together?

"Tassie and Karl said they would bring him home. Karl's going to drive the buggy here, and Tassie agreed to pick him up."

"I think she likes Dawdi."

"I know she does, but there's something about her . . ."

He didn't finish. He didn't need to. She knew exactly what he was saying, but she thought it was her granddaughter's mentality. That no one would be good enough for her grandfather. No one would be right for him. But to know someone else saw it too . . .

He fell into step beside her. "You shouldn't be alone this time of year. No one should."

"He was alone. Ethan."

"Was he unhappy?"

She smiled as they walked. "Not at all. He was one of the happiest people I know."

"Which just goes to show."

"Show what?"

"That every man's happiness is part of something more."

But what? She wanted to know. She so very desperately wanted to know. "I thought I would be happy with you and then—then—"

"We could have been happy, but we needed time to heal."

"How was that supposed to happen? You went off to Florida."

Their steps slowed as their conversation intensified. "I only left because you told me to."

Her heart fell. She had told him that she didn't need him. That she didn't want him around. But it wasn't the truth. She hadn't wanted him to stay and have all the reminders that she would have. But she couldn't leave. Too much of her life was wrapped up in Wells Landing. It was different for girls. Or at least that was what she had told herself.

And there was nothing she could do about it now.

She exhaled heavily. "That's all in the past now."

He was nearly vibrating next to her. She knew that he wanted to deny her words. But thankfully he didn't. He just walked beside her all the way back to her house.

She turned onto the drive, and he doggedly stayed at her side. All the way to the house. He started up the porch steps after her, but she faced him then. She was one step up and eye to eye with him. She put out one hand, lightly laying it against his chest to further stop his progress.

"I appreciate you walking me home and helping me with Dawdi, but it's time for you to go home."

His brow wrinkled in confusion. "What? Why?"

"Tomorrow is Christmas."

He scoffed. "That it is." He started forward once again.

Ivy stiffened her elbow. She wasn't strong enough to truly hold him back, but her resistance held him in place.

"What's wrong with you?"

"Nothing. It's simply time you went home to be with your family."

He seemed shocked still, and Ivy used it to her advantage. She marched into the house and shut the door before he could reply.

She stared at the door, thinking about locking it, then decided that was too much, even for her. Instead she trusted Zeb to do the right thing and go home. Meanwhile, she would start some coffee, maybe have a piece of pie, and pretend her heart wasn't breaking in two.

Chapter Sixteen

Zeb stared at the closed door until his eyes started to water. What was he supposed to do now? He couldn't go home. He *wouldn't*. Even though he couldn't say why the thought was so unappealing. He knew that he and Ivy were done. That didn't keep him from wanting to spend time with her. All the time he could until he returned to Florida.

He turned and plopped down onto the bench next to the front door. With a flick of his wrist, he flipped his collar up to cover the lower half of his face. It was still pretty cold, and it would only get colder as he waited for her grandfather. And he was waiting. He wasn't going home simply because Ivy told him he had to. She was hurting and in need of a friend. He was going to be that friend. Even if it was the only thing he could do for her, it would be done.

He could hear her moving around inside, most likely starting the fire back up in the fireplace. Then the smell of coffee wafted out to him. What he wouldn't give for a cup. He knew for certain she would give him one if he asked; she was just that kind of a person. But he wouldn't ask. What did they call this? A Mexican standoff? He wasn't sure exactly what Mexico had to do with any of it, but he wasn't asking for a cup of coffee. He would sit out there and freeze before he did so. But hopefully it wouldn't come to that.

He eased down a bit and tucked his nose into the folds of his scarf. Surely her grandfather would be home soon.

The wait felt a little like forever, but couldn't have been more than an hour. Zeb got up halfway through and went to the barn. There was no sense freezing when he could be working to stay warm. Besides, him doing her chores would make her all the madder.

Truth was, he loved the way her eyes sparkled when she was angry. They looked like the stars as they reflected their light into the ocean. He rolled his eyes at his own fanciful thoughts and climbed into the hayloft to toss down a couple of fresh bales.

He had to quit thinking about Ivy that way. She didn't want him like that. Their chance was gone, over, caput. And he was going back to Pinecraft. At least that was the plan, and he saw no reason to change it now. His family here didn't need him, and he had already learned that he couldn't be around Ivy and not want to hold her and touch her. And that was not okay.

He came out of the barn as Karl turned Yonnie's buggy onto the lane. He waved at the other man, wondering why he kept coming over to see Ivy if he wasn't interested in her. At first Zeb had thought that was what Karl wanted—a chance with Ivy—but now Zeb wasn't so certain. Could it be that Karl wanted to marry his mother off to Yonnie? Or was the woman herself behind all these visits?

He preferred the thought of Yonnie and Tassie over the thought of Karl and Ivy. Ivy deserved better than frowny ol' Karl Weber. Zeb didn't remember the man being quite so . . . grumpy before he'd gone to Florida—not that he kept good company with Karl or any of his friends. And he wondered what made the man so sour-faced.

Karl hopped down from the carriage, flicking a hand toward the gelding the Weavers used to pull their buggy. "He's all yours," Karl said.

Zeb wanted some way to retort, to bring the man back to the truth, but he decided that any wisdom he might impart would be lost on Karl.

Instead he nodded and started to unhitch the horse. "*Danki*." What else could he say without looking like a jerk himself?

He no sooner got the horse put back into the barn than Tassie was pulling up with Yonnie in the seat beside her.

The couple got out, and Zeb watched as Tassie walked him to the porch. As strange as it was, that was the only way to describe it. And Zeb wondered how much Tassie knew of Yonnie's memory problems. Had to be some. But her attitude toward him grated Zeb's nerves.

It's none of your business.

And that was true. It didn't concern him at all. Other than that it concerned Ivy, and he was interested in everything that happened with Ivy.

Not that she wanted him to be.

Zeb made his way toward the pair as Karl climbed into the buggy's seat.

"And we'll be by tomorrow after three."

"Tomorrow after three," Yonnie repeated with a nod.

"Can you remember that?" Tassie asked.

Something in her tone set Zeb's teeth on edge.

"Of course I can remember."

"What's going on?" Zeb asked.

"Hey, Zeb." Yonnie gave him a nod of greeting. "We were just going over tomorrow's plans. Karl and Tassie are coming back for pie."

"Is that so?" Zeb pinned Tassie with a curious stare. At

least he hoped it was more curious than accusatory. Which was exactly how it felt.

"We'll see you then." Zeb gave a nod that was both accepting and dismissing all at the same time.

"Are you going to be here?" Tassie asked.

You can bet your sweet shoes I am.

"Of course. Christmas with the Weavers. I wouldn't miss it for the world."

She didn't say as much, but Zeb could tell the idea of him being there tomorrow was not part of her plans. Her nose wrinkled just a bit, as if she had smelled something bad. Then her mouth tipped up at the corners to form a smile, but it didn't reach past her cheeks. To say the woman wasn't very happy was an understatement.

"Tomorrow," she said again, then hoisted her petite frame into the buggy behind her son.

Yonnie turned to Zeb as Karl started the buggy back down the drive. "What are you doing out here, son?"

Should he tell the truth or fabricate some feasible lie? "Ivy kicked me out."

"What?" Yonnie swung around to stare at the house, as if the answers could be found right there on the front porch.

"She told me it was time for me to go home and be with my family."

Yonnie nodded in that understanding way of his. "It is Christmas."

"*Jah.*"

"What do you want to do?"

Zeb stopped. He wanted to do so many things. He wanted to spend time with his father and brothers, Clara Rose, and baby Paul Daniel. But he also wanted to spend as much time with Ivy as possible. And Yonnie too. These last few days had been a balm to his frayed soul. Funny, but he hadn't realized how worn it was until he had returned.

He had been down in Florida hiding out, just like Ivy had said. But here, in Wells Landing, he couldn't hide any longer. He had to face the truth, and the truth was he needed healing as much as Ivy did. He needed to see her, know that she was happy, know that she had moved on. Know that she had started her life once again. But she had done none of those things. He had left, and they had both been put on hold. Only he'd thought he'd grown and gotten over their loss. He had gotten over nothing. Not the baby, not the shame of what they had done, not losing Ivy. And there was only one way to do that.

"Zeb? You still there, boy?"

Zeb stirred himself out of his thoughts. "*Jah.* Sorry."

Yonnie pinned him with a sharp stare. "What's it going to be?"

"Ivy told me to go home."

"I know. Is that what you want to do?" he asked again.

"No."

Yonnie grinned. "Good, then. Let's go inside. It's freezing out here."

Leave it to her grandfather to not care one iota about her wishes and let Zeb back in the house. It had been so hard puttering around inside knowing that Zeb was still outside, waiting. On what, she had no idea. But she had known all along that he was there. He could have easily walked back to the Detweilers' and rejoined the after-church meal. He could have asked someone else to take him home. But he had sat outside for a while, then he got up and went into the barn. She knew what he was doing, but if she went out to talk to him about it, she would have to . . . well, talk to him. And that defeated the entire purpose of making him go home.

She rested her crochet needle and yarn in her lap and glanced to where her grandfather sat. He was perched on the edge of the couch, bent over the checkerboard set up between him and Zeb.

Any stranger coming in would think the game was of earth-shattering importance, with the attention he was giving it. But she knew he was just tickled to have a worthy opponent. Or maybe it was just a willing opponent. She didn't care for checkers, at least not with her grandfather's enthusiasm, and didn't want to play with as much regularity as he preferred.

Dawdi made his move and sat back in his seat with a wide grin. "King me," he exclaimed with glee.

Zeb shook his head and did as he was told. The game was slowly slipping out of his control, and this wasn't the first one he had lost tonight. Ivy was beginning to wonder if he was deliberately letting her grandfather win. He might have been, but it didn't seem to matter to Dawdi. He smiled with boyish joy and captured two more of Zeb's red disks.

Zeb threw up his hands in surrender. "Okay, that's it. I'm not playing another game with you."

Dawdi snickered and started gathering up the pieces. "Not even tomorrow?"

"I'm not sure you should humiliate a man like that on the Lord's birthday."

Her grandfather laughed. "Okay, then. I'll give you a break. Or maybe I'll let you win."

"That wouldn't be very sporting of you," Zeb complained, but he was still grinning.

"You sure you don't want to play one game?" Dawdi asked, switching his attention to her.

Ivy shook her head. "Oh no. Not me." She placed her crocheting into the basket beside her rocking chair and stood. "Anybody ready for cookies?"

Dawdi grinned at Zeb. "That's the best part of her new job. She's always bringing home food."

"And he's always eating it." She pinned her grandfather with a playful stare. "You better watch it, or you'll end up as big as a house."

He patted his stomach. "I manage to keep it off."

Zeb stood. "Do you need some help?"

She shook her head. The last thing she needed was Zeb in the kitchen like they were a real couple, like that could ever be. "I've got it. Y'all do manly things until I get back."

She wasn't sure what that meant, and from the confused looks on their faces, neither did they.

With any luck, they would just stay where they were and let her have the small reprieve from the family playacting they had been participating in. And it was a reprieve she desperately needed. It was Christmas Eve, she had lost a good friend, and Zeb was stirring up feelings in her she had thought were dead and buried.

She heated water for cocoa, added the mix to three mugs, then placed an extra marshmallow on top of each one. She gathered the cookies, loaded everything onto the tray, and carried it into the living room.

Zeb was coming in the front door, his collar turned up against the cold. "Brrrr," he said, nudging the door closed with his foot. In his arms he carried several logs for the fire. He grinned that boyish grin in her direction, then deposited the wood on top of the pile already in the wood box. He dusted his hands and held them out to warm them at the fire.

"That should hold us till morning," Dawdi said.

She placed the tray on the coffee table.

Zeb eyed it with interest, nodding toward the steaming mugs. "Is that hot chocolate?"

"*Jah.* If course." It wouldn't be Christmas without it.

"Yum."

"Wait until you taste these cookies," Dawdi said. He plopped down onto the sofa and rubbed his hands together expectantly.

"They're not oatmeal raisin," Ivy warned.

Dawdi looked affronted. "Of course not. They better be sugar cookies. What I want to know is if you have one shaped like that Santa Claus fellow."

Zeb's gaze jerked to hers, and Ivy had to look away. Why did something like Santa Claus keep popping up in their conversations? It was strange. And secular. And seemed most inappropriate. She supposed she could play it off, since she hadn't joined the church. But it was only a matter of time before she got up her resolve and asked for forgiveness.

Ivy took up a mug and took a tentative sip. This was one of their traditions, sugar cookies and hot chocolate on Christmas Eve. A little later they would light all the candles on the mantel and read the Christmas story from the Bible. It had always been this way, and there was no reason to change it this year. Her mother might be away and her father gone, but some traditions shouldn't be broken.

She settled down on the floor near the fire and tucked her legs under her skirt. The floor was cool, even through the blanket she sat on, but she loved watching the flames, imagining she saw images in the dancing orange.

"What are you thinking about?" Zeb settled down next to her, close, but still far enough away that she would have to lean in order to touch him. That was fine. Good, even. She had no business touching him in any way.

"I've always loved Christmas," she said. Her voice sounded dreamy and far away, as if she were floating above instead of tethered to the ground.

"Me too."

She took another drink of her cocoa, not because she really wanted it, but because she needed something to do. "Where's Dawdi?"

Zeb shook his head. "He was mumbling something about shirts and combs. I figure he either had to do a load of laundry or he was getting ready for bed."

"Maybe both."

He laughed. "Maybe."

They sat quietly for a moment. Ivy watched the flames, but she could tell that Zeb was watching her. This was no good; no good a'tall.

She could turn, lean in a bit, and she would be able to press her mouth to his. It was something she had been thinking about since the first time she had seen him back in Wells Landing. Even before. Truth be known, she had never stopped thinking about his kiss, how secure she felt in his embrace, and how warm and happy his attention made her, not then . . . not now. But like it or not, that time was over. Long ago.

She shifted, more to bring herself out of her thoughts and back to the matters at hand than because she was uncomfortable. "What's Christmas like there?"

He seemed as surprised by her question as she was at herself for asking it. "In Pinecraft?"

She nodded. "Florida, *jah*."

He stared at the fire as he answered. "The same, I guess. The Gospel of Luke is the same all over, *jah*?"

"I guess." She set down her mug and picked up a cookie. It was shaped like a bell, with snow-white icing and red and green trim. It made her think of the bells in town. One of the *Englisch* churches had bells they played on Sunday mornings. Their gentle pealing could be heard all the way to Ivy's house, and it always made her smile. Christmas was no different. The bells played out "Silent Night," the notes carrying around their small community.

"There have to be some sort of differences. It's not cold there, so hot cocoa is out, right?"

He lifted his mug in salute. "Hot cocoa is always a good idea. Though I would turn the air conditioner up in order to balance it out."

"Air conditioner?" It took a moment for his words to sink in. Where there were air conditioners, there was electricity.

"Did one of the places you stayed have electricity?" She had heard of people going to Pinecraft and letting loose, so to speak. *What happens in Pinecraft stays in Pinecraft*, wasn't that what folks said? But she had never known anyone to actually do it.

Zeb fingered a spot on his trousers, his gaze downcast as if he was thinking seriously about something.

"Zeb?"

He lifted those green eyes to hers. "Every place I stayed has electricity."

She drew back just a bit, purely out of reflex. "Oh. I didn't . . . uh-huh."

"I met up with the Beachy Amish down there." As far as explanations went, it was short but telling. The Beachy Amish were less conservative than any others, certainly more liberal than those in tiny Wells Landing. The Beachys drove cars and golf carts and had electricity in their homes. They also held church in a free-standing building, but most importantly of all, they held different beliefs than Old Order. Beachys believed in saved by grace. Did that mean . . . ?

Zeb nodded as if reading her thoughts. "*Jah*," he said. "I've learned about a lot of different ideas down there."

"And you believe them?" she whispered in return.

He ducked his head and nodded, then raised it again, his chin at a defiant angle, as if he was waiting on her to argue the point with him. "I do."

"I see." Ivy didn't know how else to answer. In fact, she wasn't the one to contradict him at all. She who started rumors about herself, continued in a wild *rumspringa*, who saw fit to keep everyone away in a community that thrived on togetherness. "And you drove a car?"

"It's not about driving a car." He looked into the flames of the fire as if searching for the right words to say. "It's about Jesus and his sacrifice." He shook his head. "It's Christmas," he said. "We shouldn't talk about such things."

Ivy couldn't think of a better day to talk about Jesus other than Christmas. Maybe Easter. But she wanted to know more about what Zeb had learned in Pinecraft. She was curious, that was all. She had never been out of Wells Landing, except for the occasional shopping trip in Tulsa. She opened her mouth to ask, then shut it again as her grandfather came back into the room.

"Well, now," he said, rubbing his hands together excitedly. "Who's ready to read Luke?"

"And it came to pass in those days, that there went out a decree from Caesar Augustus that all the world should be taxed."

Zeb listened to the words as Yonnie began to read. His voice was soothing and comfortable, and Zeb wanted to close his eyes and allow the story to wash over him, swirl around him.

He couldn't say how many times in his life he had heard the story of Jesus's birth. Definitely too many to count. But somehow tonight the words held more meaning. Maybe it was the Beachy influence on his thinking. He could only imagine how Mary had felt, knowing that her son was the son of God. How had Joseph felt, knowing that his wife carried the child of another? Zeb didn't know a man who would take such news as well as Joseph had. But other things occurred to him as well.

How sad that no one could find room for a pregnant woman for the night. How pitiful that she was forced to sleep in the barn among the animals. Everyone talked about how terrible times were today, but he would have given his room up to a woman with child. Without a second thought. What did that say about those times?

And Jesus. He was just a baby, with baby thoughts and baby needs, but he would soon grow up to be a man with a higher purpose. And he accepted that purpose with more grace and dignity than any other could have. Jesus knew he came to earth to die for others. What a weight he must have carried. In that understanding, Zeb couldn't imagine how anyone could turn away from the notion of saved by grace. If they did, that would mean Jesus came and died for nothing. It was a thought not worth having.

Yet Zeb didn't feel the drive to change the minds of everyone in Wells Landing. It didn't seem right somehow. These were their beliefs, and he wouldn't want anyone trying to change them. He had stumbled upon the Beachys and fallen into the doctrine all on his own. For him it had been at the hand of God. He couldn't force the ideals onto anyone else. Not his father. Not even Ivy.

Like it would matter. He could tell her till he was blue in the face, and she could believe or not believe. Then he would go back to Florida and she would stay here. And what good would any of it be then?

"*Glory to God in the highest, and on earth peace, good will toward men.*" Yonnie closed the Bible and wiped the tears from under his eyes with one finger. The motion pushed his glasses a little higher on his nose, then they dropped back into place. "Well, now," he said, his voice rusty with emotion. "I think it's time for bed." He stretched as if to illustrate his point. "Santa Claus won't come if you're awake."

Ivy rolled her eyes, but the action seemed playful instead of exasperated. "Dawdi." Her voice held just a small beat of warning.

"Just playing, granddaughter." He bent and kissed the top of her head, then placed the Bible back in the bookcase. "Don't stay up too late." Then he disappeared up the stairs.

Yonnie's footsteps faded to silence. The fire crackled beside them. Ivy sat across from him. They had been alone before. So why was he so aware of her now?

Because this was the closest to a real date they had ever had. They had always been sneaking around, since they weren't allowed to date. If they had been allowed, they would have had many times like tonight, sitting together alone in the dark, talking about the future.

But not now.

"I'm sorry about Ethan Dallas," Zeb said. He shouldn't have brought it up, but he had to say something to break the heavy silence between them.

"I'm thinking about going over there tomorrow."

"Why? I mean, it's Christmas."

"That's why." She gestured around them with a sweep of one arm. "We have so much. Food, friends, fellowship. We should offer that to those who don't."

She was right. If yesterday was any indication, there wouldn't be many residents left at the home, but those who were would need them most of all. Why shouldn't they spend their day making others happy? In turn, it might bring them both some joy and peace. Heaven knew he could use it. "What about your grandfather?"

"He can come too. Or maybe we could go when Tassie and Karl come over."

Zeb shook his head. "I feel like she has her sights set on Yonnie."

"What do you mean?"

"She's looking to get married again," Zeb said simply.

"You think?"

He shrugged. "Sure looks that way to me."

Ivy seemed to mull it over for a moment. "I know she likes him. But . . ."

"But what?"

"I'm not sure Dawdi is up for remarrying. His memory is getting worse. I mean, sometimes he's fine, but when he forgets, it's worse than ever before. How could someone as small as Tassie take care of him?" Lines of worry creased her brow.

"Maybe that's why she keeps Karl close."

Ivy made a face. "That doesn't make me feel any better."

"I guess you could always ask him."

"Dawdi or Karl?"

He laughed. "Your *dawdi*."

"I don't know. I think I would feel weird talking to him about such things."

"Weird enough that you would chance having Tassie for your new grandmother?"

Ivy's eyes widened. "I'll talk to him tomorrow."

They fell silent for a moment, each lost in their own thoughts. The holiday, remarrying, and memory problems.

"What are you going to do when his memory gets worse?" Zeb finally asked. He could tell by the look on her face this was something Ivy had thought about time and again, but she'd never talked to anyone about it.

"I don't know. Move to Indiana, I guess."

"It gets cold up there," Zeb said.

"You've been there?"

He shook his head. "No, but I can read. Their winters are much longer than the ones here." And longer than the ones in Florida, where winter became months on the calendar instead of an actual season.

"He would hate it there," Ivy said.

Zeb knew it was pure speculation, but she was right. He couldn't imagine Yonnie Weaver in Indiana. "There are a lot of older folks in Pinecraft," he said. "It's kind of a joke, there are so many."

"A joke?"

"The tourists come down this time of year. You know, when it gets cold here and farther north. But the ones who stay year-round? Most of them are his age and older."

"The warmth is probably easier on their arthritis."

"Probably," Zeb said.

"Maybe we'll do that," Ivy mused. "Move to Indiana but spend the winters in Pinecraft."

"That'd be good." He could see Yonnie now, playing shuffleboard and riding one of the adult-sized tricycles. Yonnie would love it there. He just knew it. And he could see Ivy walking along the beach, baking cookies in one of the local eateries. At least then he could spend the winters with her. And that was a far sight better than the last two years had been.

But still he wanted more. He wanted her all the time. Every day. As his wife. His life mate. His love. And right now, he wanted to lean in and kiss her.

Instead he pushed himself to his feet. "It's getting late." He faked a yawn as if to prove his point. "I guess we should be heading to bed."

She stood up next to him. "Are you afraid Santa won't come?"

He shook his head. It was way too late for that anyhow.

Ivy sat on the edge of her bed and took the pins from her hair. She released the barrettes and then slid the elastic ponytail holder down. With her hair pulled over one shoulder, she began to brush it.

She needed to give her hair a quick detangling, then pull it back from her face and neck so she could better sleep. But there was something soothing in each stroke she took, something almost therapeutic each time she ran her fingers through the tresses in the wake of the brush.

Tonight had been one of the best she could remember in a long time. Yes, she was still grieving over Ethan, but she was doing her best to keep all things in perspective. She loved the time she got to spend with Zeb and her grandfather. For the first time in a long time, she felt . . . normal. Like her life was where it was supposed to be. But she knew it couldn't continue that same way. She could never have the normal that she had experienced tonight. And for several reasons. Zeb would be returning to Florida soon. He might not be able to say the words, but she saw the look in his eyes whenever anyone brought up Pinecraft. There was something there that was special to him. She didn't believe it was a woman. Or maybe it was that she didn't want to believe it was anything other than the place itself.

She would have to join the church, atone for her transgressions, one way or another, and pray like anything that she could reverse the damage she had done to her reputation. The problem was, she wasn't sure repairing her standing in the community was possible.

You can always go to Indiana.

She pushed that voice away. That was the last thing she wanted to do. Though she had a feeling that was exactly where her life was headed.

She dropped the brush into her lap and scooped her long hair into a ponytail at the base of her neck. Then she tied a handkerchief around the bright tresses and pulled back her covers.

For now, she would stay in Wells Landing and enjoy the time she had there with Dawdi and Zeb, for she knew that, like Christmas, it would pass all too soon.

Chapter Seventeen

Christmas morning dawned cold and bright, without a cloud in the sky. As she had done every year of her life that she could remember, Ivy raced to the window to see if by chance any snow had fallen during the night.

But alas, it was to be yet another green Christmas.

It wasn't all bad. Or disappointing. She quickly dressed and straightened her handkerchief covering. She would have to change it when they went into town, but for now, at the house, it was fine. After a short trip to the bathroom and a quick brush of her teeth, she raced down the stairs.

Someone was already up. The candles on the mantel had been lit, the smell of coffee wafted in from the kitchen, and a fire crackled merrily in the fireplace.

A rustling sound drew her attention to the doorway leading to the kitchen.

"Merry Christmas." Her grandfather smiled and handed her a steaming cup of coffee.

She took the coffee and returned his smile. "Merry Christmas." She took a sip of the strong brew, then blew across the surface. It was a little stronger than usual, but she was beginning to get used to it. "Where's Zeb?"

"He's out in the barn taking care of the chores."

"What?" She started toward the door. "He shouldn't be out there." It was Christmas, and they weren't his chores.

Dawdi laid a hand on her arm to stop her. "Girl, let him help you."

She wanted to protest. Wanted to give him all the reasons why Zeb shouldn't be helping, starting with how she was beginning to get used to having him around and going straight down to how sad she was going to be when he finally left. And everything in between.

"Pour me another one of these," she said, indicating the cup of coffee. "I'll let him help, but he's not going to do it alone."

She grabbed her coat, scarf, and muck boots, then trudged out to the barn with a cup of coffee in each hand. She pushed her way inside and quickly located him working with the horses.

He turned as he heard her approach. He smiled, and she warmed immediately. Or maybe it was the coffee.

"Merry Christmas," he said.

"Merry Christmas." She handed him one of the mugs and tried to look as if it was no big deal. This was almost as bad as waking up next to him on the couch. Bad in all the best ways.

"I'll be done here in a minute. You can go on back to the house."

"I came out to help."

He shook his head. "I want to do this for you."

She started to protest, but he took a healthy gulp of the coffee, grimacing as it slid down his throat. "What is this?" he said, effectively overshadowing whatever she had been going to say.

"Coffee," she said with a small frown.

"Are you certain?" He shuddered.

Ivy laughed. "Dawdi made it. I should have warned you. Sometimes it's perfect, and sometimes it's not. I think he either forgets that he's already added the coffee and adds more or he forgets how much to add and gives it a guess." It was just another problem for her to worry over. If he couldn't make coffee, how much longer before he started forgetting other things? And how much longer before the times all blended into one big memory loss?

She pushed the thought away. It was Christmas. There was no room for negative, worrisome thoughts today. Now, that would be a Christmas miracle—but one she hoped to make true.

"Take it slow this time," she said as Zeb raised the mug to his lips once again.

He took another sip and winced. "Not sure that helps."

"Sissy," she teased and took a big drink of her own coffee. Just to show him how it was done.

He eyed her warily. "How do I know you didn't water yours down before you came out here?"

She offered him her cup. "Want to trade?"

He shook his head, but set his coffee off to one side. He picked up the shovel and went back to work on the horse stalls.

"Tell you what," Ivy said. "You let me help you finish this, and I'll make a new pot when we get back to the house."

"Coffee?" he asked.

"*Jah.*"

"Not jet fuel."

She laughed. "Nope, just plain ol' Christmas coffee."

He handed her the shovel, grabbed the pitchfork, and started toward the loft's vertical wooden ladder. "All right, then. You got yourself a deal."

"It's time to open presents," Dawdi said once the last of the breakfast dishes had been washed and put away.

"Just a minute, Dawdi." Ivy used a damp rag to clean the table. The dishes might be done, but there was still work to do. Sweep the floor, wipe down the countertops, store the leftovers.

When she and Zeb had come back into the house, she had been grinning like a crazy fool. But she couldn't help herself. In that moment she had everything, and she knew it. How long it would last was anyone's guess, but she was going to ride it out until the end.

Just sitting across the table from him this morning was like a treat. Things she had dreamed about, but never thought would come to be. Not after everything that had happened.

They had all piled into the kitchen and cooked breakfast like they were a real family. Dawdi had fried up the bacon, Zeb had set the table, and Ivy made the biscuits by her secret recipe. And as promised, she had made a fresh pot of coffee that wasn't so hard on the taste buds.

"Can we open the presents now?" Dawdi asked a few moments later.

Ivy chanced a look at Zeb. His smile was barely controlled. Ivy knew what he was thinking. Dawdi was as bad as a child when it came to Christmas. But she knew he enjoyed the giving as much as the getting. Maybe even more.

"*Jah*," she said, somehow holding in her chuckles. "We can open presents now."

Dawdi gave a gleeful laugh and rubbed his hands together in anticipation.

They went into the living room, where they had left their presents. Each had created their own pile next to their favorite seat. Not surprisingly, Dawdi's was the largest.

"Can I start?" Dawdi asked, his eyes twinkling.

"Of course." Ivy hid most of her smile and managed not to shake her head. She loved when he was like this and hated that his slipping memory seemed to be robbing him of his joy as well. He had improved lately, but she feared it was just a matter of time . . . She pushed that thought away, unwilling to let it intrude on their Christmas cheer.

He rummaged through the packages at his side, coming up with the one he wanted. "Here you go." He handed it to Ivy. "Merry Christmas."

"Merry Christmas," she returned and started to open the package. Inside was a beautiful material of the deepest purple with a slight sheen to the fabric. Ivy had never seen anything like it. At least not in Wells Landing. She looked up at her grandfather, stunned. "Where did you get this?"

He smiled. "Your mother sent it."

Ivy looked back to the beautiful fabric. "She did?" Tears rose in her eyes. She had felt like her mother had forgotten all about her after she moved to Indiana. She knew in her heart that it wasn't true, but it was hard being left behind. Even if she hadn't wanted to go. But there in her lap was proof that her mother hadn't forgotten about her. That her mother still cared. And that was the best present of all.

"Now you." She shot Zeb a pointed look, then passed him a wrapped present.

"Me?" His eyes grew wide.

"You didn't think you'd be opening presents?"

"That's not it. Why do I have to go next?"

She got the feeling as he unwrapped his gift that he didn't like having all eyes on him. Too bad. She wanted to see his face when he saw what she had given him.

With a small sigh, he accepted the package and began to unwrap it. "Thank you, Ivy." He held up the crocheted hat and matching scarf she had made him out of dark blue yarn.

"I wasn't sure how long you are staying, but for while you're here," she said softly. While he was in Wells Landing, he would need warm things—scarves, hats, gloves—but once he went back to Florida, those would be unnecessary. And he would go back. That was one thing she was sure of.

"Thank you," he said again, his voice oddly choked.

"My turn," Dawdi exclaimed, squirming as he waited for Ivy to hand him a package to open.

She did, and he ripped into it with childlike enthusiasm. But he stopped when he caught sight of what was inside. "Ivy." He raised his gaze to hers.

"You've been complaining about being cold."

He pulled the crocheted afghan from its wrapping. "*Jah*. But this . . ." He stopped. "When did you have time?"

She shrugged one shoulder as if it were no big deal. She had worked on the afghan in the evenings after Dawdi had gone to bed. It had taken months to make what should have taken less than a week, but one look at his astonished face and she knew that it had all been worth it. "When you love someone, you find the time."

They took turns opening presents until the piles were gone. Dawdi had received a new shirt and a sweater from Ivy, as well as a calendar where he could mark his auction days from Zeb. The calendar was oversized and easier for him to read than a standard one.

Ivy had received a copy of *Alice's Adventures in Wonderland* from Zeb, along with a stack of new handkerchiefs to cover her hair when she was working and at night, and a new pair of gloves from her grandfather. But the greatest gift of all was a box containing her grandmother's German Bible. It had been given to Mammi by her grandmother and was certainly special to the family.

"I can't accept this," Ivy protested. This time the tears that threatened slipped free and slid down her cheeks. She wiped them away with the back of one hand.

"Of course you can." He smiled and patted her knee.

"I want you to have it. Your grandmother wanted you to have it."

It was something she had always admired. But to have it . . . she felt she needed to make a commitment to God, to the church. She needed to ask for forgiveness. She needed to be forgiven. She needed to take the baptism classes, join the church, get her life together. Then, and maybe only then, would she be deserving. "I can't." She shook her head.

He smiled and pressed the Bible toward her. "You can."

"Thank you," she whispered. She didn't feel worthy. She didn't want to accept it, but she wasn't going to ruin the day by arguing.

"You're welcome." Dawdi returned to his seat and retrieved the last present he had stashed there. "And this is for you." He handed it to Zeb.

The man took it and turned it over, staring at it quizzically. "You didn't have to get me anything."

"Of course not. I want you to have this."

"Thank you," Zeb replied.

"Well, come on," Dawdi said impatiently. "Open it."

Almost hesitantly, Zeb started to pull the paper. It seemed to take the longest time, but finally he held a pocket knife in his hands. "Yonnie . . ." He rolled the knife between his fingers, testing its weight and balance. "I don't know what to say."

"*Thank you* will work."

"This knife—"

"—is very old," her *dawdi* finished. "My grandfather gave it to me when I was about ten or so."

"If you've had it all these years, you should keep it."

Dawdi shook his head. "That's the exact reason why I need to give it away."

The look on Zeb's face clearly conveyed that he was confused, really confused, but he wasn't sure how to respond. Finally he settled on "Thank you."

Dawdi smiled, clearly satisfied with the exchange. "You're welcome."

Zeb pulled back the shades and looked out the front window. After they had opened presents, Ivy had gone into the kitchen, made a new pot of coffee, and gotten everyone a slice of sweet potato pie. He knew what she was doing: refueling everyone so she could leave. She was anxious to go to the retirement home and see what arrangements had been made for Ethan Dallas. Zeb had tried to convince her that a simple call would be enough, but she figured no one would give her much of an answer since she wasn't part of his family. If she went in, she could talk to the other residents, who would surely tell her everything they knew.

But now . . .

He let the shade fall back into place. The clear sky of early morning had turned into the gray clouds of afternoon. Now it was sleeting. No weather to be out running around in. Not unless it was absolutely necessary. He knew it was important to her, but it wasn't a necessity. No matter what she said.

"It's sleeting," he reported.

Ivy stopped gathering up their pie dishes and flew to the window. She peered outside, then shot him an almost accusing look. As if somehow he had made it sleet so she couldn't go into town. For a moment he thought she was going to say something, then she deflated before his eyes, crumpling under the reality.

"I'm sorry," he said. And he was. He hated that she had lost a friend. It seemed that she had so few these days. He was sorry that this was possibly the worst time of the year to lose a loved one. Not that any time would be ideal, but Christmas was supposed to be about joy and celebration.

Not funerals and eulogies. "Maybe it'll warm up some tomorrow, and we can go then."

Things like ice and snow didn't last long in the Sooner State.

"Maybe," she said. But he could see the disappointment in her eyes. Suddenly he was struck with the notion that he never wanted to see her disappointed again. How many times had he seen that look? Too many. When she lost the baby, when he told her he was leaving town, today. He wanted that expression gone from her choices. But he had no idea how to make it happen.

"What's the matter?"

He looked up, only then realizing that he had started staring at her shoes. "Oh. Nothing."

She nodded, but he could tell she didn't believe him. If he didn't want to tell her, she seemed to be okay with that. But he did want to tell her. He wanted to tell her how much he loved her, how much he had missed her, and how there were so many days that he wished he had never left.

And that would get him . . . absolutely nothing. Nothing but another one of those disappointed looks from her.

"Let's play a game," he said, hoping to take her mind off Ethan Dallas and the weather.

For a moment he thought she would tell him no, then she nodded and crossed to the china hutch. The bottom cabinets contained games of all sorts: Scrabble, dominoes, Rook cards, Uno cards, and even a machine that would shoot Uno cards at unsuspecting players. That one was always good for a laugh. "Let's play Uno Attack," he said.

Ivy shot him a look. "I thought you didn't like Uno."

"That one is different." *And maybe it will make you laugh.*

"You sure?"

"*Jah.*" He nodded.

Ivy retrieved the shiny red-and-black device and plunked

it down on the middle of the table. Then she set the special deck of cards next to it. "Are you playing, Dawdi?"

He waved her suggestion away with one hand. "Bah," he said. "I think I'll take a nap." He pulled the footrest up to his chair and settled in for a Christmas afternoon snooze.

"Looks like it's just the two of us," Zeb said.

"Uno's not as much fun with two people," she pointed out.

"Why do I feel like there's more to it than that?"

She shrugged. "I don't know. Hey. Why don't you teach me the game you and Dawdi were playing the other day?"

He shook his head. "That game is messed up."

"Y'all seemed to be having a good time playing it."

"*Jah.*"

"But?" she prompted.

She wanted to play something. He could tell. And she didn't care what. She simply needed to get her mind off of what had been going on the last few days.

"We'll play Uno," he told her. "But only if you promise to make me some more of those Christmas cookies this week."

"It'll be after Christmas," she pointed out.

He smiled. "It's always a good time for Christmas cookies."

Chapter Eighteen

Second Christmas dawned bright and clear. The sleet that had fallen the day before was nothing more than a memory.

Ivy had almost forgotten the best part about the bad weather on Christmas Day: it meant she didn't have to see Tassie and Karl. It wasn't a very Christian thought, but she couldn't help it. She had the strangest feeling that Tassie was trying to court her grandfather whether he wanted to be courted or not.

"I suppose the Webers will be over today," she said at breakfast.

Dawdi shrugged. "I don't know. Haven't been out to the shanty to check the messages."

She would guarantee there was one on there from Tassie saying she would be taking that piece of pie today. But Ivy had plans of her own. She might have missed going into town and visiting with the sweet residents of the senior home, but she wasn't going to miss it today.

"I'm going to Whispering Pines," she announced somewhere between the bacon and her first biscuit.

Dawdi stopped buttering his own biscuit and looked at her with a strange light in his eyes. "What?"

"I'm going—I would like to go into town to the retirement home today. I would like to check on the residents." She didn't say the rest. She didn't have to. They knew that she wanted to check on Ethan's things and find out about any arrangements that had been made.

"Second Christmas is for visiting," her grandfather said.

She nodded. "And that's just what I'm doing."

In the end, she left Zeb and Dawdi just after noon to drive into town. Zeb had wanted to ride with her, but she asked him to stay with Dawdi. She knew he was trying to be supportive, but this was something she had to do alone. Besides, she would feel much better knowing Zeb was there, in case her grandfather had a memory slip again.

Christmas with Zeb had been wonderful, and for a moment there, she had believed that maybe they could have a second chance. But deep down, she knew he was returning to Florida. Any second chance they might carve out for themselves would be lost along the miles.

She parked her tractor in the nearly empty parking lot and made her way inside. The Christmas music was no longer playing through the halls. Now some piano music without words wafted around. Any other time it might have been soothing, but she missed the cheery sounds of the season. She tried not to let it get her down as she stopped at the front desk to sign in for her visit.

"Hi, Ivy." Angie greeted her with a genuine smile. "How was your Christmas?"

Ivy smiled. "It was nice. Kind of quiet." Until she and Zeb had started playing games. At that point, her grandfather had put in his earplugs and headed for bed. "Yours?"

"Lots of fun, as always."

Ivy nodded. "That's good."

"There's someone here I think you should meet."

"I came to help with Ethan's room," she explained, tears pricking her eyes. She didn't want to meet any new residents today. She wanted to assist in getting all of Ethan's things packed up and ready for his family to pick them up. "Maybe next time." Would there be a next time? Or had Ethan been the only reason she had been led here? Yes, she decided. She would come again. But next time, not for her. For the residents.

"He's in Mr. Dallas's room." She nodded down the hallway toward Ethan's room.

Ivy nodded and tried not to be disappointed. She had wanted to help, not visit with some old friend from Ethan's past. Still she started down the hallway toward his room. How was she going to explain her relationship with the man? It was unique, to be sure. She would simply say that they had been friends and leave it at that.

She took a deep breath and pushed inside. But she drew up short when she saw the man standing there. This was no work colleague, no war buddy, no one from Ethan's past.

He turned at the sound of her footfalls.

She blinked at him in stunned silence.

He took a step back, obviously surprised as well.

"Who are you?" she asked.

He smiled, showing even white teeth in his sun-browned face. "I think that's my line." His sea-blue eyes twinkled as he raked his longish blond hair off his forehead.

"I'm Ivy," she said. "Ivy Weaver."

Those gorgeous eyes widened. "You are?"

She pinned him with a suspicious stare. He might be the cutest thing she had seen in a long time, but that didn't mean he was supposed to be in Ethan's room. Still, there was something oddly familiar about him. "Your turn."

He paused long enough to set the framed photograph back on the television set before meeting her gaze. "Logan

Dallas," he said. "At your service." He took a step forward and reached out a hand to shake. She took it, noting the calluses.

Ethan had told her that his grandson was in Central or South America somewhere building houses for the poor. And apparently that was so important that he couldn't come see his grandfather before he died.

She jerked her hand away. "So good of you to finally come."

He tilted his head to one side as if trying to figure her out. *Good luck, buddy. Better than you have tried.*

"I get the feeling that you're angry with something—me, actually—but I can't fathom why."

"You arrive two days after your grandfather dies when you should have been here for him long before that. You figure it out."

"I see." He smiled, once again showing those perfect teeth in that perfect face. In fact, the only thing she could see that might be an imperfection were the rough spots on his hands that he had gotten helping others. Still, his grandfather had needed him and he hadn't been there.

"He wanted to see you, you know. Before he . . . died. He wanted you to come, but you didn't." To her regret, tears rose in her eyes, but she wouldn't let them fall. She didn't want Logan Dallas to think she was crying for him. She was crying over the disappointment she had seen Ethan suffer, dying alone.

He straightened, and she knew she had hit a nerve. "I don't owe you an explanation, but I'll give you one anyhow. I was on my way here for Christmas, but I got delayed at the borders. The Nicaraguan and Honduran officials aren't exactly lovey-dovey with Americans. I spent two days at each border while they searched everything I had. More than once, I might add. And you don't even want to know what they did to my person."

She held up a hand. "Please."

Logan grew quiet, merely staring at the things on the bookcase as if he wasn't really seeing them at all. "He was my grandfather," he finally said. "And I love him very much."

Her tears rose again as his voice choked.

"I always thought that when you knew someone was going to die that it made it easier when they finally passed." He looked up at her with those beautiful sea-colored eyes. "I was wrong."

She nodded, not knowing what else to do. She shouldn't be here. Yes, she loved Ethan too, but not in the same way that Logan had. She should leave, give him time to collect his grandfather's things. She wasn't needed. "I'm sorry," she said simply. Sorry for his loss, sorry that she had accused him, sorry that he hadn't made it before Ethan died. "It was nice to meet you." She turned and hurried out the door.

"Wait," he cried.

She whirled around to find that he had followed her into the hallway.

"You must have come here for a reason." He raised his brows to make his statement seem more like a question.

She nodded, the untied strings of her prayer covering brushing across her shoulders. "*Jah.*" She lifted her chin. "I came to help pack up his belongings."

"Stay," he quietly commanded. "If you want to. I mean, you don't have to leave."

She may not have to, but she should. "This is your time with him." And she didn't want to intrude. She turned to go once again.

"He talked about you all the time," he said, effectively stopping her in her tracks.

"He did?" She slowly faced him.

"Oh, yeah. Ivy this and Ivy that. He wanted me to pray for you."

"For me?" She lightly thumped her chest. "Me?"

Logan nodded. "He was worried about you."

That was Ethan, dying himself and yet worried over the lives of others. She couldn't help but give a little smile. "He was a good man."

"Yes, he was." Logan returned her smile with one of his own. "Will you stay?" he asked. "I could use the help."

"I don't want to intrude."

He gave an understanding nod. "If you were intruding, I wouldn't have invited you."

They worked side by side boxing up Ethan's things. With only about half of it ready to transport, they decided to take a pudding break in the cafeteria.

"And you two would do this every week?" Logan asked as they grabbed their cups of pudding and found a seat.

"Without fail."

He chuckled. "That's just like him. Find the prettiest girl in the place and ply her with sweets."

She wasn't exactly sure what all that meant, but she understood one thing: Logan Dallas thought she was pretty. The idea shouldn't have thrilled her, but it did. Because he was *Englisch*? Maybe. Because he was worldly in ways she had never imagined? Perhaps. Or because he was related to someone she had fallen in love with? Even more likely. Moreover, he might be the best-looking man she had ever laid eyes on. Zeb aside. Zeb was handsome in a familiar way. Logan was exotic. He was browned by the sun, callused from hard work, and impossibly blond around his face. The back of his hair was darker, nearly a honey color, and she figured he wore a hat when he worked.

"He didn't tell me, you know," Logan said somewhere between the first cup of pudding and the second.

"Hmmm?" Ivy said in lieu of real words. Her mouth was full of pudding.

"He didn't tell me you were Amish."

She blinked, a little stunned, then somehow managed to swallow the mouthful. "He didn't?" She was *the Amish girl*. She had heard the others talking. It was simply how they remembered her.

Logan scraped the last bite from the little plastic cup, then pulled the lid off the second. "I find that strange."

"I don't." Ethan Dallas was a fair man. He didn't divide people out into parcels. He had done everything in his power to help her. He wanted her to forgive herself, go forward, begin to live again. "He was just like that." The fact that she was Amish hadn't mattered to Ethan, so he hadn't mentioned it.

"He did tell me about your red hair. And your blue eyes." Logan's expression became unreadable. Up until that point she'd been able to almost read his thoughts in those expressive eyes, but now . . .

"Is that a problem?"

He smiled, but now she wondered if he was wearing a mask to cover what he was really thinking. "Of course not. It just surprised me is all."

But he told Logan about her red hair and blue eyes. What did that mean? That her hair was more outstanding than her religion? She shook the thought away. She was overthinking things.

"I guess we should be getting back to work."

Ivy nodded and pushed herself up from the table.

They deposited their empty pudding cups in the large trash can and started for the door.

"Look, Ethel," one woman was saying as they came through the cafeteria doors. "There's the girl I've been telling you about."

Heat filled her cheeks as the woman pointed toward her.

She knew they were deep pink, most probably making her freckles stand out like little tan pepper flakes all over her face.

"Land sakes!" Ethel exclaimed, rushing toward her. Her bright red hair was styled in curls that stayed close to her head. Most of the other ladies had similar hairstyles, and Ivy wondered if the same person helped them all.

Ethel grabbed Ivy's hands, nearly dancing in place there in front of her. "They told me there was another redhead around, but I hadn't seen you with my own eyes and wasn't about to believe them. Yet here you are."

Ivy wanted to ask why they would lie about such a thing, but decided against it. "Here I am," she weakly replied.

"We could be twins," she shrieked. Except that Ethel hadn't been cursed with so many freckles. Plus she was about thirty pounds heavier and four inches shorter than Ivy. Oh, and her hair was obviously dyed. Why anyone would purposefully make their hair this color was beyond Ivy. When she was younger she had made up fantasies about turning *Englisch* just so she could dye her hair a "normal" color.

"And you must be Ethan's boy." The other lady—Alice, Ivy thought her name was—grabbed one of Logan's hands and squeezed it between her own. "So sorry to hear about your granddad. He was such a good man."

"Thank you." Logan laid his hands on top of hers as Ivy had seen some of the *Englisch* preachers in town do. She wasn't sure where she had seen it; only that she had. "He's with the Father now," Logan said with great confidence. "Happy and out of pain."

Pain? Ivy hadn't known he'd had pains. He had always seemed so upbeat and positive. She supposed he'd hidden his trials from the rest of the world.

"Amen," Ethel said, raising her hands in the air and twirling around in place.

The ladies continued to talk with Logan for a moment,

but she couldn't pay them any mind. She was too busy thinking about what Logan had said. *He's with the Father now.* As if he knew without a doubt that his grandfather had gone to heaven.

The thought was foreign to her. She had been raised to believe in Jesus, but that alone wasn't enough to secure her a place in heaven. She had to walk like Jesus, do good deeds for her neighbors and friends, even strangers. She had to be the best Christian she could be. Then, and only then, she could *hope* that she would be let into heaven when she died.

She was startled out of her thoughts as each lady leaned in and gave her a kiss on the cheek. She wasn't used to such public displays and hoped she didn't look horrified at their familiarity. They didn't seem to notice as they waggled their fingers at Logan in a gesture of goodbye, then made their way to the cafeteria food line.

Ivy and Logan walked back to his grandfather's room in silence.

"I want to thank you for helping me," he said. "Can I buy you dinner tonight?"

That sounded so much like a date, her heart pounded. Her voice was lost. She knew he didn't mean it that way, but it was shocking and thrilling all the same. She shook her head.

"You got to eat sometime."

"I—" She cleared her throat. "I have to go home and take care of my grandfather." *And Zeb,* she reminded herself. *Have you forgotten about him?*

Logan nodded in that understanding way of his. "I see. Well, that explains a great deal."

She had no idea what he was talking about.

"You don't have to stay," Logan said. "I can get it from here."

She got the distinct impression that he wanted to be alone. It was the one thing she knew she could give him, no matter how badly she wanted to stay. *But do you want to stay to help, or to gaze moony-eyed at Logan Dallas?* "Of course." She extended a hand for him to shake. He took it. There were those calluses again. "It was nice to meet you, Logan Dallas."

"Very nice to meet you as well."

He waited by the door until she was out of sight. She knew because she looked back twice.

It was better this way. After today, she would never see Logan Dallas again.

Angie flashed her a quick smile. "So?" she asked. "What did you think?"

"About what?" Ivy asked innocently. She knew exactly what Angie was talking about.

"Mr. Ethan's grandson. He's cute, huh?"

"I suppose." He was beyond cute.

"I don't know why I was so surprised when I saw him. How can he not be cute and be kin to Mr. Ethan?"

Ivy pulled the clipboard closer, checked herself out, and tried not to think too hard about Logan Dallas and how handsome he really was.

"Do you have a boyfriend, Ivy?"

Did she? What was Zeb? She couldn't really say he was anything other than a friend. And someone she almost married. Almost had a baby with.

She took so long to answer that Angie's eyes widened. "You do! Is it a secret? I heard that the Amish keep their relationships a secret. Is that true?"

"I'm not trying to hide anything." It was almost the truth. "I can't have boyfriend. I haven't joined the church."

Angie frowned.

"It's complicated," she said by way of explanation.

"I guess so." Angie straightened the papers on her desk as Ivy finished signing out. "Would you be willing to come back in a couple of days and help us get all the Christmas ornaments put away?"

Ivy looked around at the shiny tinsel. Once it had been glittery and festive. Now it seemed sad, tired. "Of course."

"Thanks, Ivy. I hope that you'll continue to come visit us. The residents love seeing your face."

Ivy gave her a small smile. "I would love to." And she would. Whispering Pines seemed to be the one place where she was always welcome.

"I can go with you if you like." Zeb studied her face with such intensity that Ivy wanted to turn away. She wasn't sure what he was seeing there, or if it was something she wanted him to see.

"No, that's okay." *I would rather go alone.*

Two more days had passed since she had met Logan Dallas at the retirement home. Today was the day they laid his grandfather to rest. Ethan had been buried at a large cemetery in Tulsa. She hadn't wanted to go to the funeral; showing up there would have been a bit too presumptuous. But she wanted to see his final resting place and wish him farewell.

Her decision had nothing to do with Logan Dallas. At least that was what she was telling herself. There was something magnetic about the man. Just as there had been about his grandfather. Ivy found herself thinking about him again and again, comparing him to the people she knew. She couldn't figure it out, so she thought it best to avoid him altogether. It wasn't like anything could happen between the two of them.

"Are you sure?"

"Positive." She smiled to reinforce her words.

From outside, a car horn sounded. "That's my ride."

Zeb studied her once more, and she squirmed under his scrutiny. "Are you sure you're okay?"

"*Jah.* Of course." But she felt different. Somehow, some-way, something inside her had changed.

"*Sei brauf,*" he said. *Behave yourself.*

She smiled. "You do the same." Though she wanted to ask him what he thought she would be doing. She was pur-posefully going when Logan Dallas wouldn't be there. She had avoided him for the last two days. But as she got into the car with her *Englisch* driver, she realized that Zeb had no idea who Logan Dallas was, because she hadn't told him. Now anything she had said on the matter would have only made her look incredibly guilty.

She had to have one of the cemetery grounds workers show her where Ethan's grave was. It was too soon to put up a headstone. She had looked at the mound of dirt that covered a man who had once been her friend, but there was no closure. Once-beautiful flowers framed the grave, but the cold air had wilted them to sad petals that dropped every time the wind blew. She hadn't thought about sending flowers. Why hadn't she sent flowers?

She wasn't sure what she had expected when she came here, but it was more than what she left with. Maybe she simply wanted answers to questions that had none.

Or maybe she wanted to know what Ethan had known about her. She could see it in his eyes each time she visited. He knew something about her that she didn't even know herself. But what?

Her tears fell, warm against her cool cheeks. She reached into the pocket of her coat for a tissue, only to find other papers in there as well. She pulled them out. It was an enve-lope. The envelope Angie had given her after Ethan had died. It was from Ethan. She had forgotten all about it. Or perhaps she had wanted to save it, this last piece of such a special man.

What better time to read it than while standing at his final resting place? She slipped the paper from the envelope and began reading.

My dear Ivy,

I can honestly say that I was well and truly blessed when you came into my life. I know we only knew each other for a short time, but you made my last few weeks very happy ones. I thank you for that more than you will ever know.

But even as you brought me joy, I could see the hurt and confusion in your eyes. I told you about Mary, Jesus, and the grace of God. Everything else is up to you. Well, it is now. If you have this letter, it's because I've passed.

Tears sprang into her eyes, but she blinked them away. The time for crying was no more.

When I first met you, I could sense the searching inside you. I don't even know if you recognized it yourself. But once you do, it may take some time, but don't give up. You will find your place. I know that as certainly as I know my own name. God is good, and He takes care of those who follow Him. In all ways.

> *Ever faithfully yours,*
> *Ethan Dallas*

She pulled the second paper from underneath and read the poem typed there.

Now Is Not the Time for Tears

Now is not the time for tears, for I have laughed . . .
I have walked through the meadows and ran
        through the fields.
I have experienced all the joy this world has to offer.
Now is not the time for tears, for I have loved . . .
And I have been loved. I never knew a stranger, only
        friends.
For every man is the face of God.
Now is not the time for tears, for I have seen . . .
The ocean blue, the mountain snow.
The beauty of this world will never fade.
Now is not the time for tears, for I have been . . .
I have joined with my fellow man,
and I pray leave this world better than I found it.
Now is not the time for tears, for I have lived . . .
In happiness and in sorrow.
When the wind brushes through your hair, I am
        there.
In every heartbeat, every breath, every joy and
        remorse.
Now is not the time for tears, for I am not gone.

He had said some of those very words to her before he
died. He had lived. He had left the world a better place. He had
left her a better person, just from having known him.

"You will be missed, Ethan Dallas." She blew a kiss
toward the mound of dirt and hoped that somewhere in
heaven he caught it. She knew he was there. How? Because
he knew that was where he was going. And that was enough
for her.

She folded the letter and poem, placed them back into
the envelope, and gently slid it into her pocket. She wanted
to save the letter, to keep it safe so she could read it again
and again. She wanted to have it when the confusion cleared,

when she found out that purpose which had eluded her for so long.

The driver had the car running by the time she walked from the grave site to the cemetery road where he was waiting.

"All done?"

"*Jah*," she said as she slid into the back seat.

"Home then?" he asked.

She shook her head. "Whispering Pines Senior Living Center, if you don't mind."

"Not at all." He put the car into gear, and down the road they went.

She contemplated why she had told him to take her to the retirement home, but could come up with no rightful answer as the miles zipped by. Maybe just to see it again, tell Angie that she would come next week and help take down all the Christmas decorations. She would read to other residents, talk with them, visit with them, anything and everything she could do to make their lives a little brighter. Because it was one thing she knew she could do. That in itself was special.

She wouldn't be able to stay long, not with a driver waiting. So perhaps just making sure it was still there was more her goal. Whatever it was, she wanted to see it before she went home.

"Can you wait for a moment?" Ivy asked. "I just need to tell a friend something, then I'll be right back out."

"Sure." He was a good driver, and she vowed to give him a healthy tip for his service.

Ivy raced to the door of the home, her coattails flapping behind her despite the chilly weather.

Angie was at her place at the desk, as usual. Just the person she wanted to see.

"Will Monday afternoon be all right for taking down the ornaments?"

Angie seemed a bit startled. Perhaps Ivy should have

said hello first. But Angie recovered quickly and gave a small nod. "Sure. They can wait until then."

"Good." She smiled and was on her way back out the door when she heard his voice.

"Ivy."

She stopped mid-stride and turned to face him. "Hello, Logan."

What was it about the man that made her feel tingly? He was handsome, sure, but so was Zeb. He was godly. Again, Zeb was too. Maybe it was the way he looked at her when she spoke, as if every word was plated in gold and more valuable than the last.

"I thought I heard you out here."

She nodded dumbly. "I thought you would be gone."

He gave a casual shrug. "These things take time, you know."

She didn't really, but she nodded again as if she understood completely. Then she realized she looked like one of those wobbly-headed statues that some people put in their cars. She stopped.

"Good luck to you," she said. This would be the last time she would see him, she was certain. "And Godspeed."

"What's your hurry?"

She jerked a thumb over one shoulder. "I have a car waiting."

"I can drive you home," he offered.

"Isn't that nice," Angie drawled. Ivy wished she could kick her. Not real hard, but hard enough to get her to shut her mouth.

"It is," Ivy agreed. "Really nice, but I should be going."

"Too bad." Logan rapped his knuckles against the receiving desk. "I was going to ask if you could come with me to get a piece of that famous Kauffman pie. Maybe we could talk a little about my grandfather."

She wanted to say no. How she wanted to say no—but even stronger was the need to say yes.

"Okay. Let me pay the driver." She refused to look at Angie as she walked away. She heard the woman stifle a squeal and knew what she was thinking. But most people didn't realize just how impossible a mixed relationship like Amish and *Englisch* could be. She might be going to get a piece of pie with Logan, but that was all it would be. Pie, nothing more.

They weren't the only ones in Kauffmans' eating pie, and she knew that word of this little get-together would be all over by sundown. She didn't care. She sniffed, stiffened her spine, and pretended this was the best time a girl could have. Not that she had to pretend very much. Logan was as sweet as his grandfather, maybe even more. He was handsome, and she could tell that all eyes were on them. Most likely on him, as the women watched under the hood of their lashes, both Amish and *Englisch* alike.

"What do you call that one?" Logan pointed to her pie with the prongs of his fork.

"Bob Andy pie." She sliced off another bite with the side of her fork and ate it with gusto.

"Why's it called that?"

She smiled. "The story goes that a farmer's wife made him the pie, and he said it was so good. It was as good as his two best horses, Bob and Andy. The name just stuck."

"For real?"

"I have no idea," she said truthfully.

"And what's it taste like?"

She grinned around her bite. "Good."

"Seriously."

"Sort of like caramel pie but not as caramel-y. A little

like pecan pie without the nuts. Maybe a little like chess pie, but not as—"

"Chessy," he supplied.

She laughed. "I was going to say boring. This has cinnamon and nutmeg to spice it up a bit."

"You think chess pie is boring?"

"It is when you compare it to this."

He looked down at his own pie, then longingly at hers. They hadn't talked about one thing of importance since they sat down. They had talked about the town, the empty shops, the home shops like Fitch's Furniture Store. The franchises. It seemed that Logan was very interested in their little town. Either that or he was trying to be polite.

"Give me a bite," he said.

"No way." She shook her head. "I told you to get something more Amish-y."

"What's more Amish than apple crumble pie?"

"Shoofly pie, buttermilk pie, peanut butter pie, vinegar pie—"

"Wait. Hold up. Vinegar pie?"

"*Jah.*"

"Will the Amish make pie out of anything?"

She smiled. "Pretty much."

"I think I'll stick with this." He took a bite of his apple pie. "Mmmm, so good and so normal."

"You don't have a sense of adventure."

He sat back looking falsely affronted. "I do so. I just got back from a year in Central America."

Okay, he had her with that one. "When it comes to food."

"I'll have you know, I eat all local food when I'm on a mission. It builds up trust and camaraderie."

"Fine. When it comes to pie. You have no sense of adventure when it comes to pie."

"I think they should be made out of something sweet," he said.

"Anything can be made into pie."

"Even vinegar?"

"Even vinegar."

"How do you take something so sour and make it into this?" He gestured toward his plate.

"I can't give away all our secrets."

"Which means either you don't know or the pie is terrible."

"Not terrible, but the best pie in town is down the street at Esther's Bakery."

"I saw that when we drove in. If they have the best, why did we come here?"

"Because you said this was where you wanted to eat."

"I could have been persuaded."

"I work there," she said bluntly. She hadn't taken him there because she worked there, and she hadn't wanted anyone to know that they'd had dessert together. *Like everyone here at Kauffmans' doesn't know.*

She pushed that voice aside. "You can be persuaded as to where to eat pie, but not what kind of pie to eat."

"That's right." His smile was so bright and warm that it almost made her forget about everything. Zeb. The baby. Forgiveness.

She ducked her head and went back to her dessert.

Almost.

Chapter Nineteen

"What's it like?" she asked several quiet moments later. Somehow the conversation had turned from playful to intense. Or was that her imagination?

"What's what like?"

"Living in another country."

He looked around at all the people, the tables in the restaurant, the cars whizzing past outside. "Different," he finally said. "At least, different than this. We're out in the middle of nothing, jungle all around, then suddenly there's a little village, but not a village. Just a group of houses in shambles."

She tried to imagine what that was like, but no picture would come to her.

"These people are so poor. They're hungry. The water supply is low or barely drinkable."

"And you correct all that?"

"We dig wells, help with crops, repair their houses, build new ones."

Ethan had told her that his grandson had built houses for the poor. He had failed to mention all the other things. They were turning villages from starving hovels into thriving communities.

"That sounds wonderful."

"It is. And hard and fulfilling."

She could only imagine.

"There are a couple of Amish boys on our team."

"Really?"

"I say Amish. I think they're more Mennonite. There's a difference, right?"

"*Jah.* There's a difference." She hid her indulgent smile.

"These boys come down from Belize. There's a settlement there, did you know that?"

She shook her head. Mennonite boys from Belize building houses in Central America for those less fortunate. "There were a couple of people from here who went to Haiti to help them."

He nodded. "There's something wonderful about helping others."

There was. She knew that from her own experience. How long had it been since she had helped her fellow man?

"You helped my grandfather," he said. "You'll never know how much that means to me."

"I didn't do anything."

"You did everything. You ate pudding with him. Played games with him, watched TV with him. You were his friend."

"And he was mine," she said in return.

"Thank you for that. Thank you for having a giving soul and giving part of it to him."

Part of her soul. She figured it was as good an analogy as any. She had given part of herself to Ethan and in return received something from him. But she still had the feeling that something else was about to happen.

"You can drop me off here," she said, pointing to the phone shanty that was a couple of houses down from hers.

"I can take you home," he said. "I may not know much about the Amish, but I know that's not a real house."

"My house is down a ways."

"Then I should take you there." He made to put the car into gear, but she laid a hand on his arm to stop him.

"Please," she said.

He sighed and got out of the car. "You know this goes against everything my mother ever taught me about being a gentleman," he said as he opened the door for her.

"It has nothing to do with that," she countered. It had to do with questions and hurt feelings, confusion and indecision. She couldn't avoid them altogether, but she could delay them a bit.

"If you say so," he grumbled.

"I do." She slipped the strap of her purse a little higher onto her shoulder and shifted in place. "Thanks for the pie."

"Thanks for going with me."

"Have a safe trip back to . . . to . . ."

"Costa Rica," he supplied.

"Costa Rica," she said, then repeated the name in her mind to lodge it there. Costa Rica.

"Thank you again for looking out for my grandfather."

She nodded. "I wish you had gotten here before . . ."

"Me too." He took a step closer, his arms opening to give her a hug. That wasn't something Amish girls did, hugging *Englisch* men on the side of the road, but she wanted that one last contact with him. It was as if he might have the answers she had been hoping to get from his grandfather.

He stepped back, but still held her arms in his hands. "Take care of yourself, Ivy Weaver," he said.

"*Sei brauf*," she returned.

He frowned.

"It means behave yourself."

"I like that." He released her then, and she was free to walk away. Except she didn't want to. Why? What sort of hold did Logan Dallas have over her? She might not ever know.

She turned on one heel and started for her house. It took everything in her power not to turn around and watch him drive away.

Her nose was numb by the time she made it to the porch. Zeb must have been watching. He bounded outside and pulled her in.

"I was worried sick about you."

"*Which of you by worrying can add one cubit to his stature?*" she paraphrased.

"Ivy." His voice lowered until it was almost a growl.

Her anger slipped away. "I'm sorry, Zeb. I didn't mean to sound callous. I'm just not used to having someone worry about me." But it was more than that. She felt almost guilty being out with Logan when Zeb was here at her house caring for her grandfather.

"Yonnie worries about you."

She looked over to where he sat on the couch, head back as he snored, feet propped up before him. He sure looked worried to her. "Uh-huh."

"Well, he does." He lifted her coat from her shoulders so she could easily slip her arms from the sleeves. In a minute he had her coat, scarf, and gloves hung by the door, ready for her next outing.

"I've got an idea," Zeb said a few minutes later.

She was warm and sitting by the fire, joyfully listening to her grandfather snore. She was thankful. He hadn't had a spell in a long while. God was good. "What's that?"

"Clara Rose and Obie are having a party tonight. Well, not really a party, more of a get-together. They want to have a Rook tournament. Couples versus. Sounds like fun, *jah*?"

It did. It sounded like a great deal of fun, but she couldn't go. If she went with Zeb to a couples tournament, she would be fooling herself that they could be a couple, when she knew without a doubt that could never happen. If she did go with Zeb, she was certain that someone would have a problem with her presence. That was the trouble with making yourself a pariah. It was hard to stop that ball rolling once it started. "I can't go," she said.

His face crumpled. No matter how badly she wanted to say yes, she couldn't do that to Zeb; she wouldn't do it to herself.

"No one will ever change their minds about you if you aren't around them so they can see you are different."

That had been the entire point. She couldn't go. She just couldn't, and yet she found herself nodding. "Okay," she said on a rumbling sigh. "I'll go."

By the time Zeb pulled up to Obie and Clara Rose's house, Ivy thought she might hyperventilate. The air wheezed in and out of her lungs, and any minute she was bound to pass out. Or throw up. Maybe both.

Zeb hopped to the ground and peered up at her. "You okay?"

Somehow she nodded. This was not good. So not good. Then a voice inside her head whispered, *Be brave.*

Be strong and let your heart take courage, All you who hope in the Lord.

Psalms, she thought. But she didn't need chapter and verse to gain strength from the words.

She reached her hand out, clasped his in her own, and hopped to the ground next to him. It was an everyday act, boring, not worthy of any attention, and yet it felt monumental. Maybe it was.

Zeb tucked her hand in the crook of his arm and turned them toward the house. "It's going to be fine, Ivy. Just fine."

* * *

"I can't believe she showed up."

Ivy was about to round the corner that would take her back into the large activity room where Clara Rose and Obie had set up the card tables. The voice stopped her cold. She couldn't tell who it was, only that it was a she.

"I think it's wonderful," another voice said. "It's about time for her to come out of her so-called *rumspringa* and get with the church."

"Coming to card night is hardly a step toward joining the church," the first voice said.

Ivy plastered herself against the wall, hoping to remain out of sight, needing to hear what they said, hating it all the while. This . . . *this* was the exact reason why she didn't want to come tonight. What had she ever done to these girls?

"Poor Zeb," the second one lamented.

"I know! It was sweet of him to take pity on her like that, but he's not helping his standing by bringing her here."

His standing? What is that all about?

"I heard he was going to leave again. Right after the New Year."

That was only a couple of days away. When was he going to tell her that?

"I guess it won't matter then."

"I suppose not."

The girls must have decided to get something to drink, or maybe they saw someone across the room and went to talk to them. At any rate, their voices continued, but faded away into the general noise of the event.

Ivy bit her lip. She would not cry. They weren't worth it. But it just proved that she would never be able to hold her head up in Wells Landing. For all the talk of Amish forgiveness, there would always be those who paid lip service to the idea, then carried on when they thought no one was looking. How could she live like that? She couldn't. It was that simple.

* * *

"When are you going back to Florida?"

Zeb jerked his head around to face her. He had been sweeping up the pine needles from the floor. While they had been at the card game, Chester had gotten into the wood box and dug out the once-upon-a-time Christmas decorations and batted them around the house. "I don't know."

"Then why is everyone saying that you're going back after the New Year?"

Zeb sighed and went back to his chore. He was in charge of the floor, while she gathered up all the yarn Chester had taken from her sewing basket and strung all over the house. Some spots were knotted together, but she was determined to save as much of it as she could. Dawdi had gone upstairs to shower and get ready for bed while Ivy and Zeb cleaned up the mess.

They had arrived back at the house only to find Tassie on the front porch looking harried. Her cheeks were flushed, her *kapp* was crooked, and some of her hair had worked its way out of her bob. Harried. *Jah*, that was the word.

"Ivy Weaver, I'm not sure what sort of monster you keep in your house, but I'll not be coming over again unless you get rid of it immediately." The last word had five distinct syllables.

After a short questioning, Ivy discovered that sometime during Tassie's visit Chester had gone a little off-kilter, as she was prone to do, and started darting through the house. It scared Tassie, who screamed, which only made it worse. Tassie ended up standing on a chair while Chester raced around and Dawdi laughed.

Needless to say, Ivy was not getting rid of her cat, and when she said as much to Tassie, the woman marched off the porch promising never to return again.

As far as Ivy was concerned, it was the perfect ending to

a not-so-perfect day. She wasn't sure what it was about Tassie, but Ivy didn't trust her intentions where Dawdi was concerned. It was possible that Ivy was being overprotective of her grandfather, thinking no one would ever be good enough for him. But it seemed obvious to her that Tassie was in the market for a new man. Her husband had recently passed, and she still had children at home to care for. Dawdi, on the other hand, had been widowed for over ten years, and as far as Ivy knew, he had never even looked at another woman. He had loved her grandmother so and seemed to have no plans to remarry anytime in the near or distant future.

"She's trying to get back at her," Ivy mumbled in awe.

"What was that?" Zeb asked.

Ivy pushed herself to her feet, her smile of discovery growing. "Tassie Weber. She and my grandmother were always at odds, but I never thought that much about it. Now Tassie wants to marry my grandfather? She's trying to get back at my *mammi*."

"Why would a woman go to such lengths to best a rival?"

Ivy shot him a look. "Seriously?"

He nodded. "Got it."

Ivy sank back to the mess at her feet. "She probably hated the cat all along," she mused.

"Cats can pick up on stuff like that."

As if she knew they were talking about her, Chester stretched from her perch on the back of the sofa and started grooming herself.

"*Jah*," Ivy agreed. Chester had probably saved them all from a lot of heartbreak.

"Did you have fun tonight?" he asked.

Ivy picked at a knot and didn't raise her gaze to his. "*Jah*. Sure."

"You had a terrible time."

She laid her hands, knot and all, in her lap and looked up at him.

He had finished sweeping and now stood, arms folded over the broom handle as he watched her.

"No, it was . . . enlightening."

"Enlightening?"

"*Jah.*"

"How so?"

She shrugged one shoulder and went back to her knot. How could she explain this where he would understand? "I'll never be allowed to be a part of this community."

"Ivy."

"No. It's true. Now I only have to accept it and go on."

"Doing what? Living your life separate from everyone else?"

"What's wrong with that?" she asked. She had been doing it for the past two years. What was another sixty or so?

"That's no life," he said gently.

He was right. She knew that. But the only solution was one she couldn't bear to think about. Moving. Sending her *dawdi* to Indiana. Maybe going there herself. Getting a fresh start.

Indiana. The thought made her stomach hurt. There was nothing wrong with Indiana itself. Not that she knew of, anyway. She had never been there. She simply did not feel in her heart that Indiana was where she belonged. It was as simple as that.

"I guess since we're doing this, we should go ahead and take the Christmas candles down. And the Nativity," Zeb said.

She sighed. It was the worst part of Christmas, taking everything down and putting it away for the year. She knew it couldn't be left up. It would lose its specialness. But putting it away made her want to cry. Why couldn't they celebrate every day?

"Is that a no?"

"Let's leave it up until the Epiphany."

"What?"

"Three Kings' Day. January sixth. It's the day the Magi came to see Jesus." One of the many things she and Ethan had talked about.

"I know what it is," he said, his tone a bit bemused.

"That should be part of Christmas too, *jah*?"

He nodded slowly. "I suppose."

"Then let's leave the decorations up until then."

"If you like." A frown creased his brow. "But the Amish don't really celebrate Three Kings' Day."

"Maybe we should petition the board to change that."

He grinned. "Just so you can keep your Christmas decorations up longer?"

She smiled in return. "There are worse things."

The bell over the door tinkled out its warning that a customer had come into the bakery. Ivy took the pan of Christmas cookies from the oven and slid them onto the cooling rack. She had convinced Esther to serve Christmas cookies year-round. Normally they would cut them into other shapes for the rest of the year—hearts for Valentine's Day, stars for the Fourth of July, and plain circles for the rest of the year. But Ivy had big plans for the cookies. They simply did not taste the same in different shapes. Zeb had laughed at her when she told him that. How long ago had that been? Years. But she knew it was true. They might not be able to celebrate Christmas in all ways all year, but cookies could always be enjoyed.

"Ivy?"

She whirled around. There, on the other side of the counter, stood Logan Dallas. She pressed the warm pot holder to her chest to keep her heart steady. "Logan. You scared me."

"Sorry." He gave an apologetic grin. "I didn't mean to."

He had only scared her because she was a million miles away. Or perhaps it was a million minutes in the past. A past that couldn't be repeated.

"I thought you had gone."

He shrugged. "I decided to stay for a bit. Get a few more things before I head back."

"Oh, *jah*?"

"That, and someone told me that the best pie in town could be found right here." He grinned.

"Of course."

"Maybe I could get a slice?" he asked.

Ivy nodded toward the small tables set up in the front. "Have a seat and I'll bring it right out."

He smiled, and her heart started that pounding again. Why? Was it because he wasn't Amish? Or because he was just plain gorgeous? Or maybe he offered her something different. Whatever it was, she needed him to leave town soon before her heart wore completely out from thrashing in her chest.

Just then Caroline came out of the back carrying a large tub of icing.

"Let me get that." Ivy took the tub from her and lugged it to the counter.

"I'm not an invalid, you know," Caroline groused. Her normally sunny disposition had disappeared as of late. She pressed a hand to her eyes. "Sorry. I didn't mean to snap. It's just that Andrew won't let me do anything at home, and between you and Esther I can barely lift a finger here."

"I'm sorry," Ivy said. "I was just trying to help."

Caroline shot her a weak, though apologetic, smile. "I know that. Which is why I shouldn't have fussed. I do appreciate you."

"Thank you." Her gaze strayed to where Logan sat at the table, patiently waiting for his pie.

Caroline followed her line of sight. "Who's that?"

"Logan." She did everything in her power not to release his name on a sigh, but even then, her voice sounded a little breathless.

"And he wants?"

"Pie."

"Then I suggest you get him some. I'll get the other pan of cookies out when the timer goes off. You take a quick break, *jah*?"

Ivy smiled her gratitude. "Thanks, Caroline."

She cut a slice of caramel pie and one of strawberry rhubarb, grabbed two forks, and headed for the table.

He smiled as she approached. "What have you got there?"

She told him as she slid the saucers onto the table. She handed him a fork.

"Both for me?" he asked with a gleam in his eyes.

She scooted into the seat across from him. "I thought we might share."

"Sounds like a perfect plan."

"This is my favorite," he claimed, two bites into the strawberry rhubarb.

"*Jah?*" she asked. "I guess this slice is mine, then." She pulled the caramel pie closer.

He snagged the edge of the saucer with his fork. "Not so fast."

"I thought that one was your favorite." She pulled her expression into the most innocent one she could muster.

"That doesn't mean I don't want to try this one. Besides," he continued, "you accepted that a little too easily. Which means this pie is probably fantastic."

She laughed and pushed the pie closer to him. "Be my guest."

He scooped up a bite of pie, shoveled it into his mouth,

then fell back against his seat as if he were in some kind of pain. "I changed my mind." He pointed to the caramel slice. "That is my favorite."

She laughed. "They can't both be your favorite."

He stopped, suddenly serious. "Why can't they be?"

Why couldn't they be? Who set up these rules? "No reason, I guess."

His expression changed and went back to its playful smile, but the question remained with Ivy as they finished their snack. The world seemed full of definitive rules that she had to follow. It had been that way her entire life. And never once had she felt like they were fair, or even valid. Why did a favorite have to be one? Why did a person only get Christmas cookies in December? Why couldn't she have shiny tinsel garland at Christmastime?

Some of the rules came from the *Ordnung,* but not all. The *Englisch* world was filled with them as well, but the price for breaking one there seemed far less severe.

"A penny for them," he said quietly.

Ivy roused herself from her musings. "What?"

"Your thoughts."

She shook her head. "Nothing worth speaking of." At least not out loud. She could fantasize all she wanted about Christmas tinsel and rules that she could believe in, but it wouldn't get her any closer to the actual thing.

Logan scraped his plate with the edge of his fork and licked off the crumbs and filling. He smiled when he caught Ivy watching him. "We don't get a lot of pie in Costa Rica."

"Is it worth it? Giving up the luxuries you have?"

"People could ask the same of you. Well, of the Amish people. Is it worth it to you?"

"But I don't sacrifice these comforts in order to help another."

He nodded. "I suppose that does make it different." He

seemed to mull it over for a moment. "It does," he finally said. "Helping others makes it all worth it. Even the lack of pie."

"He's cute," Caroline said, only seconds after Logan walked out of the bakery. Ivy was surprised he didn't hear her.

"And *Englisch*," she added unnecessarily.

Caroline gave a casual shrug. "There's nothing wrong with being *Englisch*."

Ivy whipped around so fast she almost strained her neck. Had she heard her correctly?

"What?" Caroline's eyes were wide and innocent. She turned back to her chore of cleaning the worktable. "Not all *Englisch* are bad, you know."

She knew that, but what experience did Caroline Fitch have with the *Englisch*? Ivy wanted to ask, but bit her tongue. It was really none of her business.

"And I think he likes you."

Ivy tried to play it off. "Maybe." But she thought perhaps Logan liked her a bit. Yet what could be done with such emotion? "He lives in Costa Rica," Ivy said.

"Oh, *jah*?"

"He's a missionary."

"Interesting."

"What is?"

Caroline tossed the damp rag aside and focused all her attention on Ivy. "I'm going to tell you something, and I want you to do with the information as you wish."

"*Jah*, sure."

"Sometimes the best thing a person can have is a chance to start over in a place where no one knows their name."

Then Ivy remembered. Caroline had just appeared in town a few years ago, pregnant and widowed. She had gotten a second chance in a place where no one knew who she was. Her family. Or all the rumors about her.

But what was Caroline saying? Ivy studied the woman's tired but beautiful face. Those hazel eyes were trying to tell her something, but Ivy couldn't imagine what. "Thank you," she said, her head beginning to hurt from thinking so hard. Or maybe it was the stress of a handsome man coming to see her at work. She'd never had that happen before.

"You're welcome." Caroline turned back to her work, leaving Ivy to find the meaning behind her words.

By the time Ivy pulled into the lane leading to the house she shared with Dawdi, she was certain she'd had all the winter she could take for one year. And considering it wasn't even January . . . she was in for some long months.

She parked the tractor under its place next to the hay barn and flipped up her collar before heading for the house. Despite the coat she was wearing she was shivering by the time she got inside. Maybe she should look into getting a heavier coat. And some heavier tights. Or black sweatpants, like the athletes wore.

"There you are." It was almost a happy greeting.

Ivy slipped out of her coat and hung it on the hook by the door. "Here I am," she said as she pulled the scarf from around her head. She checked the mirror to make sure her prayer *kapp* was still in its proper place, then turned to fully look at Zeb.

"What's wrong?" Something was wrong. She could see it right away. His eyes had a hard edge that she had never seen before, and a muscle in his cheek jumped as if he was clenching his teeth.

"Can I talk to you for a minute?"

Her heart gave a painful thump in her chest. "Sure. As long as I can warm up by the fire while you do."

He gave a stern nod, and Ivy moved to stand in front of the crackling flames. It was good to be home.

"What's up?" She tried to make her voice sound light and airy, as if she couldn't tell he was about to blow, but her tone was a little too high-pitched to be believable.

"Julie Ann Fitch went into the bakery today."

Ivy thought about it a moment. She didn't remember seeing Julie Ann, but that didn't mean she wasn't there. She could have come in when Ivy was eating her lunch or when she took a break. But she didn't think Zeb was asking. "*Jah*, I suppose so, I guess."

"And she saw you sitting with some *Englischer*."

Ivy nodded. "That was Logan Dallas."

He blinked at her, and for a moment Ivy was confused as well.

"Ethan Dallas's grandson."

"The man from the retirement home."

She nodded. "Right. He came by to try Esther's pie."

Zeb scrubbed his hands over his face and plunged his fingers into his hair. "What about yesterday?"

She frowned. "What about it?"

"Did you go with him to eat at Kauffmans', or is there another *Englischer* you're running around with?"

She crossed her arms and stiffened her chin. What was wrong with him? "Is something the matter?"

He scoffed. "*Jah.* I mean, you're out running around with all these guys, and I'm here taking care of your *dawdi*."

She had managed to hang on to her temper, but that grip was slipping. "No one asked you to stay here and take care of him."

"Don't you think someone should? After all, you need to work, right?"

She nodded.

"I came so you could work. Not so you could go have pie dates with other men."

Her vision blurred. She wasn't sure if it was anger alone or mixed with hot tears. "I appreciate you coming." She started for the door, nearly tripping in her haste to get there. "But you can go now. Your help is no longer needed."

"*Jah?*" His cheeks were ruddy, and for the life of her Ivy couldn't figure out what was happening. Well, she knew what was happening, but the whole encounter had a surreal quality, like it existed in a movie or someone else's dream. It was somehow removed from her, though she could see it all as it played out.

"*Jah.* And don't bother to come back over here," she continued, her voice rising to a shrill pitch. "You aren't welcome here any longer."

"Fine."

She hadn't known it was possible, but his face got even redder. He made it to the door, knocking her coat off its peg as he retrieved his own. He crammed his hat onto his head and looped his scarf around his neck before storming out the door. He didn't bother to put on his coat. The door slammed behind him. Ivy stood there wondering if any of it was real. And if it was, should she go after him?

She sank into the hard-backed chair next to the door. They sat there when they needed to take their shoes off, or put them on. She merely needed a place to collect her whirling thoughts.

She wasn't going after Zeb. It was better this way. They had been kidding themselves into thinking they could be friends, or even that they might have a second chance, but she had known from the beginning it was nothing more than a sweet daydream. And like the rest of her life, it wasn't meant to be.

But what had happened? One minute she had been so

glad to be home, out of the cold, and the next she knew, she was toe-to-toe with Zeb, arguing over . . . nothing.

"What's all the racket out here?" Dawdi picked that moment to come through the door from the kitchen. Heaven only knew if he had been waiting on Zeb to leave before emerging, or if he had even been paying attention at all. These days it could go either way.

"Nothing," she muttered, suddenly too drained to explain.

He looked around as if confused. "Where's Zeb? He was supposed to play Uno with me again."

"He left."

"Left? Why did he leave? How's he getting home? Will he be back?"

"I don't know." She hoped that answer would suffice for all his questions. She didn't want to explain. She couldn't. She didn't even understand it herself.

Dawdi propped his hands on his hips and stared off at nothing. "Huh," he said. "That's not like him."

It was exactly like him. He ran when things got rough. He had run two years ago, and he was still running now.

He was certain he was half-frozen by the time he made it to the Brenneman driveway. He was saved from being completely frozen thanks to his own anger. It had managed to keep him warm most of the way, but now the cold was starting to seep through.

Zeb stomped across the yard and onto the porch, wishing it would snow if it was going to be this cold. No sense in such low temperatures if there was no snow to help him enjoy his time. Somehow that was all Ivy's fault too. He wasn't sure how, but he was certain she had wished for no snow just to spite him.

The thought was ridiculous, and he knew it. She had

been wishing for a white Christmas. But he didn't care. He pulled off his gloves, slapped them against one thigh, and let himself into the house.

"Zeb!" Clara Rose clamped one hand over her heart as if he had startled her. "I wasn't expecting you." She let out a soft chuckle. "Nearly scared the life out of me. I didn't hear a tractor."

He gave a curt nod and headed for the fireplace to warm himself. "There wasn't a tractor."

She frowned. "Then how'd you get home?"

Zeb opened his mouth to answer, but was interrupted as Obie came through the front door.

"Was that you I saw walking down the road just now?"

"Walking?" Clara Rose squawked over Zeb's answer of "*Jah.*"

"It's barely thirty degrees out there," she continued. "You must be frozen."

Zeb shrugged and blew on his tingling fingers. He'd had on gloves, but not the sort that could combat this kind of cold. Or maybe his brother was right and he was soft. Florida winters could do that to a man.

"Actually, it's just over forty out there," Obie said.

Clara Rose sniffed. "That is still too cold with all those clouds hanging around."

Heavy gray clouds in varying degrees of darkness crowded the sky. It was cold out there. And gloomy. Perfect for his mood.

"Clara Rose," Obie started, not bothering to look at her as he spoke, "I think I heard Paul Daniel."

She looked up from her quilting to study her husband's features, then she nodded, set her sewing aside, and made her way up the stairs.

"I didn't hear the baby," Obie said after she had disappeared from view.

"I didn't think so," Zeb replied. Which could only mean one thing . . .

"You've got to pull yourself together, brother."

That.

"I'm fine," Zeb said by way of protest. Frankly he was tired of having to constantly defend his position to his family, to everybody.

"Not if you had to walk home from her house in this weather."

"I had a coat."

Obie shook his head. "You just don't get it. She's going to be the death of you."

He was so tired of defending himself that he couldn't find the words to do so. He didn't even search for them.

"You love her." Obie's words weren't a question.

Zeb nodded. At least this he could answer.

"But you're unhappy."

What could he do but nod again? He was unhappy. It was like he couldn't reach Ivy. It was like she existed on a different plane from the rest of them. She would run around with an *Englisch* man, but she wouldn't go places with him. She wouldn't be a part of the community. How could she live that way?

She loved him. Of that he was certain. But she couldn't forgive him. She couldn't forgive herself. She couldn't forgive the situation that they had found themselves in. Until she could do that . . .

Obie sucked in a deep breath, then let it out slowly. "It's time to forget about her."

His brother's words sliced through him. *Forget about her.* How could he forget? There was only one way.

"Obie, I—"

"I know," his brother interrupted. "It'll mean you going back to Florida, and I will miss you horribly, but I would rather see you happy hundreds of miles away than miserable right underfoot."

Zeb was speechless. He hated when his brother was right, and this was one of those times. He needed to move on, and the only way to do that was away from Wells Landing. Away from Ivy. Leaving her a second time would be harder than the first, but he knew he had to do it. And the sooner, the better.

Chapter Twenty

Ivy got up Saturday morning like nothing was different. Like her heart wasn't broken. She ate breakfast, got dressed, and drove into town to work. Funny how the world kept spinning even when a person didn't feel they could go on. Ivy had been feeling this way so long she hadn't realized it had eased when Zeb came back, only to return full force when she had made him leave the day before.

Who was he to tell her about going around with an *Englisch* guy? Like he had any room to talk. He'd run off to Pinecraft and taken up with the Beachy Amish for the last two years. He'd been driving a car, going to church in a building, and who knew what else, all in the name of . . . of . . . well, she didn't know what he called it. But she was sure it was something.

"You okay?" Esther asked just after noon. The cookie crowd had come and gone, and Ivy was happy to report that all the Christmas cookies were gone.

"Of course," Ivy answered, the lie falling easily from her lips.

Esther eyed her with skepticism. "You sure?"

She smiled to add some weight to her words. "What could possibly be wrong?"

The other woman shrugged and checked on a pan of dinner rolls. "I don't know, but you keep slamming around here like you're mad about something."

Ivy unclenched her jaw, only realizing in that moment that she had been grinding her teeth together. "Sorry. I must have some oil on my gloves or something." Another lie.

"If something's bothering you, you know you can talk to me. *Jah?*"

Ivy nodded. There was nothing to talk about. Not really. And there never had been.

"Ivy, phone's for you," Jodie called from the door to the office.

Ivy couldn't say the two of them had mended all the problems between them, but they had come to an understanding of sorts. Ivy didn't bother Jodie and Jodie didn't bother Ivy and a small truce was born.

"Me?" She couldn't imagine who would be calling her at work. Most of the people she knew would sooner come by than call. Who was she kidding? No one she knew who would come by would care enough to talk to her at all.

"*Jah.*" Jodie's voice gained an impatient edge, then she moved away from the office.

Ivy stripped off her thin plastic gloves and tossed them in the trash. Maybe it was Logan calling to tell her that he was leaving soon. Or . . . well, she couldn't think of an *or*.

She picked up the receiver from its resting place on the desk and held it to her ear. "Hello?"

"Ivy?"

The voice was familiar.

"This is Daryl Hicks. Your grandfather—"

A buzzing started in Ivy's ears and she missed the rest of

what he said. If Daryl was calling it wasn't good. That much she knew.

"I'm sorry," she whispered. "Can you repeat that?"

A sigh came from the other end of the line. "I can't keep doing this, Ivy. He's upsetting my mother."

Daryl's mother was ninety if she was a day and had started to lose some of her faculties.

"What's he doing?" She couldn't leave work. No, that wasn't the truth. She didn't *want* to leave work. The responsibility pressed down on her so hard she could scarcely breathe. But the other options didn't bear thinking about.

"He's on top of my barn."

"What?" Ivy dropped the phone, then hastily picked it up again.

"Are you there?" Daryl asked.

"I'm here." Ivy's voice trembled with worry. "Have you called the sheriff?" How was she supposed to get him down?

"I didn't want to involve the law. You are my first call."

She was grateful that he was thinking about them, but honestly, this was way more than she had ever dealt with.

"Call the sheriff," she instructed. "I'll be there as soon as I can."

"Okay, Ivy." She could hear the relief in his voice. "If he falls, I'm not responsible," he added.

Just like an *Englischer*, always wanting to assign blame.

"Of course not," she reassured him. But more importantly, she didn't want to think about her grandfather falling. "I'll be there as soon as possible," she said as she took her purse out of the desk drawer where Esther allowed them to stash them. "And Daryl," she added, "don't let him fall."

She hung up the phone without waiting for his response. "Esther!" she called, then grabbed her coat and rushed from the office back into the front of the store. She slowed her steps, realizing that being frantic would only make matters worse. Everyone in the bakery didn't need to know about her troubles. They would find out soon enough.

"What's the matter?" Esther met her at the entrance, clasping her hands in that reassuring manner she had.

"It's my grandfather. He's in trouble."

Esther's lips pressed together, and her eyes dimmed. "Go," she said simply. "We'll take care of things here."

Relief flooded her. She couldn't ask for better people to work for. "I don't know when I can come back."

Esther shook her head. "Don't worry about that. We've got it covered."

"Thank you." Those tears threatened once again. Tonight maybe she would allow them to fall, but now she had to take care of the most important man in her life.

Ivy barely acknowledged Helen Ebersol, the bishop's wife, as she hurried out the door. She pulled on her coat as she ran. Without a backward glance, she hopped on her tractor and headed toward home.

The drive seemed to take hours, days. She wished she had the Mustang. It would get her there in record time. But she had given it back to Luke Lambright long ago. After it'd had the desired effect on the good citizens of Wells Landing, of course. Now she wished she had it for entirely different reasons.

Finally she pulled into the drive at Daryl's house. The sheriff's deputy was already there, along with two of the policemen for the city and one from the Lighthorse Tribal Police. Great, one old man gets stuck on the roof of a barn and half the cops in the county show up. She wasn't sure whether to laugh or cry.

"There," Daryl said, pulling on the deputy's coat sleeve and pointing toward her. "She's his granddaughter."

The deputy met her halfway and tipped his cowboy hat to her. "Miss. Can you tell us why he's up there? We thought perhaps this was a jumping situation, but now we're not so sure."

Jumping?

She shook her head. "I don't know. What did Daryl say?" She inclined her chin toward her neighbor.

"He's as baffled as we are."

She nodded, unable to find any words for the situation. "My grandfather . . ." she started. "Sometimes he has problems remembering certain things."

"Like his name or who he is?"

"More like what year it is. And what's happening around him. How old he is. What time of year it is. That sort of thing." When she ran it all out in the line like that it sounded much worse than it ever had in her head.

"I see." He motioned for her to follow him. "Let's see if you can figure out what he's talking about and help him decide to come down."

She wondered if the man was passing judgment on her and her grandfather, but she only had a couple of seconds to worry about it before her grandfather came into view.

Ivy stumbled a bit when she saw him, but she recovered quickly. Daryl had told her that he was on top of the barn, but she hadn't expected him to be *on top* of the barn. Terrible thoughts raced through her mind, mixed with memories from a few years back. Chris Flaud's brother Johnny had fallen off their barn roof and broken his neck. Now the poor boy was bedridden and most likely would be for the rest of his life.

Please Lord, help me get him down in one piece.

She cleared her throat and tried to get herself together. Getting all upset would get him all upset, and that wouldn't be good for anyone involved.

"Dawdi!" She took another step forward and shaded her eyes to better see him. It was still December-cold, but the sun was peeking out in between the floating winter clouds. "What are you doing up there?" She tried her best to make her voice sound offhand and casual, as if she found him sitting on the eaves of the barn every day.

The sound of a tractor coming down the lane leading to Daryl's house floated to her. A tractor this time of year meant an Amish person was coming, but she didn't turn around to see who it was. There'd be time enough for that later.

"I'm sitting, Irene."

"Ivy," she corrected, then wished she could kick herself. She didn't need all these *Englischers* to have more problems against her grandfather than were already stacking up. "I'm not Irene," she mumbled only to herself.

"Why are you sitting on the barn?" she asked. They had been through this enough times that she knew it was better to have him realize that what he was doing didn't make sense and correct it on his own. Otherwise he would argue and sometimes turn belligerent, as he didn't understand what was happening around her.

He laughed. "It's not a barn."

"It's not?" Maybe better to play along.

"Of course not. Can't you see it's an airplane?"

The men around her shifted uncomfortably. No one knew what to do or how to respond.

"Should we call the chaplain?" one of the city officers asked.

His partner nudged him in the ribs. "He doesn't need a chaplain; he needs an Amish preacher-leader-guy."

Oh, no. The bishop was the last person they needed witnessing this. There would be enough to account for once she got him down, but until then, no one needed to know except the handful of people already witness to the matter.

Ivy ignored them all and concentrated on her grandfather. "Why are you sitting on an airplane?" she asked.

He swung his feet, and her heart dropped with the motion. All he had to do was get a little off balance, and he would come crashing down. "How else am I supposed to let the men know I'm one of them?"

She had no idea what he was talking about, but playing along was definitely better than upsetting him. "Of course." Her tone clearly conveyed *how silly of me.*

"They've done nothing but make fun of me," he said with a small pout. "My clothes, my beard. The fact that I don't have a moustache. My accent. Everything they could laugh at about me they have, but I'll show them. I'm tough."

"Of course you are."

The whole situation was beyond weird.

"You can't go halfway around the world to fight the enemy if your fellow soldier doesn't trust you. Everyone will die." He shook his head. "That's messy."

One of the city policemen took a step toward her. "Is he a vet, miss?"

She had never been asked such a question, and it took almost a full minute for his meaning to become clear. He wanted to know if her grandfather had served in one of the *Englisch* wars? "Of course not." The words were automatic. Everyone knew that the Amish were pacifists. How could a man be a pacifist and fight in a war? It just didn't make sense.

"Sure looks that way to me," another of the men said. Ivy didn't notice who he worked for, but judging by the length of his braided hair, she would think the Indian police.

Her grandfather? A veteran? The thought was baffling. It was true; she didn't know everything there was to know about him. He had lived many years before she'd been born, and though he loved to tell stories, that didn't mean he had told her all of them.

"I'd say it's been too long for it to be PTSD," one of the officers said. Ivy didn't bother to see which one. She was trying to get her mind around the scene before her.

And she wasn't entirely sure what PTSD was, only that there was a billboard with something about it on the way to Taylor Creek.

"He's been having problems with his memory lately." It should have felt good to share that burden of truth, but it only made her worry more. What would happen to him if the county services got involved? She had heard the tales of people losing their children and family members being sent to hospitals. But she had no idea how these things worked. Who decided all that, anyway?

The wail of a siren sounded far away, getting louder as the fire truck drew near. The lumbering red vehicle easing down the lane seemed too big and bright for the situation they were facing.

"What are they doing here?" Ivy asked.

Daryl took a step forward. "It was my idea," he confessed. "I thought maybe if they brought a cherry picker . . ."

Ivy had no idea how a fruit harvester could help them now, but noticed the bucket container on the extendable arm attached to the back of the fire truck. If that was what he meant . . .

She took a couple of stumbling steps forward. Her grandfather was still sitting happily on the edge of the roof, his legs swinging as if he hadn't a care in the world. At that moment, Ivy supposed he hadn't. At least he hadn't the presence of mind to know that he had any cares beyond here and now.

"Keep them back," she said, pointing to the firemen and their gigantic ladder. "Let me talk to him."

The sheriff's deputy looked a little skeptical, but nodded. Ivy supposed he must be the one in charge, for no one disputed his command.

Ivy took a couple of hesitant steps toward the barn. "Dawdi?" she called. "Why don't you come down now? You've proved your point, *jah*?"

He seemed to think about it a moment. "I'm not sure. These boys don't look convinced." He waved an all-encompassing arm toward the crowd of first responders.

"We're good," one of the men said.

"Sure. You can come down now," another one added.

"We can set you up a ladder," the lead fireman offered.

Dawdi thought about it for a moment. "You're not going to tell the CO, are you?"

The man scoffed. "Of course not. What that jerk doesn't know won't hurt him."

Dawdi chuckled as Ivy wondered how he knew her grandfather's CO was a jerk. "I can do it." He started to stand, and all the men on the ground leaned toward the barn.

"No, don't," the deputy said. "This nice MP is going to set up a ladder." He motioned to the fireman.

Ivy's head swam with all the letters being tossed around. She had no idea what any of them meant.

"MP, huh?" Her grandfather's eyes narrowed. "Not so fast." He shifted as if to stand.

The fireman kept coming with the ladder, but in the blink of an eye, Dawdi lost his balance and fell from the roof.

Chapter Twenty-One

"Dawdi!" The scream was unrecognizable, though she knew it to be her own. He fell entirely too fast, yet in slow motion. The two images superimposed on each other, until she didn't know what was fact and what was fiction. "Dawdi."

She slid to her knees beside him.

He groaned, and she touched his face, unwilling to do more, though she wanted to scoop him into her embrace. At his age, a fall like that . . .

"Stand aside." Gentle hands circled her arms and eased her to her feet.

"But—" She started to protest, then realized these were EMTs who had come on the fire truck. Thank the Lord they were there. She allowed them to put her aside and looked on as they started to examine her grandfather.

Lord, please let him be okay, she prayed. *I know I've made more than my share of mistakes, but he's a good man and deserves better than this.*

Though why he believed he was on an airplane was a mystery to her. She had never thought about it, but she knew her grandfather had lived a life she hadn't known everything about. But she had always imagined farming and singings and courting pretty girls. Not wars and airplanes. She just prayed now that she had the opportunity to ask him about it.

One of the uniformed men brought a stretcher to the edge of the throng around her *dawdi*, and before she knew it, they had him loaded into the back of an ambulance.

"Come on," Cephas said, lightly touching her elbow. "This kind man has offered to take us to the hospital." He indicated the sheriff's deputy standing just behind him.

Ivy nodded. She hadn't thought about that. She was still reeling over the accident. How she would be getting to the hospital hadn't even crossed her mind. But now it wasn't just her, but her and the bishop.

She followed them over to the white patrol car and slipped into the back seat while the bishop took the spot next to her. She had hoped he would sit in the front with the deputy, but she wasn't that lucky.

"It's time, don't you think?" He spoke Dutch; she was sure it was so the officer wouldn't understand. She had some explaining to do, but Cephas was fair and wouldn't embarrass her in front of a stranger.

"Time for what?" she asked. She was stalling, and they both knew it. But maybe if she put this off, even by a few minutes, the Lord would give her the solution she needed.

"Ivy," he said in that gentle, caring way of his. But that only made it harder.

"I don't want to call her," she said, satisfied when her voice didn't crack. "We don't need her."

"I understand that you're hurt, but you have to do what's best for Yonnie."

He didn't have to say the rest. Next time Dawdi might injure himself worse than today. She had heard talk of a possible concussion and maybe a broken arm and leg. He wouldn't be able to stand another fall like that. He shouldn't have to.

Ivy had mulled over the words for the rest of the trip to

the hospital in Pryor. Now she was sitting in the front seat of Bruce Brown's sedan as the miles to Wells Landing streaked past the window. Her grandfather was stretched out across the back seat, his leg in a cast from the top of his thigh to the tips of his toes. His arm was in a sling and some sort of brace. The break in his wrist was worse than the one in his leg, and they would have to wait for the swelling to go down before they could cast it. Thankfully, he didn't have a concussion and wouldn't require surgery. The Lord had been looking out for him after all. But what of Ivy?

Was she just being prideful? Had her pride nearly killed her grandfather? This had all been about what she wanted. She hadn't even bothered to ask him. If Dawdi wanted to move to Indiana, he could have gone when her *mamm* left, but he hadn't. Ivy just assumed that he hadn't wanted to go. Had she been wrong? Did her grandfather even know his mind?

She shook her head. She wasn't being fair. He needed to decide for himself, and after that, she would figure out her place. But Costa Rica with Logan Dallas was looking better and better. What a place to start over. What a place to begin again. Helping others, shedding the responsibilities that Wells Landing held for her. No one would know her there. And even if they did, they wouldn't find her behavior as scandalous as the good Amish citizens back home.

Her heart thumped at the prospect, part excitement, part anxiety. If she knew her mother at all, there would be a message for her at the phone shanty just down the road. Mamm would tell her that she would come and get Dawdi and take him back to Indiana to live with her and Alan Byler. And Ivy should come too. But she wouldn't. She might allow Dawdi to be uprooted for his own safety, but she wouldn't be able to look at him knowing that she had quit him when he needed her the most.

But do you want to go to Costa Rica?

It didn't matter. Hadn't she learned that the hard way? What a person wanted and what they ended up with were sometimes miles apart. This was one of those occasions.

Getting Dawdi through the night was a chore in itself. It wasn't that he was a bad patient, but he had trouble getting comfortable. The pain medicine that the doctor warned them might make him sleepy had the opposite effect, and he seemed to be having weird daydreams throughout those darkened hours. By the time sunrise came, Ivy was exhausted and more than grateful that it was a non-church Sunday. She would have to call the doctor and have him get her *dawdi* a new pain medication, but in the meantime she had eased his suffering with one of those nighttime pain relievers that eased aches and helped a person sleep. He had finally conked out, but for how long was anybody's guess. Right now all she wanted to do was catch a nap before heading over to Daryl's house. She wanted to give him the update and hopefully use his phone to take care of the outstanding hospital business.

She settled down on the couch, lying on her side and covering herself with an afghan her *mammi* had made years ago. Chester curled up in the crook of her knees, purring and kneading, so thankful that things were settling down.

Ivy stared at the fire, watching the flames dance across the logs. She had decisions to make, too many and too important to make on little or no sleep, but they needed to be resolved, and immediately. All she had to do was say the word, and her mother would come after Dawdi.

It was Sunday, December 31, New Year's Eve. The last day of the year. How ironic, or maybe it was befitting, that she had to make these decisions, these life-changing decisions, on the last day of the year. Tomorrow everything would change. Like it or not.

She jumped when a knock sounded at the door. She blinked, not realizing until she was awakened that she had been asleep. Was someone knocking? Or was she dreaming? Maybe it had been Dawdi. She paused, listened, then the knock came again.

Ivy hopped to her feet and hustled to the door as Chester followed behind her. She placed one hand on the knob to open it, then checked the mirror to make sure her kerchief was still in place.

Logan Dallas was standing on the other side of the threshold. Perhaps he was the last person she had expected to see.

"Logan." She couldn't keep the surprise from her voice.

"Can I come in?"

She took a step back to allow him entrance. "*Jah*. But we'll have to be quiet. My *dawdi* is sleeping."

He smiled. "I thought the Amish were up before the sun."

"Usually." She led the way to the living room, Chester following behind. "We had a little accident yesterday." They settled down, him on the sofa and her in the rocking chair just next to it, and she told him about Dawdi's fall.

"I'm glad he wasn't hurt worse," Logan said when she had finished her tale.

"Me too."

He nodded, and a moment of silence fell between them. "We're leaving tomorrow."

"Leaving?" Her heart jumped in her chest. She had been able to think of nothing else, all night long. Starting over in another country, a chance to be someone else, someone who wasn't dragging around a suitcase full of sins. But she hadn't thought it would be tomorrow!

"That's sudden," she finally managed. "I thought you were going to stay awhile."

He clasped his hands between his knees and looked into the fire. "Yeah, me too, but the guy I came with is ready to go back." He chuckled. "He's originally from the Caribbean and not used to such weather. He's ready to be warm again."

Ivy tried to smile, but her lips stuck to her teeth. This was her chance. *Take me with you.* That was all she had to say. So why were the words stuck in her throat? Her mother would come soon and take Dawdi away. She wouldn't be able to stay in this house and live off what she made at the bakery. She would have to find a roommate. Or move. Maybe both. But if she went with Logan, it wouldn't matter. She could stay in a tent, help those less fortunate. Do God's work. And maybe then He would forgive her.

But the words wouldn't come.

Be brave. It was the only instruction she had. But brave about what? Telling Logan she wanted to tag along? Going to Costa Rica? Moving to Indiana? Staying in Oklahoma? What? What was she supposed to be brave about?

If only she knew.

But she couldn't go with Logan. He was perhaps the most handsome man she had encountered, with his streaky blond hair and enticing grin, but he seemed to think that the two of them could have something special. And maybe they could, except for one thing: She was in love with Zeb. Always had been. Always would be. It wouldn't do to give a false hope to Logan, or even one to herself. Whether she went to Central America, stayed in Wells Landing, or made her way to Indiana with her *mamm* and Dawdi and Alan Byler, she would be a spinster, because she had hurt the man she loved one too many times.

Logan stood, and she followed suit. "I just came by to thank you for being so kind to my grandfather in his final days. It means a lot to me that he had a good friend at his side before he passed." He shot her a teary smile. "I can't thank you enough."

Ivy blinked back her own tears. "There's no need. I'm a better person for having known him." The words of his poem jumped to her mind. She couldn't remember them all and vowed to read it again before going over to call the doctor. "Are you sure you won't stay for a while longer? Maybe have a piece of pie?"

"It's nine thirty in the morning."

She shrugged. "I guess it's an Amish thing." She had grown up eating pie at all hours of the day.

"That may be something I have to adopt for my own, but I do need to be going." He reached into his coat pocket and pulled out a little card. It was about the size of a regular business card. "That's my sat phone number," he explained.

She wasn't sure what a "sat phone" was, but didn't ask.

"I wanted you to be able to get in touch with me." He shrugged as if it was a stupid idea, but he had followed through regardless. "Just in case . . . whatever, you know?"

She looked at the number and swallowed the lump in her throat. Was now the time to be brave? She didn't know.

"I know the Amish don't have a lot of phones, but I know you can use one, and if you need me . . ." He tapped the card with one finger. "You can find me."

"*Danki*," she choked, then cleared her throat. "Thank you."

He smiled and shoved his hands into his coat pockets. "It was nice knowing you, Ivy Weaver."

"Same to you," she murmured.

Then he leaned in and kissed her cheek, then stepped out onto the porch. He waved once before Ivy shut the door and leaned against it.

That wasn't her brave time. At least she didn't think it was. She wasn't sure. She needed more sleep. Or to drink some coffee. Maybe have a piece of pie. She needed to call the doctor, check on her grandfather. So many things.

Instead she looked at the card in her hand. The number was scrawled there in bold black letters. Strong, unapologetic. *Here's my number. Call me if you need anything.* How about a new life?

She pushed off the door and walked toward the kitchen. Sleep wasn't an option, so coffee was the next best thing. She had to get down to Daryl's and call her *mamm*. Maybe that was her be-brave moment: to own up to God's will. To stop fighting for the things she wanted and accept what was to happen.

She started the coffee and sat down at the kitchen table. Chester wove around her legs, in and out and back in again, rubbing her face against Ivy's calves and purring all the while.

Ivy set the card on the table as she waited for the water to boil. Then she picked it up again. She turned it over and discovered that Logan had written his number on the back of a witness card. At least that was what she thought they were called. She had heard some of the members of the *Englisch* churches talking about them. They were printed so that the church members could hand them out to people who needed God. At least that was what she had gotten from her eavesdropping. But she had never seen one. It was pretty. The background was blue, like the noon sky on a summer day. Clouds floated behind the black lettering and a cross stood proudly in one corner. *John 3:16*, it read. *For God so loved the world, that he gave his only begotten Son, that whosoever believeth in him should not perish, but have everlasting life.*

Everlasting life. Heaven. That was what that meant.

On the stove, the water started to boil, but she could only stare at the words printed on the card.

Whosoever believeth.

That included her. She believed. Then Zeb's words came back to her. They had been talking about Florida, and he'd shared about the church he had been going to, how they believed that all a person had to do was believe in Jesus and they were saved. Saved by grace. The concept was as foreign to her as Costa Rica, but it sent a pang through her heart. Excitement, anxiety. Longing.

She believed. This could be her. She could have everlasting life. She didn't have to worry. She didn't have to confess her sins. She believed, and because she believed, God loved her and forgave her. It was as simple as that.

A warmth came over her. It started in the vicinity of her heart and spread through her until it reached the ends of her fingers and the tips of her toes. God forgave her.

She bowed her head and prayed. She might be forgiven, but she asked for it. She held her own little confession, nothing like what Ethan had talked about, but she could see how they were beneficial. God might know everything she had done, but to recount it to Him was cleansing somehow. She felt refreshed, her soul revived. God loved her. He forgave her. She couldn't have asked for a better gift.

Tears rolled down her face as the warmth inside was replaced with joy. The sweetest and purest joy she had ever experienced, and she wanted to feel this way for the rest of her life.

It took a couple of hours, but she managed to get ahold of the doctor and get her grandfather's prescription changed. It wasn't normally allowed to transact business on Sundays, but Ivy knew that her slip would be accepted. This was a special situation, and Cephas was fair.

She hitched up the buggy and started into town. The tractor would have been so much quicker and easier, but she figured one transgression a day was enough. But she didn't want to leave her grandfather alone for so long. Thankfully Daryl agreed to come sit with him until Ivy got back. He figured it was the least he could do since her grandfather had fallen on his property, but Ivy guessed that he was just thankful the Amish didn't sue.

Be brave rang in her ears as she drove back from town. She had her grandfather's new medication and a new hope that everything was going to be just fine.

But brave . . . brave about what? She had turned away from everything she had been taught growing up. She remembered reading the passage of John 3:16 when she was a kid, but not how it played into their beliefs. Now it held so much importance. Now it had freed her.

Almost.

There was still the matter of being brave and loving Zeb.

Realization shot through her with such a force that she pulled back on the reins. Her horse whinnied and shook his head, blowing out his disapproval.

She could be brave. She should be brave. And she should tell Zeb how she felt about him. Only then would she be able to continue on this path of healing. But first she had the little matter of Dawdi and how he felt about the whole situation.

"How are you feeling?" Ivy eased into the room, a glass of water in one hand and the new bottle of pills in the other.

Her grandfather was in the bed, propped up on pillows and blankets to help ease the pressure on his broken bones and bruised body.

"Like I fell off a barn." His bad attempt at humor brought a small smile to her lips. This could have turned out so much worse than it had. And it had turned out bad enough, to be certain.

She handed him the water glass and opened the bottle of pain pills, shaking a couple into her hand and offering them to him. "This is something different. Hopefully they'll help you sleep."

"Bah." He popped the pills into his mouth and washed them down with the water before handing the glass back to her.

"Dawdi," she said slowly, easing into the chair at his bedside. "What do you remember about yesterday?"

He rubbed his chin and eyed her with a look she had never seen before. "You think I'm going crazy, don't you?"

She drew back. "Of course not, but . . ."

"But what?"

"It was a little unnerving seeing you up on that barn."

"I suppose it was." He did that chin-rubbing thing again, and Ivy wondered if perhaps it was his way of distracting her.

"Do you remember how you got up there? Or maybe why you climbed up there?"

He nodded. "Of course I do."

She waited, but no other explanation was forthcoming. "Why is that?"

"You want to know about the war."

She wouldn't have been more shocked if he had burst into song. "The war?"

He shook his head. "I won't tell you about it. Never told anyone."

"Dawdi, what were you doing in a war?" She didn't have to tell him that fighting was against everything the Amish stood for.

"There are a few things a man is called to do in his life. Mine was to accept the notice when I was drafted and sent to Vietnam."

"But . . . but . . ." He could have explained that he was a conscientious objector. Many men were called up in the wars that had activated the draft, but there were jobs other than combat. The Amish might not study so much of

Englisch history, but this was one thing they all knew. So why had he . . .

And why had he never mentioned it until now?

But she knew those were answers he would carry with him always. Answers she might not ever know.

"Did Mammi know?"

He nodded. "She was the only one. Her and Tassie."

And there was some connection between this war and the grudge between Tassie and her *mammi*. She didn't know how she knew it; she just did.

"Mammi—"

He held up one hand to stop the stream of her words. "You're right. These pills are making me sleepy."

Ivy nodded and stood, pulling on the sleeves of her sweater as she did so. "Just one more thing," she started.

"*Jah?*"

"What do you think about Florida?"

"To tell the truth, I don't think about Florida much at all."

"How would you feel about moving there?"

His eyes took on a bright twinkle despite the glaze the medication had caused. "Are you talking about you and Zeb?"

Her breath hitched in her throat. She had better get used to saying the words. *Be brave.* "If he'll have me."

"He'll have you. That boy loves you more than anything in the world."

How she hoped he was right.

"What does this mean for me? You go to Florida, and where will I be?"

"That's up to you, I suppose. You can go to Indiana, or maybe stay here."

"What about Pinecraft?"

"You would want to go to Florida with me . . . with us?"

He smiled even as his eyes grew heavy. "Someone's got

to keep the two of you out of trouble." And on that note, he fell asleep.

Zeb was sitting next to the front window as a buggy hurried down the lane.

"Clara Rose," he called. "Someone's visiting." But he had no idea who. In the time that he had been gone to Florida, buggies had switched hands from fathers to sons and daughters. New ones were bought, old ones sold. It was a never-ending cycle.

Clara Rose bustled down the stairs, cheeks pink. "Who is it?" she asked.

He shrugged. And if he wasn't mistaken, he saw the light of disapproval in her eyes. He knew he hadn't pulled his weight these last couple of days, but he couldn't motivate himself to do the things he knew needed to be done. It should have been easy, but Ivy's flushed and angry face kept circling inside his mind. She had been so angry when she told him to leave.

He had seen hurt from her, something close to betrayal, but this was pure anger. Well, no matter. He had made up his mind. He was going back to Pinecraft just as soon as he could make the arrangements. It was Sunday, and he put off leaving out of respect for Obie and Clara Rose. But tomorrow, first thing, he was going into town and getting on the first bus out of there.

The thought should have made him happy. But it didn't. It made him . . . pensive. He wanted to see Yonnie one last time before he went. Who knew when he would ever get back out this way. But Ivy had made her position very clear. He had been worried about her, concerned that she had been out with people she shouldn't have been out with. Okay, and maybe a little jealous that she would run around with an

Englischer and not even pretend to give him the time of day. And after all that he had been through. It was a knife to the heart.

One thing his time back in Wells Landing had taught him was that he belonged in Florida. He belonged with like-minded people. He had been fooling himself to think that he could come back and live—even for a time—the way folks lived in Wells Landing. Ivy included. For a while there he had thought he had seen a kindred light in her eyes when he talked about the beliefs of the Beachy Amish, but he hadn't forced the issue. That wasn't his place. But he knew that if she tried, the different beliefs would set more easily on her shoulders. It was a lesson he'd discovered soon after setting foot in Pinecraft. And whether she wanted anything to do with him or not, it was a peace he wished he could give her now.

Clara Rose made her way to the window and looked out while Zeb pretended to read. The words jumped around on the page and made no sense at all. But he had discovered that his courteous sister-in-law wouldn't bother him if she thought he was reading.

"It's Ivy Weaver."

The words sliced through him. "Ivy?" He did his best to make his voice sound like nothing, but it hitched on the end. Hopefully Clara Rose didn't notice. Zeb didn't want to explain why he and Ivy could have nothing though he loved her so.

Clara Rose made her way to the door and opened it before Ivy even had the chance to knock. "Ivy Weaver, come inside here. It's freezing out. Obie will get your mount."

Zeb didn't have to look up to know what was playing out before her. Ivy was unhitching her horse, and Obie was coming out of the barn on his wife's cue.

"No," Ivy said. Just the sound of her voice made his

fingers tingle, made his heart happy. Yet another reason why he needed to get back home, to Florida. He couldn't live in the same town with someone who only had to say one word and he was like half-set gelatin. "I came to talk to Zeb," she said.

His heart soared, then sank. He couldn't keep doing this with her.

"Zeb?" Clara Rose took a step back from the door as if he was about to get up and come walk through it. Not happening. The last person he wanted to talk to was Ivy Weaver. Okay, maybe not truly, but he had no business talking to her. Why break his heart into more little pieces when he could avoid her altogether? Until tomorrow, even after. Once he got on that bus he was not looking back. Not even for her.

"I don't want to talk to her."

"Why don't you come on inside where it's warm?" Clara Rose invited.

"Clara Rose," he hissed under his breath. That was not what he had told her to do. But Clara Rose had always been something of a stubborn girl.

"I just need to tell him something."

"Zeb." Clara Rose cut her eyes toward him. He shook his head. "Really? You can't even talk to her?"

She wasn't going to let the matter rest. Zeb shut the book and slid it onto the table next to the window, only then realizing that it had been so hard to read because he had been holding it upside down. When had that happened?

He released a long breath out his nose, something akin to a bull snorting, then stepped in front of the threshold. There she stood, Ivy Weaver, still holding the reins and waiting for him. She shouldn't have looked so good.

"What is it, Ivy?" He did everything he could to make his voice sound bored and apathetic. He couldn't have her knowing how she affected him.

"I came to tell you that I love you."

Behind him Clara Rose gasped. He wasn't sure if the sound was a happy one or not, but it didn't matter. Their love hadn't been able to grow. Not two years ago, and certainly not now. "That doesn't matter, Ivy."

She didn't even flinch from his harsh words. He had expected her to take a step back, but she held her ground as if she knew he was lying. But how could she know that? "I beg to differ. It matters a great deal."

"Is that all?" He had to get back into the house, away from her, before those blue eyes captured him and he got lost in the spaces between every sweet freckle on her even sweeter face.

"Yes." She stammered, stuttered, tried to find the words. He knew she wanted to say more. "No. I need to tell you something, Clara Rose."

"Me?" She stepped out onto the porch, pointing at herself just to make certain.

Ivy nodded. "And Obie too." She waited until Obie came around and stood next to his wife. "Zeb and I . . . well, before Zeb went to Florida, I discovered that I was pregnant."

Clara Rose gasped, but Obie merely nodded as if he wasn't surprised at all.

"We found out early, and before we could make any plans about what to do, I lost the baby."

Clara Rose murmured something he was sure was meant to be consoling, but once again Obie merely nodded. Zeb hadn't told his brother any of this, so he could only assume that Obie had known as twins often do that something big had been bothering Zeb. And when the time was right Obie would know what it was.

"Zeb went to Florida, and I—"

"Tried to keep everyone away by making up stories about yourself." The words slipped from Zeb unbidden. He hadn't meant to say anything. He wanted no part of this. Any role he could play would only draw him in. He was struggling enough now as it was. "I'm leaving tomorrow," he said, the words like bullets, fast, staccato.

"When were you planning on asking me to go with you?"

His heart pounded wildly in his chest. "What?"

"I said, when were you planning on asking me to go with you?"

Chapter Twenty-Two

Her heart seemed to stop, her mouth to turn to ash, and she waited for what Zeb was going to say. *Please Lord,* she silently prayed. *I've done everything You've asked of me. I was brave.*

"You want to come with me?" His words were quietly spoken and gave away nothing as to what he was feeling inside. Had she made a mistake?

"*Jah.* Me and Dawdi. If you'll have us."

"And if I won't?"

Those words sent her heart back to stuttering, erratic life. "I hope that you will."

"I think this is where we leave," Obie said.

Clara Rose looked about to protest, but Obie shook his head and directed his wife into the house. The front door shut behind them, and Zeb and Ivy were left alone.

She looked at him, studying his expression, though he was giving her no hint as to his thoughts. She had been brave. But what if this wasn't what God was talking about? What then?

She had been more than brave. She had been downright forward. And still he merely stared at her.

"Why?"

"What?" He had taken so long to answer that she had almost forgotten the question.

"Why do you want to go with me?"

"I told you that I love you. Is that not enough?" She swallowed back the tears clogging her throat.

"Pinecraft is different," he said.

She nodded. "I know. And I want to embrace those differences. I want all of that and more."

"And Dawdi?"

She shook her head. "He fell yesterday. He might not be ready to travel for a while, but I think he would enjoy Florida."

He only nodded, but the action didn't seem to be in agreement to anything she had said. "Is he okay?"

"He will be."

"And this is what you want?"

She frowned at him. "Why do you keep asking me that?"

"Because . . ." His voice choked. "Because I'm afraid that you don't really mean what you say. That you're going to change your mind and walk away."

She held her arms out at her sides. "I'm not going anywhere."

"You mean that?" A piece of his mask chipped away, leaving the residue of hope behind it.

"More than anything I've ever said before."

He still seemed to hesitate.

"I let you leave me once before. I will not do that again." She started toward him. If she could touch him, run her fingers down his face, maybe she could show him how much she meant what she was saying.

"If I say yes, you can't change your mind."

"Why would I do that?" She took another step.

"I don't know. I just—"

She drew even with him. And placed one finger on his lips.
Be brave.

She raised up on her toes and pressed a kiss where her finger had been.

A small sound escaped him as she stepped back. Bravery could only take a girl so far.

"If you go to Florida, you'll have to marry me," he said.

"Okay."

"And there are no white Christmases in Pinecraft."

"I think a sandy Christmas will suit me just fine."

This time he stepped toward her and swept her into his embrace. He kissed her there on the porch while his brother and sister-in-law peeked out the window. But that was okay. There was no more hiding the love they held for each other, and like sandy Christmases, that was just fine with her.